The Loner
BOOK ONE

The Loner
BOOK ONE

J. A. Johnstone

PINNACLE BOOKS
Kensington Publishing Corp.
www.kensingtonbooks.com

PINNACLE BOOKS are published by

Kensington Publishing Corp.
119 West 40th Street
New York, NY 10018

All Kensington titles, imprints, and distributed lines are available at special quantity discounts for bulk purchases for sales promotions, premiums, fund-raising, educational, or institutional use. Special book excerpts or customized printings can also be created to fit specific needs. For details, write or phone the office of the Kensington special sales manager: Kensington Publishing Corp., 119 West 40th Street, New York, NY 10018, attn: Special Sales Department; phone 1-800-221-2647.

ISBN-13: 978-0-7860-2151-2
ISBN-10: 0-7860-2151-9

First printing: May 2009

10 9 8 7 6 5 4 3 2 1

Printed in the United States of America

Chapter 1

The cantina had no name, only a reputation for vice and violence. It was a squat adobe building in a squalid, sun-blasted village in the Four Corners area. Most of the inhabitants were uncertain whether it lay in Arizona, New Mexico, Colorado, or Utah. Most of them didn't give a damn. Such designations were legal matters, and here the only law that mattered was the law of the gun.

Three fine horses were tied up at the hitch rail in front of the cantina. In a place such as this, where most people tried to scratch a meager living out of the arid soil, horses such as these could only belong to outsiders. The only outsiders who passed through the village were those who rode the lonely trails, men who had heard the owl hoot on dark, blood-soaked nights. In fact, it was known among the community of such men that they were welcome here. The cantina's proprietor, Gomez by name, could provide whiskey, tequila, beer, tortillas, beans, *cabrito,* a place to sleep, all for a reasonable price, *señor.*

And women, ah, yes, women, too, although at the

moment Gomez had only a few to offer, ranging
from his rather buxom wife to a half-breed Navajo
girl barely old enough to be considered a woman.
The men who patronized Gomez's place were, as a
rule, not too picky about such things.

The three men who owned the fine horses were the
cantina's only customers at the moment. All the villagers were drowsing in the midday heat except for
Gomez, who was behind the bar, and the Navajo girl,
who brought drinks to the men when they called for
them. Each time when she set the tray on the table
where the men were, they laughed and pawed at her
and said things that she didn't understand. She didn't
particularly want to understand them. Their rough
hands made their intent clear enough.

The oldest of the three men was middle-aged, with
a face to which time had not been kind. Gray hair stuck
out from under a flat-crowned black hat with turquoise-
studded conchos on its band. He wore a sour expression, along with a black vest over a shirt that had once
been white, black whipcord trousers, and twin gunbelts
that crossed as they went around his hips.

Across the table from him was a stocky, bearded
Mexican whose sombrero was pushed back so that it
hung behind his head by its chin strap. He carried
only one gun, an old Colt Navy in a cross-draw holster. He had three knives of varying lengths and
styles concealed around his body.

The third and final man was big and young, with
a moon face under a high-crowned white hat and a
gut that stretched his gray shirt. He had only one gun
as well, a long-barreled Remington. Despite his
youth, his face already showed the marks of cruelty
and dissipation.

In an impatient, high-pitched voice, he said, "We're gonna have to come up with some money pretty soon, Buck. We're about to run out. Time we buy a few more drinks and a roll in the hay with that gal, we'll be broke."

"What do you expect me to do about it?" the oldest of the trio asked. "Did you see a bank when we rode in?"

"No. There ain't much to speak of in this town."

"Well, we can't very well rob a bank that don't exist, now can we?" Buck asked. He took a swallow from a mug of beer. "I swear, Carlson, if you didn't have me around to do your thinkin' for you, I think you'd forget to wake up in the mornin'."

"Carlson is right," the Mexican said. "What will we do when our money runs out?"

"You let me worry about that, Julio. We've done all right with me runnin' the show so far, haven't we?"

Julio shrugged. "I cannot argue with that, amigo."

"Well, I can," Carlson said. "I can argue with any-thing."

Buck grunted. "Tell me about it. I think you'd argue with a tree stump, boy."

"I'd win, too," Carlson said with a grin.

Buck picked up one of the shots of tequila sitting on the table and tossed it down his throat. He wiped the back of his hand across his mouth. A look of in-tense concentration had come over his face. He turned to gaze at the bar, where the Navajo girl stood talking quietly to Gomez, who spoke her native tongue.

After a moment, Buck said, "I'm thinkin' we ought to ride down to Gallup. That's where Baggott and Hooper said they were headed. Maybe we can hook up with them and find some job to pull down there. It's been long enough since that other business."

"They have banks in Gallup," Julio said.

"That they do," Buck agreed.

"Wait a minute," Carlson said. "What are we gonna do for money between here and there? I told you, time we settle up with Gomez, we ain't gonna have any more."

"That ain't a problem. We just won't settle up with Gomez."

He said it loudly enough, and the gloomy, low-ceilinged room was small enough, so that Gomez heard. He protested, "Señor, you must be joking."

"I never joke," Buck said. Casually, he drew his left-hand gun and shot Gomez.

The gun was loud in the close quarters, loud enough to make Julio and Carlson wince. The girl had thrown herself aside, out of the line of fire, when she saw Buck pulling iron. She fell to her knees on the hard-packed dirt floor in front of the bar and screamed as Gomez stumbled backward under the bullet's impact. His stubby-fingered hands pawed at his chest where a crimson stain spread slowly on the front of his dirty shirt. He opened his mouth and tried to talk, but nothing came out except a trickle of blood. With a gasp, Gomez fell forward, landing across the bar with his arms flung out in front of him. He stayed that way for a second before gravity took over and hauled his body down behind the bar. He slid off the hardwood and landed with a heavy thud.

The girl kept screaming. "Shut her up," Buck said.

Carlson grinned as he got to his feet and lumbered toward her. "I got just the thing."

Before he got there, a large figure burst through the beaded curtain that hung over the door leading to the living quarters in the rear of the cantina. "Carlson, look out," Julio snapped as he leaped up out of his chair. His hand went to a sheath at the back of his neck, under the hanging sombrero, and came out with a throwing knife. The blade flickered across the room and lodged in the throat of the woman who had come through the curtain, yelling curses in Spanish and brandishing a shotgun.

The curses turned into an agonized gurgle as blood flooded the woman's throat. She was Gomez's wife, and she had heard what was going on in the cantina as she rolled tortillas in the back room. Too late to prevent her husband's murder, she had snatched up the scatter-gun and rushed out to avenge his death. To be sure, he frequently sold her to the men who stopped here at the cantina, but he was still her husband after all.

Choking and drowning in her own blood, she managed to pull both triggers on the shotgun, but the twin barrels had dropped so that all the double charge of buckshot did was blow a hole in the dirt floor. She leaned forward. The shotgun held her up for a second as its barrels struck the floor, but then she toppled to the side.

"You are a lucky man, amigo," Julio said. "If not for me, that cow would have blown your head off."

"Yeah, I owe you my life," Carlson said. "You want to go first with the girl?"

Julio started across the room to retrieve his knife. "No, you go ahead," he said. "I am in no hurry."

Carlson grinned. He was looking forward to this.

The girl had stopped screaming. She cringed away, scuttling across the dirt floor as Carlson reached for her. She had been with many men in the time she had been here at Gomez's place. Some of them had been bad men and treated her rough. But these three were different, she sensed. These three would not leave her alive when they rode away from here.

Julio pulled his knife out of the dead woman's throat and used her skirt to wipe the blood from the blade. "Do you think anyone will come to see what the shots were about?" he asked Buck.

"Not likely," Buck replied with a shake of his head. "Those villagers'll be too scared to come outta their holes, like the rabbits they are." He downed another shot of tequila. "Now, we don't have to settle up with Gomez. I'll bet there's even some money in his till that we can help ourselves to. We'll have enough to make it to Gallup."

"*Sí,* I believe you're right."

"Damn it, girl," Carlson said, "don't run away from me. You'll just make it worse for yourself." He chuckled. "Not that it could get a whole lot worse'n what I got in mind for you."

Like a giant cat pouncing on a mouse, the big man suddenly lunged forward. A hamlike hand at the end of a thick, heavy-muscled arm wrapped around the girl's slender arm. She cried out in horror as Carlson jerked her toward him.

From the door of the cantina, a voice said, "I'd let her go if I was you."

The three outlaws looked toward the door. They hadn't heard a horse come up, but the man who stood there had to have gotten to the village some way. He wasn't one of the villagers, that was for sure. With the brilliant sunlight behind him, they couldn't make out anything except his tall, broad-shouldered silhouette, topped by a flat-crowned hat. His accent was American. Not very Western maybe, but still American. His voice held hints of culture and education. Despite that, the hard menace it contained was also obvious.

"Mister, you are a damned fool," Buck drawled. Despite his casual tone, he was tense and ready for trouble now. Men on the run could never let their guard down for too long. "If you've got any sense, you'll turn around and walk away from here. Hell, if you're smart, you'll run."

The stranger laughed softly. "That's one thing nobody's ever accused me of," he said. "Being smart." His head turned slightly as he looked at Carlson again. "I said let her go, fatty."

Carlson shoved the girl against the bar and took a step toward the newcomer. "Why, you son of a bitch—"

"I think I'll kill you last," the stranger mused. "Those two bastards with you strike me as being more dangerous."

The voice was so smooth it took a heartbeat for the three hardcases to grasp the implication of the words. Then Buck yelled, "Get him!" as he exploded from his chair, clawing at both guns.

The stranger went for Julio first, and it was a good thing he did, because the Mexican was a lightning-fast knife man. As it was, he barely beat Julio's throw. The Colt that appeared in the stranger's fist seemingly by magic blasted out a shot just a hair before the knife left Julio's hand. That was enough to throw off the Mexican's aim. The knife thudded into the wall just inches to the right of the door, the handle quivering as the blade stuck in the adobe. Julio was already crumpling to the floor, the stranger's bullet in his belly.

Buck had both guns out, their barrels rising. The stranger shot him twice. The slugs drove him backward as they punched into his chest. He tripped over the chair that had overturned when he leaped to his feet. The guns in his hands roared as his fingers jerked involuntarily on the triggers. The shots went into the cantina's ceiling.

That left Carlson. He had succeeded in dragging out his Remington while the stranger was disposing of Julio and Buck. He even got a shot off that knocked chips of adobe from the edge of the door as the stranger crouched. The Colt spouted flame again. The bullet hit Carlson just between his nose and his upper lip, traveling at an upward angle that sent the deadly chunk of lead boring deep into his brain. Carlson's head jerked back, but he managed to stumble ahead a couple of steps as the knowledge that he was dead slowly penetrated his piggish brain. His knees hit the floor; then he pitched forward on his face.

The stranger didn't pouch his iron. He stalked into the cantina with a pantherish stride and held the gun ready as he checked the bodies to make sure they were dead. Buck and Carlson were, but breath still rasped in Julio's throat as he lay there with his arms crossed and pressed to his bleeding stomach. The stranger bent down and plucked the gun from Julio's holster, placed it on the table. He took the knives he could see, too. It was possible Julio had more hidden on him somewhere, but gut-shot as he was, it was also possible he would never regain consciousness.

He'd probably be lucky if that turned out to be the case. Dying from a bullet in the belly was a bad way to go.

The stranger moved to the bar, where the Navajo girl still cowered. "Are you all right?" he asked as he holstered his gun.

She stared up at him in disbelief. Like an angel, he had swooped in to save her, drawing his gun and firing with a speed the likes of which she had never seen before—and she had witnessed several gun-fights here in Gomez's cantina.

Although it wasn't Gomez's anymore, she thought. He was dead, and so was his wife. She didn't know what would happen to the place now, or to her.

"Are you hurt?" her angel asked.

No, not an angel, considering that he was dressed all in black from head to toe. Devil was more like it. He had the Devil's own skill with a gun. He would have been handsome, the girl thought, with that long, sandy hair and close-cropped beard, if not for the coldness in his eyes.

Yet despite that coldness, the chilly glint that said he cared for nothing and no one, he had risked his life to save her. Julio and Carlson had both come within a whisker of killing him. The fight could have turned out very differently.

But it hadn't. Struggling to form the words in En-glish, she whispered, "Yes, I . . . not hurt."

He nodded. "Good." His eyes went to the woman. "Was she your mother?"

"No, she . . . Gomez's wife."

"Gomez?"

The girl pointed behind the bar. The stranger took a look, shook his head. "Sorry," he muttered. "You just worked here?"

The girl nodded.

"Well, I reckon it's your place now, unless Señor and Señora Gomez have any relatives who want to claim it."

Her place? The girl couldn't imagine owning

anything other than the dress she wore, let alone having her own business. The idea was . . . interesting, though.

"I'll find someone to help get these bodies out of here." He turned toward the door.

The girl plucked at the sleeve of his shirt. "Señor? You leave? If you stay . . . I be . . . very good to you."

"Sorry," he replied with a shake of his head. "I had business with those three, and now it's done. I'm just sorry I didn't get here in time to save Señor and Señora Gomez."

"You knew . . . those bad men?"

He nodded. "I knew them."

"But they not act like . . . they knew you."

A hint of a smile played around his lips. "I've changed a mite since the last time they saw me."

"S-Señor . . ."

That hoarse voice came from Julio. He had regained consciousness in time to hear what the stranger said. As the man came over to him, Julio fought off the incredible pain in his belly and went on. "Who . . . who are you?"

"Morgan," the man said as he hunkered on his heels next to the gut-shot Mexican. "Some call me Kid Morgan."

"I never . . . heard of you."

"You knew me by another name. Remember when you were in Carson City a while back? You remember Black Rock Canyon?"

Julio's eyes widened. "No. *Dios mio, no!* We heard . . . you were dead."

"You heard wrong."

"You came . . . all this way . . . to find us . . ."

"You three were just the first. You won't be the last."

A wave of agony began in Julio's midsection and washed through the rest of his body. "Ah," he breathed through clenched teeth.

"Hurts like hell, doesn't it?"

"*Sí* . . . Señor, I have no right . . . to ask any favors of you . . ."

"You sure don't."

"But . . . I beg you . . . in the name of El Señor Dios, who will send me to Hell . . . end it now. Spare me . . . this pain."

"You didn't spare me any." The Kid straightened and drew his gun. "But I reckon I can give you what you want . . . if you give me what I want." He looked over his shoulder at the girl, who watched with wide, dark eyes. "Run along for right now. Go find somebody to help you. And tell the people in the village that it'll be all right. I'll be gone soon."

She hesitated, then started tentatively toward the door. She was running by the time she went through it. A moment later, a shot blasted behind her in the cantina.

Kid Morgan walked out, untied the reins of a buckskin horse from the hitch rail, and swung up into the saddle. He turned the horse and rode at an easy pace out of the village.

Although he was glad he had caught up to the three men in time to save the girl from whatever they had planned for her, their deaths didn't ease the pain inside him. He wasn't sure anything could do that unless he could figure out how to turn back time. To go back to a better place, a better time, to the world he used to know . . .

To the man he used to be.

Chapter 2

Six weeks earlier

Nevada was beautiful this time of year. But then, any setting would be beautiful as long as Rebel Callahan Browning was in it, Conrad Browning thought.

"Here's to you, my dear," he said as he raised a fine crystal champagne flute. "You make a lovely view even lovelier."

"Why, Conrad, what a sweet thing to say." His wife smiled at him. The sunlight filtered down through the branches of the pine tree under which Conrad had spread the blanket he'd taken from the buggy. The golden glow struck highlights from her blond hair where it fell in thick waves around her shoulders. Her face was flushed with happiness. Or maybe it was just the champagne, Conrad thought.

She clinked her glass against his, and they both drank. He didn't need alcohol to become intoxicated these days. His wife's beauty and the clear, high country air were more than enough to cause that.

The remains of a picnic lunch were spread out on the blanket in front of them. Conrad had packed the lunch in a wicker basket, placed it in the buggy along with the blanket, and then surprised Rebel with his suggestion that they take a drive up here into the hills overlooking Carson City, Nevada.

"What about work?" she had asked with a puzzled frown.

"I'm the boss, aren't I? I think I can take half a day, or even a whole day, off if I want to."

"Yes, of course," Rebel had said. "But it's just so . . . unlike you."

"I'm not myself since we moved out here."

It was true. Conrad had felt himself changing ever since they'd left Boston behind and come to Carson City. He wished they had made the move earlier. He slept better, breathed easier, and was coming to realize that even though he had been raised in the East, this was now home to him.

It was all Frank Morgan's fault. Or perhaps it was better to say that Frank deserved the credit, although for a long time Conrad had been unwilling to give his father the least bit of credit for anything. All he had done was blame him for his mother's death.

Conrad Browning was practically a grown man before he found out that his father was Frank Morgan, the notorious Western gunfighter known as The Drifter. Frank hadn't known he had a son either, because Conrad was the product of a brief marriage when he was a young man, a marriage that his beloved Vivian's father had ended abruptly. Vivian had gone on to marry again and to found a business empire that stretched across the continent. She and her second husband had raised Conrad, who had taken his step-father's last name.

Several years earlier, during a trip West, outlaws

had murdered Vivian. Those same outlaws had kidnapped and tortured Conrad. He had Frank Morgan to thank for saving his life. Conrad had been in no mood to thank the man, however. He had found out by then that Frank was his real father, and he didn't care for that news at all. He had been a bit of a prig in those days, he often thought now.

More than a bit actually.

Frank hadn't given up on him, though, and over the course of several adventures they had been drawn into, Conrad had come to respect his father, even to feel genuine affection for him. They worked well together.

It was during one of those adventures, in fact, that Conrad had met and fallen in love with Rebel. After their marriage, they had gone back to Boston, but circumstances kept pulling them westward. They had spent some time in Buckskin, a mining community in the mountains southeast of Carson City, where Frank had served as the marshal for a while. Seeing how Rebel thrived in the frontier atmosphere had convinced Conrad to move out here permanently. With telegraph wires and railroad lines stretching all across the country now, there was no reason why he couldn't manage the Browning business holdings just as effectively from Carson City as he did from Boston.

"Well, whoever you are these days, I like him," Rebel said. She finished her champagne, placed the glass in the basket, and lay down on the blanket, stretching her arms above her head so that her breasts rose enticingly.

Conrad couldn't resist the temptation. He set his glass down and moved alongside her, propping himself up on an elbow so that he could lean over her and press his lips to hers. The kiss was sweet and gentle at first, but it grew rapidly in intensity. Passionate urgency surged through Conrad's body. Rebel wrapped her arms around his neck and pulled him tighter against her. Their bodies molded together, her breasts flattening under the pressure of his muscular chest.

She was breathless with desire when he pulled back and broke the kiss. He slid his left hand between them to caress her right breast through her dress. "Conrad," she said in a husky voice, "it's broad daylight, and we're right out in the open . . ."

"And there's no one but us around for miles," he said. He didn't know that for a fact, but he felt fairly certain it was true. He wanted it to be true. He kissed Rebel again.

Her hands clutched at him. He reached for the hem of her skirt and drew it up, exposing sleek, bare, beautiful legs. His fingers stroked the softness of her thighs.

Somewhere not far off, hoofbeats thudded on the ground.

Rebel gasped and started pushing Conrad away. He went willingly, but not happily. He didn't particularly want anybody riding up on them like this either. He rolled off Rebel and sat up. Beside him, she hastily tried to tug her skirt down. She didn't manage to cover herself completely before half a dozen men rode out of the trees and into sight. They had to have gotten at least a flash of her bare legs before she finally got her skirt over them.

As the men reined in, Conrad's eyes darted from them to the picnic basket. A short-barreled Colt .45 revolver was in the basket, within reach if he needed to grab it. When he and Rebel set out on this excursion, he certainly hadn't anticipated running into any trouble, but one of the things he had learned from being around his father was that it was best to be prepared.

The gun had only five rounds in its cylinder, though; the hammer rested on the empty sixth chamber. Something else he had learned from Frank. Five bullets, six men . . . that could present a challenge.

Stop jumping to conclusions, Conrad told himself. These men probably meant them no harm. He was sure they hadn't even known that he and Rebel were here.

He got to his feet, brushed off his trousers, and nodded to the strangers. "Gentlemen," he said. "It's a beautiful day, isn't it?"

"It sure is," one of the riders replied. He gestured with his left hand toward the blanket and the wicker basket. "We didn't mean to interrupt your picnic."

"That's quite all right. We were finished anyway." Conrad held a hand down to Rebel. "Weren't we, my dear?"

"That's right," she said as she grasped his hand and let him help her to her feet.

The man who had spoken before grinned and said, "Don't let us run you off, folks." He was a narrow-shouldered man with a ginger beard and a cuffed-back hat. The well-worn walnut grips of a revolver jutted up from the holster on his hip. The men with him were similar sorts, all dressed in range clothes. Some were bearded, some clean-shaven, but they all had hard-bitten faces. Conrad had seen plenty just like them, men who were no better and no more honest than they had to be. Just like the outlaws who had sliced off the top of his left ear to torture him while he was their prisoner. He wore his sandy hair long to cover up that disfigurement.

Conrad tried to ignore the cold ball of fear that had

formed in his belly. He wasn't afraid for himself so much as he was for Rebel. Outnumbered as the two of them were, if the men decided to attack them, they could probably overpower him and do whatever they wanted to her.

Some of them would die in the process, though. He made that vow to himself, even as he tried to keep what he was feeling from showing on his face.

"That's all right," he said as he reached down to pick up the basket. "We were leaving anyway. Got to get back to town."

"Live in Carson City, do you?"

"That's right." Conrad felt a little better now that he had the basket in his left hand where his right could swoop into it and snatch out the Colt. There was a Winchester in the buggy. He wondered if Rebel could reach it while he gave her some covering fire. If she got her hands on the rifle, they could give a better account of themselves. Rebel was a better shot with a Winchester than he was, and she had the fighting spirit of a girl who had grown up on the frontier.

If those varmints started any trouble, they'd get a warmer reception than they likely expected, Conrad thought.

But then the spokesman surprised him by reaching up, tugging on his hat brim, and nodding pleasantly. "Guess we'll be ridin' on then," he said. "You folks have a pleasant day." He turned his horse, hitched it into motion, and jerked his head at the other men to indicate that they should follow him.

Conrad slipped his right hand into the basket and closed it around the butt of the Colt, just in case this was some sort of trick. That didn't appear to be the case, though. The men rode on around the shoulder of the hill, soon going out of sight.

Rebel reached down, grabbed the corners of the blanket, and gathered the whole thing into a bundle with the leftover food inside. Conrad took the revolver out of the basket. Rebel crammed the blanket in to replace the gun.

"Let's get out of here," she said.

"Indeed," Conrad said. He tucked the Colt behind his belt. "Those men could still be lurking around."

Rebel shuddered. "Did you see the way they were looking at me? Especially that big, ugly one?"

"Not really," Conrad admitted. "I was watching their shoulders most of the time." That was where a tiny hitch could be seen just before most men went for their guns. Frank had taught him that. With some men, the tell was in their eyes, but experienced gunfighters could control that. Not the shoulder hitch, though.

"Well, it wasn't good," Rebel said. "I thought for sure they were going to—" She stopped and shook her head. "Let's just say I was trying to figure out how fast I could get to that Winchester in the buggy."

A grim laugh came from Conrad as he set the basket in the back of the buggy. "I must admit, the same thought was going through my mind, my dear."

Moments later, he had the vehicle rolling back down the hill toward Carson City, behind the big buckskin horse hitched to it. There was still no sign of the six riders. Conrad sighed with relief as he glanced over at his wife. That encounter had turned out much better than he had feared it might.

Although he was still disappointed that he and Rebel had been interrupted just at that particular moment . . .

* * *

"Damn it, Lasswell, we should've waited another few minutes before we rode up. Then we could've seen 'em goin' at it. That gal'd be worth watchin', I'll bet."

Clay Lasswell leaned to the side in his saddle and spat. "And then what would you fellas have done?" he demanded. "You're tellin' me you could've seen Mrs. Browning buck nekkid and not wanted to jump on her?"

The giant, moonfaced Carlson nudged the older man riding beside him and laughed. "Buck nekkid," he said. "I don't want to see that! You get it, Buck?"

"Shut up," Buck said without any real rancor. Carlson was an idiot most of the time. Buck had learned to make allowances for him. Julio Esquivel was the same way. He just shook his head at Carlson's comments.

Ezra Harker, the man who'd been complaining to Lasswell, said, "What would it have hurt if we'd gone ahead and shot the dude and taken the girl?"

Lasswell raked the fingers of his left hand through his ginger-colored beard. "Well, for one thing," he said, "that ain't what we're bein' paid to do. For another, did you see the way the boy kept eyein' that picnic basket? I'd bet a hat he had a gun in there."

"What if he did? You worried about bein' shot by some pasty-faced gent from back East?"

Lasswell squinted at Harker and said, "Do you just not pay attention to anything, Ezra? That boy didn't look too pasty-faced to me. And have you forgot that his pa's Frank Morgan?"

"Just because his pa's a gunfighter don't mean that he is. Anyway, Morgan's an old man now."

"Not that old," Lasswell said, thinking of some of

the stories he'd heard about Frank Morgan in recent years. The Drifter might not be as young as he once was, but his gun hand hadn't slowed down any. He was still tough as whang leather and dangerous as a wounded wildcat. Sure, the boy was different, but if he'd inherited even part of his pa's skill with a gun and pure cussedness . . .

"We'll do things the way we were told," Lasswell went on. "That's the best way of bein' sure we get paid like we were promised."

The sixth man in the group, the dark, saturnine Ray Duncan, said, "We'd better get paid. If we don't, I'll be lookin' to even the score with some hot lead."

The riders kept moving gradually higher in the mountains. Off to the west, surrounded by pines, lay the blue depths of Lake Tahoe. It wasn't far from here to the California line. This was silver country, but large ranches abounded in the area, too. Several railroad lines passed through Carson City and Reno to the north. If a man wanted to rob a mine payroll or an ore shipment, hold up a train or rustle some cattle, this corner of Nevada was the place for him to be. Opportunities for lawlessness were everywhere.

Right now, those opportunities included kidnapping a rich man's wife.

"Anyway," Lasswell went on to Harker, "if we killed the boy, who'd pay the ransom for his wife?"

"Frank Morgan?" Harker suggested.

Lasswell spat again. "Morgan? You ever know a gunman to have a lot of money? Hell, it runs through our fingers like water, you know that. That's why we can't go too long between jobs. Not to mention the fact that if we was to kill Morgan's boy, I don't reckon he'd be too disposed to handin' over any ransom money to us. Likely, he'd come after us and try to kill us all instead."

"Well, then, what about the girl's family?"

Lasswell shook his head. "From what I understand, she don't come from money. Browning's got all of it. And he'll pay handsomely to get her back once she's in our hands."

"A woman like that'd be worth damn near anything," Duncan said.

"Sí," Julio agreed. "She is very lovely."

Carlson said, "I don't care what else we do, long as I get a turn or two with her 'fore we send her back to the dude. Lord, I'm lookin' forward to that."

Lasswell frowned. He was going to have his hands full keeping this bunch of mangy coyotes under control, and he knew it. If he had to, he could afford to shoot one or two of them, he supposed. That would still leave him with enough men to do the job, assuming that the others were waiting like they were supposed to be.

A few minutes later, the six riders came to a large clearing. Lasswell had been smelling wood smoke for a while, so he wasn't surprised to see that the men waiting for them had built a campfire. They even had a pot of coffee brewing.

"Lasswell?" one of the men called as he strode forward to meet the riders. He was tall and barrel-chested, with a face that looked like it had been hacked out of an old log with a dull ax.

Lasswell reined in and nodded. "That's right."

The man stuck a hand up to him. "I'm Vernon Moss. You sent me a wire, told me to gather up as many good men as I could and meet you here."

Lasswell shook hands with Moss, then swung

down from the saddle. The men with him dismounted as well. Lasswell looked around the clearing, saw that there were nine men in addition to Moss.

"That's Jeff and Hank Winchell," Moss said, pointing to two tall, skinny hardcases who looked as much alike as two peas in a pod. "Don't bother trying to tell them apart. That's Clem Baggott next to them, then Abel Dean, Jim Fowler, Titus Gant, and Spence Hooper. The old-timer's Rattigan, and the breed is called White Rock."

"You vouch for all of 'em, Moss?" Lasswell asked.

"I do."

Lasswell studied the men intently for a moment, then chuckled. "You're about as evil-lookin' a bunch of hombres as I ever seen. Good job, Moss."

"What is it we're after?" Moss wanted to know. "With sixteen men, we can hold up a train or knock over a bank easy."

"Our job will be even easier than that. We got to kidnap one woman."

Moss frowned at Lasswell, who heard several surprised mutters from the other men. "One woman?" he repeated. "Why do you need this many men to snatch one woman?"

"Because snatchin' her ain't the problem. Hangin' on to her until we get the ransom is."

"Must be one mighty special woman," Moss said. "Who is she anyway?"

"It ain't who she is. It's who her husband's father is. You ever hear of Frank Morgan?"

The worried look that suddenly appeared on Moss's face answered that question. "The woman we're after is Frank Morgan's daughter-in-law? The payoff had better be damned good! I won't take a chance on going up against Morgan if it's not."

"How does fifty thousand dollars sound?"

"Split between sixteen men?" Moss did some quick ciphering in his head. "That's a little over three grand apiece."

"It'll be even more if some of us don't live to claim a share," Lasswell pointed out.

"You reckon that's liable to happen?"

"If Frank Morgan gets involved," Lasswell said, "I think you can damned well count on it."

Chapter 3

Conrad didn't exactly forget about the encounter with the six men on the hillside, but he had plenty of other things on his mind, so he didn't dwell on it. Keeping up with all the far-flung Browning business holdings required a great deal of time and attention. When he and Rebel had first moved to Carson City, he had rented an office in one of the bank buildings downtown and hired a private secretary, as well as several bookkeepers and stenographers. All of them stayed busy as information flowed into the Carson City office over the telegraph wires from Boston, New York, Chicago, Denver, and San Francisco.

Conrad was at his desk a few days later when Edwin Sinclair, his secretary, came into the office. Most people thought of secretaries as frail and bookish, but Sinclair hardly fell into that category. He was taller and heavier than Conrad and fancied himself an amateur pugilist. The only thing typical about him was that he had to wear spectacles at times, as a result of years of doing close work on ledgers and files.

Sinclair had a stack of papers in his hands. Conrad

groaned at the sight of them and said, "Not more reports?"

"The wheels of the business world are lubricated with ink, Mr. Browning," Sinclair said. "You know that."

Conrad chuckled. "You're right, of course, Edwin. Set them down here, and I'll start going through them." He pulled his watch from a vest pocket, flipped it open, and checked the time as Sinclair placed the stack of papers on the desk. "And a start is all I'll be able to make. There are too many to finish this afternoon. I wonder if I should take the others home with me."

"I'd be glad to come to your house and help you go through them this evening, sir," Sinclair volunteered.

Conrad considered the offer for a second, then shook his head. "I'm sure you have better things to do with your evenings than help me wade through paperwork," he said. "But I appreciate the offer."

"I really don't mind—" Sinclair began.

"No, that's all right." Conrad pulled the papers closer to him. "That's all, Edwin, thank you. And as late as it is, you and the boys might as well go on home."

"Well, all right, if you say so, Mr. Browning," Sinclair replied with a shrug of his broad shoulders. "I'll see you in the morning."

Conrad nodded, already distracted by the summaries of the business dealings conducted by the companies covered in the reports.

Not so distracted, though, that he didn't look up with a frown a few minutes after Edwin Sinclair had gone. He knew he was probably wrong to feel this way, but he didn't want Sinclair spending a lot of time around Rebel. The secretary had come to their home a few times in the evenings to help Conrad when the press of work threatened to become overwhelming. Rebel had insisted that he have dinner with them on those occasions. Western hospitality and all that, Conrad supposed. And he had to admit that Sinclair had been as polite and charming as he could be. Conrad thought he had seen something in Sinclair's eyes, though, when the man glanced at Rebel . . . It was nothing overt, and of course he wasn't the least bit worried about Rebel ever being tempted to return the illicit affections of another man, but still . . . Conrad was just more comfortable keeping his dealings with Sinclair strictly at the office.

He worked a while longer, then finally pushed the papers away, rubbed his eyes, and yawned. When he stood up, it felt good to stretch muscles that had stiffened from long hours spent bent over a desk. As Conrad began getting ready to leave for the day, he thought about how good it would feel to climb up into a saddle and ride out into the mountains, to breathe some air that hadn't grown stuffy from being confined inside four walls, to see something besides those walls.

He had really enjoyed that excursion with Rebel a few days earlier, he thought, at least until those men interrupted them. They ought to spend more days like that.

His father would certainly be surprised to hear him say such a thing, he told himself with a smile as he gathered up the papers he was going to take home.

A few minutes later, carrying a case with the reports fastened securely inside it, Conrad left the building. His house was half a mile away. It was a good walk, and today he was looking forward to it.

He thought about how Rebel had looked, stretched out on that blanket with an inviting smile on her beautiful face, and his stride lengthened in his eagerness to get home.

In a café located across the street from the bank building where Conrad Browning had his office, Edwin Sinclair watched through a window as Browning walked away. Sinclair had a cup of coffee in front of him, but he had barely touched the brew. His hands clenched into fists on the table as he watched Browning.

"Something wrong, sir?"

The unexpected question made Sinclair give a little start. He looked up and saw that the waitress had paused beside him, a coffeepot in her hand. She looked slightly startled, too, and he supposed that was because of his reaction.

He forced a smile onto his face and said, "No, I'm fine, thank you."

"Some more coffee, Mr. Sinclair?"

She knew him because he ate lunch here fairly often. It was convenient to the office. But it had been a mistake for him to come in here this afternoon, he told himself. He didn't want the waitress or anyone else remembering—afterward—that he had been here today, watching Conrad Browning leave the bank building.

Still smiling, he shook his head and said, "No, thank you. In fact, I must be going."

"You hardly touched your coffee. Is there anything wrong with it?"

He wanted to yell at the stupid woman and tell her

to stop badgering him with questions. Instead, he said, "No, it's fine as always. I guess I just wasn't thirsty after all."

What he was thirsty for was a shot of whiskey. That was all right. He could get one at the place he was going to next.

He left a bill on the table to pay for the coffee and placate the nosy waitress, then left the café and strode off in the opposite direction from Browning. His steps led into a rougher part of town. Although Carson City was the state capital and a bustling, modern city, it wasn't all that many years removed from the mining boomtown and cattle town it had once been. The frontier was still alive here, just not quite as visible as it used to be.

That was why Sinclair felt almost as if he were stepping into a dime-novel illustration as he entered the Ace High Saloon a short time later. Frock-coated gamblers, cowboys in boots and spurs and tall hats, painted doves in gaudy dresses and rolled stockings . . . Sinclair was the one who was out of place here in his gray tweed suit and soft felt hat.

He spotted the man he was looking for at a table in the rear of the long, smoky room. He had met with the man once before, nearly a week earlier. At that time, Lasswell had been alone. Tonight, the gunman had a companion, a large man with a florid, rough-hewn face. A bottle and three glasses, one of them empty, sat on the table.

Sinclair tried to ignore the raucous talk and laughter around him as he made his way through the crowded saloon. When he was halfway across the room, one of the women who worked there blocked his path. "Buy me a drink, honey?" she asked as she smiled up at him.

The heavy perfume she wore wasn't quite strong enough to cover up the smell of unwashed flesh. The neckline of her spangled dress gaped so low that he could see the upper edge of one nipple.

"No, I don't believe so," he replied with a shake of his head.

"You could buy something else if you wanted to," she said, putting a mock pout on her rouged face. "Big handsome fella like you, it'd be a pleasure, not just a chore."

Sinclair just wanted to get away from her. "Maybe later," he said, and reached around her to give her rump a squeeze. That made her laugh and jump and say, "Oh, you!" Mainly, though, it got her out of his way.

Lasswell grinned at him when he reached the table. "Thought you was gonna stop for a little slap an' tickle," he said.

Sinclair pulled back a chair, sat down, and nodded at the empty glass. "Is that for me?"

"Yeah." Lasswell picked up the bottle, splashed some of the amber liquid into the glass, and then pushed it across the table toward Sinclair. "Bottoms up."

Sinclair followed that suggestion, tossing back the drink and savoring the fiery path it traced down his throat and into his stomach. He returned the empty to the table with a thump.

"Is it all set?" Lasswell asked.

Sinclair didn't answer. Instead, he asked a question of his own. He nodded toward the other man at the table and said, "Who's this?"

"Name's Vernon Moss," the man said, "and I can answer for myself and everything."

"I meant no offense, Mr. Moss. I simply wanted to know if it was all right to speak frankly."

"Vernon's in on the plan," Lasswell said. "I reckon you'd say he's my second in command. Anything you can tell me you can tell him." Lasswell leaned forward. "Now, is it set up? Are you gonna be at Browning's house tonight?"

"No," Sinclair said, aware of the bitter edge that crept into his voice. "He refused when I suggested that I come over to help him with the paperwork."

He had held back reports all day so that there would be a thick stack of them by late afternoon. He had done the same thing several times in the past, whenever he felt that it would be impossible to live through one more day without the sight of Rebel Browning. Since the trick had worked before, it should have worked again. Damn the luck anyway, Sinclair thought.

Lasswell frowned. "You was supposed to be there, so you could put Browning out of the picture."

"I know that," Sinclair snapped. He had played the scene over in his head time after time, figuring out how he would make some excuse to leave the room, then sneak back in behind Browning and knock him unconscious. Later, after Lasswell and his men carried off Rebel, he would have pretended that they had attacked him first, so that he had no idea what had happened while he was out cold. No one would have been able to dispute his story. But now it wouldn't happen that way.

Lasswell scratched at his beard. "That means we'll have to deal with Browning."

"For God's sake, you have at least a dozen men at your disposal, don't you? Isn't that enough to handle one man?"

"Me and some of the boys took a look at Browning the other day. I got a hunch he's tougher than you give him credit for, mister. When we bust in, there's liable to be shootin'."

"You can't kill him," Sinclair said. "You know that."

"I know what the orders are. I also know that bullets don't give a damn about orders when they start flyin' around. I can't guarantee that Browning won't be hit."

"That would ruin everything." Without waiting for Lasswell to pour, Sinclair grabbed the bottle himself and filled his glass. He drank half the whiskey and then said, "Let me think."

There had to be some way to salvage the plan. Everything had been carefully thought out. It couldn't collapse just because of one minor obstacle.

He wasn't sure who had come up with the scheme. His only contacts with his mysterious benefactor had been through letters, letters that he had been careful to burn after committing them to memory. So he had no idea why the man wanted Rebel Browning kidnapped. It was enough to know that he, Edwin Sinclair, was going to be her savior.

Once the ransom had been paid, he would slip into the isolated cabin where the outlaws had confined Rebel and "rescue" her before they could return to kill her, as they would make plain was their intention before leaving to collect the ransom. Then, grateful to him for saving her life, Rebel would finally see that she should be with him, not Conrad Browning. It was foolproof, Sinclair thought, even though certain elements of it did smack of a bad stage melodrama.

An idea began to come to him. He wrestled with it for a few moments while Lasswell and Moss drank and watched him with their dull eyes. Finally, he said, "How about this? I'll show up at Browning's house this evening with a telegram. I can tell him that it's an urgent wire from the San Francisco office or some such, and claim that the messenger delivered it to me rather than him by mistake. That will get me in the door, and then I can say that as long as I'm there, I might as well go ahead and give him a hand with all the paperwork he took home from the office."

Lasswell looked over at Moss. "What do you think?"

Moss's beefy shoulders rose and fell. "It might work, I reckon."

"It *will* work," Sinclair said. "For one thing, once I'm there, Mrs. Browning will insist that I at least stay and have a cup of tea with them. I'll find a way to get Browning alone and knock him out."

"That's the only way we can be sure he won't get ventilated," Lasswell said. "You better have it done by eight o'clock, though, because that's when we're comin' in the back. You're sure there won't be any servants there?"

"They only have a woman who does the cooking and cleaning, and she goes home by six. It'll be just the two of them . . . and me."

Lasswell nodded. "There's one more thing we been wonderin' about. Do you have any idea where Frank Morgan is these days?"

"Browning's father?" Sinclair asked with a frown. "Why do you want to know?"

"You know who Frank Morgan *is*, don't you?"

"Of course I do. He's some sort of dime-novel gunman."

Lasswell gave a harsh laugh. "Not hardly, mister. Morgan's the genuine article. If he's anywhere around these parts and hears that his daughter-in-law's been kidnapped, he'll come a-runnin' to get on our trail. And we don't want that. We don't want no part of it."

Sinclair suppressed the impulse to sneer. "You're that afraid of one man?"

"It's not a matter of bein' afraid. It's a matter of bein' careful."

Sinclair sighed. "I don't know where Morgan is, but I can tell you that not long ago he was in California, down around Los Angeles. Browning mentioned that his father was lending a hand to one of their lawyers."

"That don't make no sense at all," Lasswell said with a frown. "Morgan's a gunfighter, not a lawyer."

"All I know is what Browning said. It had to do with some sort of dispute over oil wells, or something like that."

"Oh," Lasswell said. "Some kind of ruckus. Gun work, more'n likely. I can see Morgan bein' mixed up in something like that."

Moss said, "California's too close. I wish he was over in Texas, or way the hell and gone up in Montana or the Dakotas."

"It'll be all right," Lasswell said. "The whole thing won't last long. It'll be over and done with, and we'll be gone before Morgan can ever get here."

"You hope," Moss said.

"Damn right I do."

"All right, it's settled," Sinclair said, not bothering to try to keep the impatience out of his voice. "I'll do my part. You do yours."

Lasswell poured himself a drink. "You can count on us."

"One last thing . . . Under no circumstances is Mrs. Browning to be hurt in any way, shape, or fashion, do you understand? No one lays a finger on her except to restrain her and bring her along."

"Sure, sure," Lasswell said. "We know we got to be careful with her."

"Good." Sinclair gave them his best steely-eyed glare. "Because anyone who harms her will answer to me."

When Sinclair was gone and Lasswell and Moss were sitting there polishing off the whiskey, Moss chuckled and said, "That young fool don't have any idea what's really goin' on, does he?"

Lasswell shook his head as he emptied the last drops from the bottle into his glass. "No, he don't," he said. "Not one damn bit."

Chapter 4

Conrad enjoyed dinner with Rebel, as he always did. A cloth of fine Irish linen covered the table in the dining room. The china and the crystal sparkled. The meal prepared by Mrs. O'Hannigan was delicious. But of course, it was Rebel's company that really made the meal special. She sat at the other end of the table in a white blouse and dark gray skirt, with her blond hair pulled up on top of her head in an elaborate arrangement of curls this evening.

Conrad could hardly wait to pull loose the pins that held Rebel's hair and allow it to tumble freely about her shoulders. *Bare* shoulders by that time, he hoped.

But of course, he had to show some restraint and decorum. He wasn't an animal after all, consumed by his lust. Almost, but not quite. And he had brought home that pile of work from the office, he reminded himself. He needed to get at least some of it done before he and Rebel retired for the evening.

He mentioned that as he lingered over a snifter of cognac following dinner. "If I don't take care of some of it, I'll be too far behind when I start in the morning," he said. With a smile, he added, "Then I'll never get caught up."

"You should have had Edwin come over to help you with it," Rebel said. "I'm sure he wouldn't have minded. He's such a hard worker."

Conrad hesitated. Over the past few years, he had learned a great deal about the sort of natural caution that most Westerners practiced. Living in an often harsh and unforgiving land ingrained that in a person. Rebel was no different. She was probably more suspicious of people as a rule than he was.

Like everyone, though, she had her blind spots, and Edwin Sinclair was one of them. She seemed never to have seen the things that Conrad had, and he had never mentioned them to her.

Now, he said, "He offered to help, but I told him it wasn't necessary."

"Why would you do that?" Rebel asked with a frown. "Helping with paperwork is part of his job."

"Not after office hours it isn't."

"Yes, but if he doesn't mind . . . Anyway, you could always pay him a little bonus for extra work like that, if he's not too proud to accept it."

"I suppose." Conrad didn't want to argue with her, not tonight, so he smiled and promised, "I'll certainly keep that in mind next time." He swirled the cognac left in the snifter, then tilted it to his lips and drank the last of it. As he got to his feet, he said, "I won't work for more than an hour or so."

"I suppose I can be patient," Rebel said. "I'll clear away these dishes and then go upstairs to read for a while."

On several occasions, Conrad had suggested that they ask Mrs. O'Hannigan to stay in the evenings until after dinner, but Rebel had insisted that she was perfectly capable of cleaning up. Not only that, she said, but Mrs. O'Hannigan needed to get home to her own family as well.

That was another point Conrad hadn't argued. He knew that Rebel would be just as happy sitting next to an open campfire out on the trail as she was in the dining room of this big, two-story house on the outskirts of Carson City. Maybe even happier. So it was best, he thought, to let her do just as much as she wanted to do.

As he left the dining room and started down the hall toward his study, the image of Rebel in boots and jeans and a buckskin shirt drifted through his mind. Maybe if he could get ahead on his work, he could take some time off and they could head up into the high country on an extended trip. They could go on horseback, just the two of them, taking along enough supplies to last for a week or two. They wouldn't have to worry about fresh meat; the mountains were full of game, and Rebel was a superb shot with a rifle. Conrad could handle a long gun fairly well, too. They would be fine.

It was such an appealing prospect that Conrad stopped just outside the door to his study and sighed in anticipated pleasure.

A knock on the front door broke that reverie and put a puzzled frown on Conrad's face. They weren't expecting any visitors tonight. He had no idea who could be at the door.

"I'll get it," he called to Rebel as he started toward the front of the house. He didn't know if she had heard the knock, but in case she had, she would know that he was answering it.

When he swung the door open, the light from the foyer revealed Edwin Sinclair standing there on the porch, his hat in one hand and what appeared to be a yellow telegraph flimsy in the other. Conrad was surprised and not very happy to see Sinclair, especially after he had told the man not to come to the house this evening. But the telegram in Sinclair's hand meant that something important might have happened, so Conrad supposed he had to hear him out.

"Hello, Edwin," he said. "What are you doing here?"

Sinclair held up the yellow paper. "I received this wire that was intended for you, sir. I'm not quite sure how the messenger boy managed to make a mistake and deliver it to me instead, but that's what happened."

Conrad took the telegram and scanned the words printed on it in a bold, square hand. "Your name is on it as well as mine," he pointed out. "I'm sure that's what caused the mix-up." He continued reading as he spoke, then exclaimed, "What? Has Kirkson lost his mind? Did you read this, Edwin?"

"I did, sir. I was worried about the news, too."

"If Kirkson goes ahead with this plan, he'll cost us thousands of dollars." Ronald Kirkson was the manager of a steel plant in Pennsylvania owned largely by Conrad and his father. Conrad was no engineer, but even he could see that the changes in the manufacturing process Kirkson proposed would be tremendously inefficient.

"I imagine you'll want to wire him first thing in the morning to hold off on implementing the changes," Sinclair said. "In the meantime, since I'm already here, I'd be glad to help you go through some of that paperwork—"

"In the morning, hell!" Conrad broke in. "I'm

going to wire Kirkson tonight. Right now, in fact. I'm going to write out a message, and you can take it to the Western Union office and send it as a night letter."

"That will cost more," Sinclair said.

"Penny-wise, pound-foolish," Conrad quoted. "Come with me."

"Where are we going, sir?"

"To my study. I want to sit down while I'm figuring out the best way to tell Kirkson that he's a damned fool."

"Oh. All right."

Conrad closed the door and then stalked down the hall toward his study. Sinclair was close behind him.

"What about that other work?" Sinclair asked as they entered the study. "Those reports?"

"They can wait," Conrad snapped. "They're nothing but an annoyance. This is a crisis, or at least it will be if we don't avert it." He went behind the desk. "Pull up one of those armchairs, Edwin. This may take a little while."

"Perhaps I should go out to the kitchen and brew some coffee for us."

"No, that's all right," Conrad said. Rebel was probably still in the kitchen, and the last thing he wanted was for her and Sinclair to spend even a few minutes alone in such an intimate setting. He was probably wrong to distrust Sinclair, but wrong or not, he wanted to keep the man where he could see him.

He sat down behind the desk, pulled a blank sheet of paper in front of him, took up a pencil, and started composing a strongly worded message. "What do you think about this?" he asked Sinclair, then read the sentences to the secretary as he scrawled them on the paper. He might not fully trust Sinclair where Rebel was concerned, but the man was a good secretary and knew the business.

"That's very good, sir."

"Do you think it's clear enough that Kirkson will regret it if he goes through with this?"

"Oh, I think so, Mr. Browning. Quite clear." Sinclair paused. "I hope all this uproar doesn't disturb Mrs. Browning."

Conrad shook his head. "It won't. She's upstairs." He didn't know if she had gone up or not, but he wanted Sinclair to think she had.

Sinclair started to look uncomfortable, shifting around in the chair like a man with something bothering him. Conrad frowned at him and asked, "What's wrong?"

"I'm sorry, sir, but, I'm not feeling well. If I could use the, ah . . ."

Conrad waved a hand toward the door. "Of course, of course. You know where it is." Despite not fully trusting Sinclair, Conrad couldn't deny him the use of the facilities. He stood up and began to pace back and forth, reading the message over to himself as he did so. "I'll have this ready to go by the time you get back."

"Of course." With a vaguely embarrassed expression on his face, Sinclair slipped out of the room.

The thought crossed Conrad's mind that Sinclair might run into Rebel while he was gone, but he decided that was unlikely. When she was finished cleaning up in the kitchen, Rebel would probably use the rear stairs to go up to their room. She'd said she was going to read while Conrad worked on the reports from the office.

He didn't care about the reports now. As he'd told Sinclair, they weren't really urgent. This telegram from Kirkson had upset him, and he wasn't going to worry about the paperwork anymore. As soon as he'd sent Sinclair off to the Western Union office with the scorching reply, Conrad intended to do his best to forget all about work for the rest of the evening.

He went back to the desk, stood in front of it, and leaned over to cross out several words and substitute others. There, he thought as he straightened. That made the message even stronger. All he needed to do now was recopy it with all the corrections made. Or perhaps he'd get Sinclair to do that. The man had excellent handwriting.

Suddenly, Conrad frowned. He put down the message he'd been writing and picked up the telegraph flimsy he had dropped on the desk. Something about the printing on it was familiar. He had assumed that a telegrapher from the Western Union office had printed the message, but something about the bold strokes of the letters reminded him of Sinclair's writing.

That made no sense. Sinclair had said that the message was delivered to his room at a boardinghouse several blocks away. He couldn't have written it.

The secretary had left the door partially open when he left the study. Conrad heard it swing open behind him now, and he started to turn so that he could ask Sinclair what was going on here.

He didn't make it. A swift step sounded behind him, and something crashed into his skull. The blow's impact sent Conrad slumping forward. He dropped the telegram and caught himself by slapping his hands down flat on the desk. Groggy, half-stunned, he tried to push himself upright again.

The intruder hit him a second time, and this time his knees buckled. He couldn't hold himself up. The floor leaped up to smack him in the face. Conrad felt the rough nap of the rug in front of the desk scraping his cheek. He let out a groan that sounded to his ears as if it came from far, far away.

Then the sound faded out entirely, along with everything else, as Conrad lost consciousness.

It would have been easy to finish him off, Edwin Sinclair thought as he stared down at Conrad Browning, who lay on the study floor, out cold. A few more blows from the bludgeon he had carried into the house, concealed under his coat, and Browning's head would be a shattered, misshapen mess. He would never have Rebel again.

But he wouldn't be able to pay the ransom either, and without that, Lasswell, Moss, and the other hired gunmen wouldn't carry out their part of the plan. It was vital that Conrad Browning live through this night. That was why Sinclair had gone to the trouble of forging the message from Kirkson on a telegraph flimsy he had lifted from the Western Union office.

He didn't think that Browning would recognize his hand if he printed the words in as blocky a style as he could manage, and sure enough, the ruse had worked. Browning had accepted it as a genuine message from Kirkson. For a while, Sinclair had worried that there wouldn't be an opportunity for him to strike down Browning without being seen, but in the end, luck had been with him.

Now all that was left to do was to let Lasswell and the others into the house through the rear door. Sinclair slipped his watch out and checked the time. Five minutes until eight. He had almost shaved it too close.

As he put his watch away, he glanced down at Browning. Maybe it would be a good idea to tie him up. That was what real kidnappers would do, wasn't it? Of course, Lasswell and the others *were* real kidnappers, he reminded himself. They just had help that no one else would ever know about.

Sinclair yanked down one of the cords from the drapes and used it to bind Browning's hands behind his back. He wasn't any too gentle about it either, jerking Browning's arms around without worrying about whether or not he injured the bastard. He had hit Browning twice, so he didn't think there was any chance he'd regain consciousness any time soon, but just in case he did, this would take care of the problem. Sinclair used Browning's own handkerchief to gag him, tying the ball of cloth in place with another piece of drapery cord.

There, Sinclair thought as he straightened from his work, all trussed up like a pig on its way to market.

But now there was really no time to waste. He almost broke into a run as he hurried from the study and down the hall. His heart pounded heavily in his chest as he pushed open the door into the kitchen. He didn't know if it was from fear or anticipation or just sheer excitement at being part of something so audacious. He stepped into the room . . .

And his heart seemed to leap into his throat and freeze there as he saw Rebel standing at the foot of the rear stairs.

"Edwin!" she said, obviously surprised to see him. But then she smiled, like the sun coming up and chasing away the shadows of night, and went on. "I didn't know you were here. Did you come to help Conrad with all that paperwork after all?"

Before he could answer, a soft knock sounded on the rear door.

Judging by Rebel's expression, she was even more surprised by that than she was by Sinclair's unexpected appearance in her kitchen. She said, "Who in the world can that be at this time of night? Maybe Mrs. O'Hannigan forgot something."

She started toward the door, clearly intending to answer it.

Sinclair sprang forward. "Let me," he said. "You seemed to be on your way upstairs. You should go ahead. It's probably a tradesman at the door. I'll deal with him."

"Nonsense," Rebel said. "This is my house. I can answer my own—"

Lasswell must have run out of patience. A boot heel crashed against the door just below the knob, springing it open. The door flew back. Rebel let out a startled cry as she jerked herself out of its way.

"Edwin, run!" she shouted. "Get Conrad!"

Shocked, struggling to figure out what to do next, Sinclair stayed rooted to the floor. A couple of hard-faced men rushed into the kitchen with guns drawn. Sinclair had never seen either of them before, but he knew they must be some of Lasswell's men.

Rebel reacted with the sort of blinding speed that Sinclair would have expected from that gunfighter father-in-law of hers. She snatched up an empty coffeepot from the stove and swung it at one of the men, crashing it against the side of his head. He stumbled into his companion and dropped his gun. Rebel was on it like a hawk, scooping it up before it hardly had a chance to hit the floor. She shot the second man at such close range that the flame licking out from the gun muzzle scorched the man's shirt as the bullet punched into his chest.

Sinclair had made it clear to Lasswell and Moss that Rebel wasn't to be hurt, but he didn't know if the gunmen would be able to control themselves when someone started shooting at them. They might return her fire. He couldn't let that happen. He leaped toward her, wrapped his arms around her from behind, and said, "Rebel, no!" He got one hand on her wrist and forced the gun toward the floor.

More men burst into the room, among them Lasswell and Moss. Lasswell's bearded, leathery face creased into a grin as he said, "Looks like you decided to jump right in there and grab her yourself, Sinclair."

Sinclair bit back a groan of despair. Now everything really *was* ruined. He had hoped for a second that he could pass off his actions as merely fearing for her safety, but now Rebel had to realize that he was part of the plan. Otherwise, Lasswell wouldn't have known his name.

He would just have to make the best of it. If he disappeared along with Rebel, Browning and everyone else would believe that the intruders had kidnapped him, too. He could go with Lasswell and the others, and once the ransom was paid and he had his share, he could take Rebel and leave Carson City far behind. They would go to Mexico, he thought. She would go with him, and in time, she would learn to love him.

He twisted the gun out of her hand and threw it on the floor, then shoved her toward the outlaws. "Here," he snapped. "Get her on a horse, and let's get out of here."

Two of the men grabbed her. One of them was a giant with a moon face. Sinclair didn't like the leer the man wore as he looked at Rebel.

She twisted and struggled in their grip, but she had no chance of getting away. Turning her head, she looked straight at him and said, "You son of a bitch. Conrad will kill you for this, and if he doesn't, I will!"

Lasswell chuckled. "Better be careful, boys, she's a wildcat. Hurry up now. That shot means we ain't got time to waste."

One of the men pointed at the one Rebel had shot and said, "What about Ray?"

"Get him on his horse, too," Lasswell ordered. "Maybe he'll make it." He looked at Sinclair. "You talked like you was comin' with us, mister."

"Of course I'm coming with you," Sinclair snapped. "I can't stay here now. She knows I was part of it."

In fact, Rebel was still glaring murderously at him as the two men dragged her out of the house. Sinclair hoped they wouldn't treat her too rough.

"Well, here's the problem," Lasswell said. "We ain't got a horse for you."

"I'll ride double with someone, then." Sinclair took a step toward the door. "Let's go. As you said, there's no time to waste."

Lasswell put out a hand to stop him. "Sorry, Sinclair. Your part in this is over here and now."

"What? You're insane! I can't stay here. *She knows.*" Sinclair shook his head impatiently. "I realize we can't follow the original plan now, with me pretending to rescue her and everything—"

"That was never the plan," Lasswell said.

Sinclair frowned. "Of course it was. I was going to rescue her—"

"Nope. You were just here to knock out Browning, so we could grab the gal without havin' to worry about hurtin' him. Like I said, you're done."

"I most certainly am not!"

Lasswell looked past Sinclair and said, "Julio."

Sinclair hadn't realized that one of the men was behind him. He'd been so upset about his part in the plan being revealed to Rebel that he hadn't been paying much attention to anything else. Now as he started to turn, he felt a sudden, sharp, white-hot pain in his back. He gasped.

A second jolt of agony lanced through him. Someone had stabbed him, he realized as he stumbled forward. Then Moss stepped up and hit him in the belly, causing him to double over and fall to his knees. An icy chill that coursed through his entire body replaced the hot pain in his back.

"When Browning comes to and gets loose, he'll figure you got yourself killed tryin' to defend his poor wife," Lasswell said as he loomed over Sinclair. "He won't know better until he gets her back . . . *if* he gets her back."

"You . . . you can't . . ." Sinclair gasped.

Lasswell looked past him again and nodded. Someone grabbed his hair and jerked his head back, and he felt something tug at his throat, followed instantly by a hot, wet gush.

"Your throat's just been cut, you damn fool," Lasswell told him. "You're so stupid, you had it comin'."

Sinclair blinked. He couldn't talk, couldn't breathe, and he suddenly felt incredibly sleepy. There was surprisingly little pain. Someone shoved him from behind, and he fell facedown. He wasn't sure, but he thought he smelled the coppery scent of his own blood pooling around his head.

It wasn't fair, he thought. He was going to die on the kitchen floor of Conrad Browning's house. He was going to die without ever seeing Rebel again. He was going to die . . .

He did.

Chapter 5

Conrad heard someone groaning, and gradually became aware that it was him. He was adrift in a deep, black sea, the waves jolting him back and forth. After what seemed like an eternity, he realized that the waves were actually the pulsing of blood in his head.

He was alive.

That knowledge brought strength and determination with it, but they seeped slowly into his body and brain. Finally, he tried to move his arms, but they were pulled behind him in an awkward position and wouldn't budge. Someone had tied him up, and the uncomfortable, soggy lump in his mouth was a gag of some sort. He moved his head and felt his chin scrape against something rough. He knew that he was lying on the rug in front of his desk.

Then it all came flooding back to him.

Sinclair. That bastard.

Sinclair had to be the one who had hit him and knocked him out. Conrad wasn't sure *why*, but he was certain it had been Sinclair. In that instant before everything had fallen in on him, he had realized that the writing on the telegraph form was his secretary's. Sinclair had printed the message in an attempt to disguise his hand, but it hadn't worked. Conrad had recognized those decisive strokes.

So the telegram was a lie. Kirkson wasn't going to change everything at the steel manufacturing plant. Sinclair had dreamed up the whole thing so he'd have an excuse to get into Conrad's house. But why?

Rebel!

The answer shot through Conrad's veins like a jolt of that newfangled electric current. And like that electric current, it galvanized his muscles into action. Conrad lurched up onto his knees, ignoring the fresh pain that pounded in his skull like the sound of distant drums and the agony in his shoulders. He leaned against the desk to brace himself and shoved with his legs until he was on his feet.

He had to free himself and get to Rebel.

Easier said than done. The room spun crazily around him as he turned his back to the desk. His hands had gone numb enough that he could barely feel them as he fumbled around for the letter opener he knew was on the desk. At last he found it, and struggled to turn the blade so that he could use it to saw through the cord binding his wrists. Luckily, the cord wasn't very thick and parted within a few minutes. Even so, those minutes seemed like an eternity to Conrad, because all he could think of was that something terrible might be happening to Rebel.

When his wrists were free, he pulled his hands in front of him again and took a moment to massage some feeling back into them. Then he ripped the gag out of his mouth and took a step toward the door.

He reeled, and would have fallen if he hadn't managed to grab the back of the chair where Sinclair had been sitting earlier. Conrad dragged a deep breath into his body and waited a few seconds. No matter what was going on, no matter what danger threatened, he couldn't do Rebel any good if he passed out again. He had to stay awake and on his feet.

Even though he stumbled a little, his stride was stronger when he started for the door again. He grasped the jamb to steady himself as he stepped out into the hall. "Rebel!" he shouted. His voice sounded distorted to his ears. "Rebel, where are you?"

No answer. In this case, maybe the worst answer of all.

She had said she was going upstairs. Conrad wasn't sure he could manage stairs just yet. If he took a tumble down them, he might break a leg, or hit his head and knock himself out again.

The rear stairs, he thought. They were narrower than the main staircase. He could press a hand against each wall and brace himself. He staggered toward the kitchen.

As soon as Conrad shoved the door open and stepped into the room, he recognized the smell in the air. He had seen enough gruesome death to know what freshly spilled blood smelled like. He stopped in his tracks and stared down stupidly at the figure lying on the floor in front of him.

It was Edwin Sinclair, Conrad realized. The secretary lay facedown. A large pool of reddish-black blood had formed around his head and was slowly soaking into the hardwood floor. Several large crimson stains marred the back of his suit coat. In the middle of one of those stains, the handle and part of the blade of a knife protruded from Sinclair's body.

And pinned to the corpse with that knife was a piece of paper.

Conrad lurched forward. He saw his name written on the paper and knew it was meant for him. He dropped to his knees beside Sinclair and reached for the knife. He wrapped his fingers around the handle and pulled it free. The blade made an ugly sound as it came out of Sinclair's lifeless flesh.

Conrad heard other sounds, but they meant nothing to him. A door slamming, voices shouting, heavy footsteps . . . He ignored all of them. Every bit of his attention was focused on the words crudely printed on the paper, which Edwin Sinclair's blood had stained in places. Sinclair hadn't written this note.

WE HAV YUR WIF. DO WHAT WE SAY OR WELL KILL HER. YULL HERE FROM US.

Rebel was gone, taken from their house by strangers, intruders who had killed the secretary. Had he been wrong about Sinclair? Conrad asked himself.

"Good Lord!" a gravelly voice exclaimed. "Put that knife down, mister. I've got you covered."

Numbly, Conrad looked around. Carson City had an actual police force now, not just a local marshal and deputies, as befitted the capital city of the whole state. Two uniformed officers stood just inside the kitchen, revolvers in their hands. They pointed the guns at Conrad, and he realized that he was still holding the knife. Not only that, but he was kneeling beside the bloody corpse of his own secretary.

"This isn't . . . what it looks like," he managed to rasp after a moment.

"What is it, then?" one of the officers demanded. "It looks to me like you stabbed that poor son of a gun."

Conrad held the paper out so the man could read it for himself. Suddenly, he was too tired to explain.

Too tired, and too filled with fear for his wife.

The presence of the note made it clear that Conrad hadn't killed Edwin Sinclair. The chief of Carson City's police force admitted that as he sat in Conrad's study an hour later.

"Your secretary must have tried to fight off the kidnappers," the chief said. "He paid for it with his life, but at least he tried."

Conrad rubbed his temples as he sat behind the desk. The dull, throbbing ache in his head hadn't gone away.

But it wasn't as bad as the ache in his heart.

"I misjudged poor Sinclair," he said. "To tell the truth, I wasn't sure I trusted the man. In business, yes, but not that much around my wife."

The chief raised his eyebrows. "You shouldn't say things like that, Mr. Browning," he advised. "Some folks might figure that was a motive for murder. Of course, in this case, we know the kidnappers are to blame for Sinclair's death."

"Chief, do you have any experience with things like this?"

"Well . . . no, sir, I don't. This is the first kidnapping I remember ever taking place in these parts. But I've heard about such things, and I reckon it's only a matter of time before you hear from those varmints again. They'll have to tell you how much money they want, and where and how you're supposed to deliver it."

"Do you think they'll want me to bring the money in person?"

The chief scratched his jaw. "That wouldn't surprise me. They'll figure you'd be less likely to try some sort of trick that way." He hesitated. "You *are* going to pay?"

"Of course," Conrad snapped. "I'd pay any amount of money to get my wife back safely."

But that didn't mean he was going to let those bastards get away with what they had done, he thought. They had to pay for taking Edwin Sinclair's life, and for the ordeal they were putting Rebel through.

Conrad wouldn't let himself think about what might be happening to her. Rebel was strong and smart. She would do whatever she needed to do in order to live through this. For the moment, her survival was all that mattered.

Vengeance would come later.

Even though he was willing to wait, Conrad had taken the first step toward settling the score with the kidnappers. He had written out a wire and prevailed on one of the police officers to take it to the Western Union office. The urgent message was addressed to Claudius Turnbuckle in San Francisco, a partner in one of the law firms that represented the Browning interests. The last time Conrad had seen his father, Frank Morgan had been on his way to Los Angeles to lend a hand to Turnbuckle's partner, John J. Stafford. Conrad didn't know if that affair had already been settled, but Turnbuckle would. The lawyer might have at least an idea of how to get in touch with Frank.

Because Conrad didn't mind admitting that he needed his father's help again.

"We'll do everything we can to help," the chief

was saying now, "but our job is really keeping the peace here in town. You might want to give some thought to hiring the Pinkertons, or some outfit like that, if you want to track down the men who did this."

"I know someone who can find them," Conrad said, thinking of Frank.

The chief must have understood what he meant, because he nodded and said, "Oh. Yeah, you're probably right about that."

The problem was that it might take days to locate Frank, and even longer for him to get here. Conrad didn't think the kidnappers would wait that long to make their demands. They would move quickly, in hopes of getting their hands on the ransom and making their getaway before anyone had a chance to corral them. He would probably have to handle that part himself, without Frank's help.

The chief put his hands on his knees and pushed himself to his feet. "If there's anything I can do for you, Mr. Browning, don't hesitate to let me know," he said. "In the meantime, I don't reckon there's much any of us can do except wait. Maybe you should try to get some rest."

"Yes, of course," Conrad said, even though he had no intention of resting again until Rebel was at his side once more. He shook hands with the chief of police and thanked him. Then, the chief left, and he was alone.

He had never been alone in this house, he realized. Rebel had always been with him. He felt a sharp pang of loss as that sunk in on him.

Staying busy would help, he thought. A cabinet on one side of the room held several Winchesters, a double-barreled shotgun, a long-range European sporting rifle, and half a dozen Colt revolvers. Checking and cleaning all those weapons would take time. Conrad wanted to be sure he had plenty of ammunition on hand for all of them, too.

There was no telling how many guns he might need before this was over.

By morning, Conrad still hadn't slept. The ache in his head had faded some but was still there. He went into the kitchen to make some coffee, but stopped short when he saw the large, dark stain on the floor. The undertaker's men had cleaned up the blood as best they could when they came to collect Edwin Sinclair's body, but nothing would get rid of that stain. The floor would have to be replaced. Once Rebel was back, the two of them could go on that trip to the high country, Conrad thought, and while they were gone, someone could come in here and do the work on the house that needed to be done to cleanse it of every reminder of what had happened.

A knock on the front door as he stood there contemplating the bloodstain made him jerk around. His long legs carried him quickly to the door. He had to force himself not to run.

When he opened the door, he found a boy about twelve years old standing on the porch. He looked like a typical frontier youngster in boots and overalls and with a round-brimmed hat. He gazed up at Conrad and asked, "Are you Mr. Browning?"

"That's right," Conrad said.

"An hombre told me to give this to you." The boy held out a folded piece of paper. "He said you'd give me a nickel."

Conrad took the paper. When he unfolded it, he saw that the words on it were printed in the same crude block letters as the message that had been left for him the night before. He recognized that before the actual meaning of the words sunk in on him.

BRING 50 GRAND TO BLACK ROCK CANYON TONIGHT MIDNIGHT COME ALONE.

Conrad's heart pounded hard in his chest. Fifty thousand dollars was an incredible amount of money. Most men wouldn't earn that much in a lifetime. He had it, though, and he didn't mind spending it if that would insure Rebel's safe return.

Unfortunately, there were no guarantees that the kidnappers would keep their word.

"How about that nickel, mister?" the boy who had delivered the message prodded.

Conrad reached in his pocket and brought out a double eagle. The boy's eyes widened at the sight of it.

"I'll do better than that," Conrad said. "This is yours if you can give me a good description of the man who gave you the message for me."

"Sure! He was older than you, and sort of skinny. He had a reddish-colored beard that sort of poked out from his chin."

"How was he dressed?"

The boy frowned. "Well, I never paid much attention to that. Like a cowboy, I'd say. I know he had on boots and an old Stetson."

"Anything else you can tell me about him?"

"Not really," the boy said with a shrug. "He was just a fella."

"Was anybody with him?"

"Nope. He was by himself. I know that."

"Where did you see him?"

The boy turned and pointed toward the road that led northwest out of Carson City. "He was up yonder, about half a mile, I reckon. He was just sittin' on his horse in some trees when I walked by and he called me over. He asked me if I knew you or where you lived. When I said I didn't, he told me how to find your house and gave me the paper."

"What about his horse?"

"It was a big chestnut gelding."

Conrad's heart had started to beat faster as the boy described the man who had given him the note. The description of the horse was the last bit of evidence Conrad needed. He remembered both man and horse from the encounter on the hillside overlooking the city several days earlier. He had no doubt that the kidnappers were the men who had interrupted the picnic he and Rebel had been enjoying.

Which meant that the encounter probably wasn't a coincidence. Those men had been following them, probably plotting their crime even then. Conrad suspected that they had wanted to get a good look at him and Rebel.

They must have decided it would be easy to steal her away from him, he thought bitterly.

"Mister?"

Conrad looked down at the boy and forced a solemn smile onto his face. He held out the double eagle.

"Here. You've earned this."

The youngster snatched the coin and bit it to make sure it was real, obviously a habit with him. He grinned and said, "Thanks, mister." He started to run away, then stopped and looked back at Conrad. "That note I brought you . . . was it bad news?"

"I don't know yet," he said honestly.

He wouldn't know—until midnight tonight.

Chapter 6

Despite the vow he had made to himself earlier about not resting until Rebel was safe again, Conrad knew he couldn't afford to be groggy tonight from lack of sleep. He would need to be alert, with all his senses functioning at top efficiency. For that reason, he went upstairs and forced himself to lie down on the bed in the guest room. He couldn't bring himself to stretch out by himself on the bed he normally shared with Rebel.

Exhaustion overwhelmed him, and he fell asleep with surprising ease even though he hadn't taken off his clothes. His dreams were haunted, though, by nightmares in which shadowy, faceless, evil figures were chasing Rebel through a dark, seemingly endless forest. More than once he jolted awake, only to fall back almost right away into a stupor that turned into yet another of the horrible dreams.

It was the middle of the day when he woke up and stayed awake. As he stumbled down the stairs, he spotted a Western Union envelope on the floor just inside the front door. He had sent instructions with the message to Claudius Turnbuckle that Western Union was to bring any reply to him right away, no matter what time it was, day or night. He supposed he had been sleeping so soundly that he hadn't heard the messenger knocking on the front door.

Conrad practically pounced on the telegram. He tore open the envelope and pulled out a yellow flimsy like the one Sinclair had brought to the house the previous night. This one read:

MORGAN'S WHEREABOUTS UNKNOWN AT
PRESENT STOP WILL ATTEMPT TO LOCATE WITH
ALL URGENCY STOP ANYTHING ELSE I CAN DO
TO HELP STOP TURNBUCKLE

Conrad heaved a sigh and suppressed the urge to crumple the telegram in his hand. That wouldn't do any good. He couldn't help but be disappointed, though. He had hoped that Frank was somewhere close by.

It looked like Conrad couldn't count on his father's help with this problem.

He took the telegram into his study and left it on the desk. Then he cleaned up a little, shaving and changing clothes. He had to pay a visit to the bank, and he didn't want to look like he had slept in his clothes—which, of course, he had.

Conrad did business with the bank in the same building where his downtown office was located. He went there now, hitching up the buggy horse and driving the half mile. When he walked into the bank, he carried a good-sized carpetbag with him.

A clerk ushered him into the bank manager's office without delay. The man stood up and shook hands with Conrad, smiling with the same eager affability that he used to greet any large depositor.

"What can I do for you, Mr. Browning?" the man asked.

"I need fifty thousand dollars," Conrad said.

The manager prided himself on being unflappable, but even he gaped at that unexpected statement. For a moment, he couldn't speak. Then he said, "But . . . but that's a great deal of money, Mr. Browning!"

Conrad nodded. "I know that. I need it anyway."

"But why?"

Conrad allowed his tone to grow chilly. "No offense, but that's not really any of your business, is it?"

The bank manager clasped his hands behind his back and squared his shoulders. "Actually, it is," he said. "I have a responsibility to the depositors to protect their money. You don't have fifty thousand dollars in this bank, sir, so I'd be giving you other people's money."

"You know perfectly well I'm good for it," Conrad snapped. "You can wire my banks in Boston and Denver and San Francisco if you don't believe me."

"Oh, I believe you," the manager said quickly. He had been taken by surprise, but he didn't want to offend Conrad if he didn't have to. "It's just that there are procedures we normally follow—"

"I don't have time for normal procedures." Conrad placed the carpetbag on the manager's desk. "When I leave here, I need to have fifty thousand dollars in this bag."

The man ventured a nervous laugh. "You sound almost like a holdup man, Mr. Browning."

Conrad's face remained impassive as he said, "If that's what it takes."

The manager swallowed hard. "No . . . no, of course not. You're well known to be a man of sterling reputation. Of course you're good for the money. It won't be necessary to wire any of your other banks." He went to the door of his office, opened it, and called to the clerk who had announced Conrad a few minutes earlier. Quietly, the manager said, "Joseph, I want you to begin putting together a package of cash for Mr. Browning. Fifty thousand dollars. And be discreet about it."

The clerk's eyes widened. "Did you say—"

"You heard what I said," the manager snapped. "Hop to it!"

"Yes, sir!"

The manager closed the door again and turned back to Conrad. "We're more than happy to help you with this, Mr. Browning," he said. "But if there's anything else I can do . . . I mean, if you're in some sort of trouble . . ."

"What makes you think that?"

The manager looked solemn as he said, "Whenever someone needs a great deal of money in a hurry, there's always some sort of trouble."

The chief of police had promised to keep the news of Rebel's kidnapping quiet. Obviously, he had kept his word. If the story had leaked out, the bank manager would have heard about it by now.

Conrad smiled. "I appreciate your concern, but this is something I have to handle myself. I can promise you, I won't forget about how you're cooperating with me."

"We'll do anything we can to help, Mr. Browning. You know that."

A short time later, the clerk came back to the office carrying a box that contained bundles of twenty- and fifty-dollar bills. He placed it on the manager's desk and said, "Will there be anything else, sir?"

The manager looked at Conrad, who shook his head.

When the clerk was gone, Conrad and the manager both counted the money to be sure the amount was correct; then Conrad placed the bills in the carpetbag. The bag was fairly heavy when he was finished. He signed a receipt for the money, then said, "I'm sure that I can count on your discretion?"

"Of course," the manager answered. "No one will hear about this from me."

"I'll replace these funds, one way or another, within forty-eight hours." If the ransom payoff went off without a hitch and he got Rebel back safely, he would have fifty thousand sent to the Carson City bank from one of his other banks. If it didn't . . .

Conrad wouldn't allow himself to think about that.

As Conrad started to leave the office, the bank manager said, "Surely, you'd like one of our guards to go with you, Mr. Browning. That's a great deal of money to be carrying around with you."

"I'm aware of that," Conrad said. He pulled back his coat so that the manager could see the butts of the Colt .45s tucked behind his belt on each hip. "That's why I'm taking precautions of my own."

The manager didn't say anything to that. He just stared at the man in his office as if he had never seen Conrad before.

And it was true—he had never seen *this* Conrad Browning. This Conrad Browning had appeared only a few times in the past, when faced with danger to himself or someone he loved. This Conrad Browning was his father's son.

Conrad carried the carpetbag with him when he

stopped at a clothing store on his way home. He came out half an hour later with a paper-wrapped bundle under his other arm. One more stop, at a local gunsmith's shop, and then he went back to his house to continue getting ready for that night.

Black Rock Canyon was northwest of the city, well off the road to Reno and not far from Lake Tahoe. Conrad had been there once, when he was investigating some land he was thinking about buying, just over the state line in California. One trail led through the canyon, which was steep-sided and covered with pines. No one lived there; it was dark and desolate, and above it loomed a huge bluff that gave the place its name. An appropriate lair for the sort of evil bastards who would abduct a man's wife, he thought.

When he had awoken from his troubled sleep earlier in the day, the beginnings of a plan had been in the back of his mind. First and foremost was Rebel's safety, of course, but once that was assured, he planned to go after the men who had taken her, with all the forces at his command. Also, he knew better than to assume that the gang would return her even if he paid the ransom. The chances that they would try to pull a double cross were high. If that happened, Conrad was going to be ready for them, or at least he was going to try to be. He would have felt a lot better about his chances if he'd had his father siding him.

But he had known for years that he wouldn't always have Frank Morgan to help him. The time had come for him to grow up and handle his own problems. Stomp his own snakes, as Frank would put it.

He opened the bundle he had brought from the clothing store and laid out his purchases on the bed in the spare room. He had bought a pair of black whipcord trousers and a black bib-front shirt, as well as a flat-crowned black Stetson. He already owned a pair of black, high-topped boots. At the gunsmith's shop, he had picked up a holster and cartridge belt of fine black leather. If it was necessary, he wanted to be able to blend into the shadows. The black outfit would make that easier. He planned to wear it underneath his regular clothes. The gunbelt would be in the buggy, along with a Winchester and his shotgun.

The kidnappers would be expecting a scared, inexperienced Easterner. That was what Conrad would give them—up to a point. But if they went back on the deal, or if Rebel was hurt in any way . . .

Then the man they would have to deal with would be someone else entirely.

Lasswell was beginning to wonder if the payoff would be worth it. He'd hardly had a moment's peace since they'd snatched that crazy bitch out of her house the night before.

At the moment, she was tied and gagged, the first time she had been quiet for more than a minute or two. For a gal who was married to a rich businessman from back East, she could cuss like a Texas cowboy who'd been following a trail herd and eating dust all the way to Kansas. Lasswell knew that for a fact, because he had been a cowboy just like that, years earlier as a kid, before he'd decided that following the owlhoot trail was more to his liking.

It was dangerous to get too close to her, too. Clem Baggott had made that mistake. Mrs. Browning had gotten her teeth fastened on his left ear and damn near ripped it off his head before Carlson pulled her away from him. Carlson had taken advantage of the opportunity to run his hands over her breasts, and she had repaid him by twisting around and kicking him in the balls. Howling in pain, Carlson had back-handed her and knocked her a good ten feet. When Abel Dean and Spence Hooper rushed over to grab her and keep her from getting away, she'd hauled off and punched Spence in the face hard enough to break his nose. Gant and White Rock had had to pile on as well to bring her under control.

And that was just getting her out of the house and onto a horse.

By the time they were able to ride away from there, Lasswell had gotten pretty worried that the law would show up. That didn't happen, though, and he started to think that maybe nobody had heard that shot after all.

Their camp was at the foot of the bluff that loomed over Black Rock Canyon. Finding the place in the dark was difficult, but Lasswell had been over the ground enough in the past few days so that he was able to do it. Once they got there, he had told Mrs. Browning that they would leave her legs untied and not gag her if she would promise to behave. Not only had she not made that promise, she had told him to go to hell and then do something physically impossible once he got there. Lasswell had never run into a woman quite like her.

Her hair had come loose from its upswept curls and hung in disarray around her face. Her eyes burned with anger and hatred, and Lasswell knew by looking at her that if she had been loose and had a gun in her hand, he'd be a dead man by now. They'd all be dead if she had her way.

If he had been thirty years younger, he thought, he

could come damn near falling in love with a woman like Rebel Browning.

Sure made him sorry about what was going to happen. But he had his orders, and he intended to carry them out; otherwise, he might not get paid. A man didn't have to be young to be in love with money.

All day long she had carried on, tied hand and foot and lying under a pine tree. Lasswell had finally gotten fed up and told a couple of men to gag her. Rattigan had almost lost a finger trying to follow that order.

Moss came over to Lasswell and said, "Duncan just died."

Lasswell grimaced. "Damn. Ray was a good man. He hung on longer'n I expected him to really."

"If he was a good man, he wouldn't have let a girl shoot him."

Lasswell felt a flash of anger toward Moss. "I rode with him for a long while, you didn't," he snapped. "I reckon I know how good he was. Anyway, that ain't no regular gal. She's a hellcat if ever I saw one."

Moss shrugged and then lowered his voice. "Carlson's gettin' some of the boys stirred up. He wants to have a go at her, and the others think they ought to have a turn, too."

"I never said anybody could do that."

"You never said they couldn't either."

Moss had a point. But Moss didn't know the rest of the plan. Nobody did except Lasswell. He was the only one who had actually talked to the boss. The orders he had were very specific, and they didn't include molesting Mrs. Browning. But he had allowed the other men to believe they might get a chance to have some fun with their captive, thinking that might make them more inclined to go along with what he wanted. He saw now that might have been a mistake.

"All right," he said with a weary sigh. "I reckon we'd better clear the air."

The sun was low enough in the sky so that thick shadows were gathering under the trees. Lasswell strode through them to the center of the camp and called, "Everybody gather 'round. I got somethin' to say."

The men formed a rough circle around him. Lasswell looked at them and thumbed his hat back on his head. Then he lowered his hand and hooked his thumb behind his gunbelt, so that his fingers hung near the butt of his Colt.

"There's been some complainin' around the camp because you fellas ain't had a chance to get more . . . friendly-like . . . with Mrs. Browning."

"Damn straight," Carlson said.

"Well, I'm here to tell you, that ain't gonna happen."

The men stared at him in surprise. Some of them, like Rattigan, didn't seem to care all that much. Others, like Titus Gant and the Winchell brothers, looked mad.

Carlson was the most upset, though. "What the hell are you talkin' about?" he demanded. He waved a big hand toward Rebel. "She's right there, and she can't do a damned thing to stop us. Why can't we take turns with her?"

"Because I say you can't," Lasswell said. "I'm the boss of this outfit, and what I say goes."

"Is it because you want her for yourself?" Gant asked. He wore a black frock coat and a string tie, and when he wasn't holding up banks or trains—or kidnapping women—he dealt faro in saloons. His voice was soft, but Lasswell recognized a dangerous quality in it. Maybe Carlson *wasn't* the one he ought to be worrying about the most.

"That ain't it," he said. "We took Mrs. Browning for the ransom money. That's all I'm thinkin' about."

"Her husband won't know that he's not getting her back in exactly the same condition as he saw her last until after he's paid the money," Gant pointed out.

"Yeah, well, what if he won't hand over the loot until he's talked to her? If she tells him that you fellas molested her, he might not pay."

Gant shook his head. "That's loco. He won't be calling the shots. If he tries anything like that, we'll just kill 'em both and take the money anyway."

"Not if he's hidden it somewhere." Lasswell was trying to think of arguments he could use to convince them without having to tell them the truth. "I'm tellin' you, we got to be careful and cover all our bets."

Gant sneered and brushed his coat back. "And I'm telling you I intend to have that woman before we give her back to her husband."

Lasswell sighed. He read the challenge on Gant's face and in the gambler's stance, and he knew that he couldn't let it go unanswered.

With a flickering move that filled his hand and gave Gant no chance, Lasswell drew and fired.

He was close enough so that the bullet drove Gant back a couple of steps as it thudded into his chest. Gant tried to draw, but his body was no longer following his commands. He weaved to the side and then spun off his feet, crashing to the ground.

Lasswell stood there, apparently as casual as he had been a couple of heartbeats earlier, when Gant was still alive. Smoke curled from the barrel of the gun in his hand.

"Let's make it simple," he said. "None of you are gonna bother Mrs. Browning because I say you ain't. That plain enough for you?"

Nobody argued, not even Carlson. A few of the men muttered agreement, and the gathering broke up, the men drifting away to see to their horses or roll a smoke or get a card game going. Lasswell told the Winchell brothers to grab some shovels and start digging. They had both Gant and Ray Duncan to bury.

Moss came over to Lasswell, who had replaced the spent shell and pouched his iron. "I remember you now," he said quietly. "You were part of that big feud in Texas about twenty-five years ago. Seems like I recall hearin' something about a shoot-out in a saloon in Comanche. Fella named Lasswell downed four of the other bunch even though he had a couple of slugs in him."

"I'm still carryin' around one of those slugs," Lasswell said, "and it hurts like the dickens whenever it's about to rain."

"Hell, man, you're a gunfighter!"

Lasswell shook his head. "Not to speak of, not when there are men like Frank Morgan still alive. That's why I wouldn't go into this job with just me and the boys who'd been ridin' with me. Just the chance we might have to go up against Morgan is enough to make me mighty careful."

"Well, I reckon you won't have to worry about any of them comin' at you head-on," Moss said. "After seein' that draw, they won't want to do that. Gant was a pretty slick gun-thrower, and he didn't even clear leather." A shadow of a smile crossed Moss's granite face. "All you'll have to do is watch out behind you."

"I always do," Lasswell said.

Chapter 7

After night had fallen—after what had been the longest day of his life, without a doubt—Conrad went out to the carriage house and hitched the big buckskin horse to the buggy. The animal was more than just a buggy horse; Conrad had used him as a saddle mount before and knew the buckskin had plenty of speed and stamina. He stowed his saddle in the back of the buggy, along with the Winchester and the shotgun and the coiled shell belt.

He hoped he wouldn't need any of those things. He hoped that he would turn the money over to the kidnappers and that they would give him Rebel in return. But if it didn't work out that way, he was going after them. He would kill anyone who got in his way, until his wife was safe again.

It would take about two hours to reach Black Rock Canyon, Conrad estimated. He drove out of Carson City a quarter of an hour before ten o'clock, to give himself plenty of time. The carpetbag with the fifty thousand dollars in it was at his feet.

On his way out of town, he stopped at the Western

Union office to see if there were any more messages from Claudius Turnbuckle concerning Frank Morgan, but of course there weren't. Conrad had known there wouldn't be. But he had checked just to·make sure.

The kidnappers had picked a good night for their evil purposes. The moon was only a thin sliver of silver in the sky, so the night was at its darkest, lit mostly by the millions of stars. They wouldn't do much good in Black Rock Canyon.

Conrad's thoughts were a confused, frightened jumble in his head. Most of the fright was for Rebel's safety, of course, but he knew he was nervous about how he would handle himself tonight as well. Danger had tested him in the past and he had always come through, but that was no guarantee he would again. He had big footsteps to follow, the footsteps of Frank Morgan.

That's loco, Conrad, he seemed to hear his father saying. *Follow your own trail, not mine, and don't walk in fear. You'll be all right. You'll do just fine. Do your best, and don't back down.*

Conrad took comfort from the words. A flesh-and-blood Frank Morgan would have been better, but right now he would take what he could get.

He was able to find the trail to Black Rock Canyon without much difficulty, although a time or two he worried that he had taken a wrong turn. Eventually, though, he spotted the huge rock formation that loomed above the canyon and knew he was in the right place. The bluff towered eighty or a hundred feet above the canyon floor, and formed a patch of even deeper darkness because it blotted out some of the stars. Conrad saw it above the tops of the pine trees that bordered the trail.

He didn't know when or how the kidnappers would stop him and demand the ransom, but he assumed they would whenever they were good and ready. He didn't bother taking out his watch to check the time. He would have had to strike a match in order to see it, and he didn't want to do that.

Every muscle in his body was taut with tension. His heart pounded, causing the blood to pulse in a frantic drumbeat inside his head. He had trouble catching his breath. He imagined this must be what it felt like to be drowning.

Suddenly, a voice called out, "That's far enough, Browning!"

Conrad hauled back hard on the reins. He was glad the kidnappers were confronting him at last. Anything was better than just driving slowly along in the buggy and waiting for them to show themselves.

What happened next surprised him. Several torches blazed into life along both sides of the trail. The harsh light from them washed over the buggy so that Conrad couldn't make a move without the kidnappers being able to see what he was doing. They were smart. They didn't trust him any more than he trusted them.

A man stepped out into the middle of the trail, in front of the buggy. Conrad half expected to see the ginger-bearded man, but this fellow was one he'd never seen before. He was tall and burly, with a deeply tanned, rough-hewn face.

"Are you alone, Browning?" he asked.

"Your note said for me to come alone," Conrad snapped. "I'm cooperating. I want my wife back."

"You'll get her, if you do as you're told. If you don't . . ." The man waved a hand toward the trees alongside the trail. "There are a dozen rifles trained on you right now. Try any tricks, and you'll wind up ventilated."

Conrad looked toward the trees. Enough light from the torches penetrated into the shadows underneath them for him to be able to see the barrels of those rifles the kidnapper had mentioned. He also caught glimpses of some of the men holding the weapons. He recognized several of them from the previous encounter, including a huge, moonfaced man who was so big, he stuck out from both sides of the tree trunk he was using for cover, a bearded Mexican with a steeple-crowned sombrero, and an older, ugly man in a black vest and with black sleeve cuffs. Conrad stared at them over the barrels of their rifles and committed each face to memory in turn.

He would never forget any of them. Their images would be burned into his brain until the day he died.

Which might be today, he reminded himself. He was badly outnumbered, if it came down to a fight.

A wry smile tugged at his mouth. "You should hope your men are good shots," he said to the spokesman.

That comment put a frown on the man's face. "Why the hell do you say that?"

Conrad nodded to the right of the trail, then the left. "You've got six men on each side of the trail. If they shoot at me and miss, they're liable to hit some of the men on the other side."

The spokesman frowned. "Never you mind about that. You got the money?"

Conrad didn't even glance down at the carpetbag at his feet. Nor did he answer the man's question. Instead, he asked coolly, "Do you have my wife?"

"Oh, we got her, all right. Don't you worry about that."

"Let me see her." Conrad supposed that Rebel was somewhere back in the trees, with at least one of the kidnappers guarding her.

Instead, the kidnappers' spokesman took him by surprise by pointing at the sky and saying, "Look up."

For a terrible moment, Conrad thought the man was saying that Rebel was already dead and was pointing toward heaven, but then as he lifted his eyes, he saw another torch flare into life. This was on top of the rocky bluff that overhung the canyon. Conrad gasped as he saw the two figures illuminated by the torch's glare.

Rebel was one of them, standing perilously close to the bluff's edge. The other one, right behind her, was the bearded man Conrad had pegged as the leader of the kidnappers. He had hold of Rebel's arm with one hand. The other pressed the barrel of a revolver into her side.

"Oh, my God!" Conrad cried. "Rebel! Rebel, can you hear me?"

"I hear you, Conrad!" she called down to him. "And I love you!"

"I love you, too!"

The craggy-faced man in the trail said, "That's touchin' as all hell. Let's see the money, Browning."

Conrad had to tear his eyes away from Rebel. It wasn't easy. He glared at the man and said, "You don't get the money until my wife is safely in this buggy with me."

The man shook his head. "You ain't givin' the orders. Here's how it's gonna work. You give us the money and then stay right where you are. We leave, and our man leaves your wife up on top of that rock. There's a trail down. She can make it if she's careful. She climbed up there after all. Once we're gone with the money, she can climb down, and the two of you can go back to Carson City. You'll never see us again. Sound good?"

"The part about never seeing you again does," Conrad lied. He planned to see each and every one of them again, either at the end of a hangman's rope, or over the barrel of a gun.

But that would come later, after Rebel was safe.

"All right," he said. "I'll turn over the money. But I want your men to pull back, so that I don't have all those guns pointing at me." He paused. "They make me nervous."

The man thought it over, then shrugged. He drew his Colt and called, "All right, you fellas heard the man. Back off so it's just him and me. That all right with you, Browning?"

"Let's see them do it first," Conrad said.

One by one, the kidnappers stepped out from behind the trees and moved along the trail, withdrawing until they were about fifty yards behind their spokesman. That gave Conrad an even better look at their faces. He would know them when he saw them again, that was for sure.

"Now, damn it," the craggy-faced man said. "We've done what you wanted. Turn over the money, or we'll just kill you both and take it."

Conrad knew he had to risk it. He bent over and reached down to pick up the carpetbag, and as he did so he felt the pressure of the gun that was tucked into his trousers at the small of his back, under his coat. He hefted the carpetbag and stood up in the buggy. With a grunt of effort, he tossed it over the buckskin horse's head. Dust puffed up around the bag as it landed in the trail, almost at the man's feet.

He took an eager step forward and reached down to unfasten the catches on the bag. As he threw it open and saw the packets of bills inside, a grin creased his face.

"You can count it if you want," Conrad said coldly.

"I don't reckon that'll be necessary. You've played square with us. Now we'll play square with you." The man closed the bag, fastened it, and picked it up. He carried it over to where one of the torches was stuck upright in the dirt beside the trail. He wrenched the torch free and waved it over his head. Conrad supposed that was the signal to the man on the bluff with Rebel that they had the money.

Maybe now they would let her go, he thought. No tricks, he prayed. Please, no tricks.

"Browning!" the man on the bluff shouted.

Conrad's head jerked back as he gazed upward. He hoped to see the man let go of Rebel and retreat, but that didn't happen. Instead, as the man stepped behind her, he called, "What happens now is on your head! Welcome to hell!"

"Noooo!" Conrad screamed.

Rebel must have realized what was going to happen next. She twisted and tried to strike at the man, but she was too late. Muzzle flame spurted as the man fired. Rebel cried out in pain as the bullet tore into her and knocked her backward.

Right off the bluff.

Conrad couldn't believe his horror-stricken eyes as he saw Rebel stumble back into empty air and then plummet toward the base of the bluff so far below. Even though it took only the blink of an eye for her to disappear into the trees, the fall seemed to last an eternity.

Instinct sent Conrad's hand flashing to the gun at the small of his back. He whipped it out and tilted the barrel upward, blazing away at the man atop the bluff, the man who had just shot Rebel. The bastard was already gone, though, having leaped back out of Conrad's line of fire.

He jerked his eyes back down and saw that the man in the trail was still standing there, apparently dumbfounded by what had just happened. Evidently, it had taken him by surprise just as much as it had Conrad. But he recovered quickly from the shock and clawed at the gun on his hip.

Conrad grabbed the reins, yelled, "Hyaaah!" and sent the buckskin leaping forward. The kidnapper had to leap to one side to avoid being trampled by the big horse. He couldn't get out of the way of the buggy, though. The vehicle clipped him and sent him spinning off his feet. He screamed as he fell, and from the lurch Conrad felt, he was pretty sure one of the wheels had passed over the man's legs.

Standing in the buggy, holding the reins with one hand and the Colt with the other, Conrad sent the buggy racing toward the rest of the kidnappers. He emptied the revolver as he charged them, and between the flying lead and the racing horse and buggy, the men were forced to scatter. They fired back at Conrad as they scurried out of the way. He heard some of the slugs whine past his head, but he ignored them.

He didn't care if they killed him. He was sure that Rebel was dead. Shot at close range like that, followed by the fall off the bluff . . . There was no way she could have survived. So, actually, they had already killed him. His heart might still beat and his lungs might draw breath into them, but he was dead, right along with his beloved Rebel.

He charged through the kidnappers and kept the buggy moving, not stopping until he had gone a couple of hundred yards, well out of reach of the light from the torches that still blazed alongside the trail. Then he hauled the horse to a halt and leaped out of the buggy. He tore off his outer clothing, revealing the black garb that would be impossible to see in the shadows. Moving swiftly and efficiently, he reached behind the seat, picked up the gunbelt, and strapped it on. The holster already held a loaded Colt. The black Stetson was next, tugged down on his sandy hair. Then he retrieved the Winchester and the shotgun and loped off into the darkness, carrying one in each hand.

Shots roared, but the kidnappers had to be firing blindly because they couldn't see him in the shadows as he circled back toward them. After a moment, a man bellowed, "Hold your fire! Hold your fire, damn it!" Conrad thought the voice belonged to the ginger-bearded man. "Forget Browning! Leave him alive! *Just get that money!*"

They had all charged after him, determined to kill him, and had forgotten momentarily about the ransom. Conrad hadn't forgotten, though. That money was the bait that would bring them to him, so that he could kill them. He reached the trail and dashed out into the light. The carpetbag still lay there, close to the man he'd run over with the buggy. That man had pulled himself to the edge of the trail, dragging what appeared to be two broken legs behind him. He was

whimpering in pain, but he let out a shouted curse as
he saw Conrad coming.

"He's here! The son of a bitch is here! He's after
the money!"

Men came running from the other direction, but
they were too late. Conrad dropped the Winchester
next to the carpetbag and whirled toward them, using
both hands to brace the shotgun as he eared back the
hammers and pulled the triggers. The double charge
of buckshot exploded from both barrels with a thunderous boom.

Conrad heard yells of pain, but didn't know
how many of them he'd hit or how badly they were
wounded. He dropped the scattergun, snatched the
rifle and the carpetbag from the trail, and darted past
one of the torches into the trees again.

"Get that money!" the leader yelled. "But don't
kill Browning!"

That was strange, Conrad thought. Why did the man
want his life spared? So that he could be tormented
that much longer by the knowledge that he had failed
his wife, that she was dead because of him?

Before he could ponder that any further, a crackling in the brush near at hand warned him. One of the
kidnappers burst from behind a tree and tackled him.
Conrad went down hard, but he managed to hang on
to both the carpetbag and the Winchester.

"I got him!" the man yelled as he tried to pin
Conrad to the ground. "Over here! I got him!"

Conrad swung the carpetbag and smashed it
against the man's head. The kidnapper fell off him
and sprawled to the side. Conrad lurched to his feet
and pressed the Winchester's barrel to the man's

head. In the faint light from the torches, he saw the man's eyes widen with fear.

"Help! He's gonna—"

Conrad pulled the trigger.

This man had helped murder Edwin Sinclair, had helped kidnap Rebel. He was partially responsible for her being dead. There was no mercy in Conrad at this moment. Barely anything human remained inside him. He took no pleasure in blowing this bastard's brains out. It was just something that had to be done.

The sound of the shot set them off again, despite their leader's orders. Guns roared, and bullets whipped through the trees around Conrad, thudding into trunks and clipping off branches. Conrad crouched and ran, trusting to luck or fate to keep him safe, at least until he could kill the rest of them. After that, he didn't care what happened to him.

Something slammed into him and knocked him off his feet. The carpetbag's handle slipped out of his hand as he fell. A burning pain in his side sent waves of weakness through him. He got a hand under him and pushed himself to his knees. He felt around for the carpetbag but couldn't find it.

As a young man back East, before he'd ever come West and met Frank Morgan for the first time, Conrad had taken part in several fox hunts. He was reminded of those times now as he heard the outlaws crashing through the brush toward him, yelling to each other like hounds baying after the fox.

And he was the fox.

He had no doubt they would tear him apart if they ever got their hands on him, just like the hounds did when they caught up with the fox. The wound in his side had put him at a disadvantage. He felt his strength deserting him, and since he no longer had the money, he couldn't use it to lure them on and kill them at times and places of his choosing.

They outnumbered him by too much. He had to admit it. He couldn't kill them all tonight. So he had to get away. Sooner or later they would die at his hand, but in order for that to happen . . .

He had to live.

That knowledge burned through him with a fiercer heat than the bullet that had gouged his side. The need for revenge that filled him could only be satisfied if he survived this night of blood and death.

He forced himself to his feet and stumbled through the trees. Behind him, somebody shouted, "Hey, it's the money! Hot damn, I found the money!"

"Let's get out of here!" That was the ginger-bearded man again, the one who had shot Rebel. It was all Conrad could do not to lift the Winchester and spray the remaining rounds in the direction of that voice as fast as he could work the rifle's lever.

But he couldn't hope to kill all of them, and even though the bearded man was the one who'd pulled the trigger, they had all played a part in Rebel's death. He wouldn't be satisfied until all of them were dead.

"What about Hank?" another man demanded. "He killed Hank!"

"Sorry. There's nothin' we can do about it now. My orders were to leave Browning alive."

There it was again. Conrad huddled against a tree trunk and wondered who could have given such orders. He had seen the reaction of the man in the trail when the bearded man shot Rebel. He hadn't known that was going to happen, and Conrad thought that the rest of the kidnappers hadn't either. They had expected to collect the ransom and turn Rebel back over to him.

That meant the bearded man had been playing a different game, a game of his own. And only he had the answers that Conrad needed.

The voices faded. A few minutes later, Conrad heard hoofbeats in the night. They were leaving. Taking the money and riding away from the place where Rebel had died. Where a huge hole had been ripped out of Conrad's heart. No one could live with damage like that. *I'm dead,* he thought again. *Conrad Browning is dead.*

His head jerked up, and he realized that he had lost consciousness. He had no idea how long he'd been out. He blinked and looked through the trees, thinking that he might catch a glimpse of the torches if they still burned, but nothing met his eyes except darkness.

The canyon was quiet now. The place was far enough from town, isolated enough, that no one would have heard the shots. No one was going to come and help him. He shouldn't have tried to handle this alone, he thought. He should have asked for help, from the law or the Pinkertons or someone. But time had been short, and he had honestly believed that he stood the best chance of saving Rebel by following his instincts.

A sob wracked him. His instincts had betrayed him, and Rebel was dead.

He was no Frank Morgan, that was for damned sure. Frank wouldn't have let this happen. Frank would have found a way to save her, to save Rebel and kill all the bastards who had kidnapped her.

Conrad sat there stewing in self-loathing for long

moments, before he finally braced his back against the tree trunk and began struggling to his feet. The least he could do was to find Rebel and take her body back to town so that she could have a proper burial. He owed her that much, after failing her so spectacularly.

The pain in his side had faded to a dull ache. He placed his hand against his shirt and felt the blood that had soaked into it. He couldn't tell how badly he was hurt, but he could walk, so he hoped the wound wasn't too bad.

Eventually, he stumbled onto the trail. He whistled, hoping that the horse was still somewhere around. A moment later, he was rewarded by the sound of hoof-beats moving toward him. A second after that, he heard the faint creaking of the buggy wheels.

The buckskin brought the buggy to him. Conrad caught hold of the horse's halter and leaned against him. The horse shied a bit, no doubt from the smell of blood. Conrad patted his shoulder, murmured to him until he calmed down. Then Conrad found the suit coat he had tossed behind the seat and dug out a box of matches from one of the pockets.

He made a torch of his own, ripping the lining out of the coat and wrapping it around a branch he found. Then, holding the torch above his head, he stumbled toward the spot where he thought Rebel's body had fallen. His head was spinning by now, and he couldn't be sure he was going in the right direction, but he would search all night if he had to.

His instincts were true this time. He found her only minutes later, lying in a huddled heap between two trees. Her body was broken from the fall, and her white blouse was dark with blood from the gun-shot wound. Conrad fell to his knees beside her and jabbed the torch into the ground so that it would stand up as he gathered her into his arms. She was limp, lifeless. He cradled her against his chest and sobbed as he searched in vain for a pulse, a breath, even the faintest sign of life. But of course, there was none. Rebel was gone. And her last words, he realized, had been to tell him that she loved him.

That horrible, bittersweet thought was in his mind as he held her and cried, and then he felt the cold ring of a gun muzzle press against the back of his neck as a man said, "Don't move, Browning! I figured you'd come back for that bitch."

Chapter 8

Conrad stiffened as the man went on. "That was my brother you killed back yonder! My twin brother! Shot him like he was no better'n a damn dog! You know what that feels like?"

Forcing the words past the huge lump in his throat, Conrad said, "I'm holding my wife's dead body in my arms. And men like you and your brother killed my mother. So, yeah, I know what it feels like."

The response seemed to throw the kidnapper for a loop. He must have expected Conrad to beg for his life. It would be a cold day in hell before that happened, even though Conrad wanted desperately to live now, so that he could have his revenge on Rebel's murderers.

Even as he spoke, he was moving one hand carefully toward the makeshift torch stuck in the ground beside him. His fingers touched the branch. He pushed on it, gently and slowly, so the kidnapper wouldn't notice what he was doing.

"Well, now you're gonna find out what it feels like to get your brains blown out, just like my brother."

Before the man could pull the trigger, the torch tipped over, falling straight at his legs. The flames coming at him caused him to jump back instinctively, and even though he jerked the trigger of his gun, Conrad had already rolled to the side, taking Rebel's body with him. The gun still blasted painfully close to Conrad's ear, but the bullet thudded harmlessly into the ground.

Conrad wound up lying on his back, with the kidnapper looming above him. He brought his right leg up and buried the toe of his boot in the man's groin. The kidnapper screamed in agony and doubled over, but he didn't drop his gun. He managed to get another shot off as Conrad flung himself to the side. The bullet plucked at the sleeve of the black shirt, but didn't touch Conrad's flesh.

Conrad whipped a leg around and caught the kidnapper behind the knees, sweeping the man's legs out from under him. The man fell heavily and curled up into a ball as he clutched at his injured privates. Conrad came up on his knees and pulled his Colt, then lunged forward. The gun barrel thudded against the man's head. He shuddered and then straightened out, unconscious.

Out cold like that, at least he wasn't thinking about how bad his balls hurt anymore.

A sudden glare caught Conrad's attention as he knelt there, breathing heavily. He looked around and saw that the carpet of dry pine needles on the ground had caught fire where he'd shoved the torch over. A fire like that would spread quickly in these woods, and for a second he thought about leaving the kidnapper there to roast alive.

Something inside him wouldn't allow him to do

that. He had thought that all vestiges of his humanity had died with Rebel, but maybe that wasn't completely the case. He pushed himself to his feet, hurried over, and stomped out the flames before they could spread. That plunged the canyon into darkness again.

Conrad tried to ignore the pain of his own bullet wound as he knelt next to the unconscious kidnapper once more and used the man's own belt to lash his hands together behind his back. He didn't want the fellow going anywhere just yet. Conrad realized that he might be able to make use of him.

Then, using matches to light his path, he made his way back to the buggy and retrieved a blanket from the area behind the seat. The same blanket he had spread out on that hillside so they could sit on it to enjoy their picnic, he thought as another shred of his soul peeled away. He had never carried it back into the house. Now he took it into the woods and gently wrapped Rebel's body in it.

Once he had placed her in the buggy, he went back for the kidnapper, who was beginning to stir. Conrad hit him again with the gun to keep him still. He took hold of the man's feet and dragged him through the woods, back to the trail where the horse and buggy waited. He didn't worry about how scratched up the bastard got along the way either.

Conrad knew he had lost quite a bit of blood. He could feel the insidious weakness creeping through him. Grunting from pain and effort, he lifted the unconscious man and toppled him onto the buggy's floorboard, in front of the driver's seat. Conrad would have to ride back to Carson City with his feet resting on the man. It would be uncomfortable, but there was no way he was putting the kidnapper in the back of the vehicle with Rebel.

Conrad never remembered all the details of the drive back to town. By that time, he was functioning largely on instinct and sheer determination. He recalled that a time or two, the kidnapper started to move around a little, and each time, Conrad kicked him in the head. In the back of his mind, he hoped the man wouldn't die from the punishment before they got back to town.

The kidnapper knew things that he needed to know. Conrad intended to have answers.

The moon was down by the time the buggy reached Carson City. The darkest hour of the night lay over the town. No one was in the streets, and there was no one to challenge Conrad or even see him as he drove around the house and into the carriage house.

The kidnapper was still breathing, but hadn't budged for a while. Conrad hauled the man out of the buggy and stood him up against one of the posts that supported the roof, tying him in place with some rope that was in the carriage house. Then, he lifted Rebel and carried her into the home that they had shared for all too short a time. Just having her in his arms seemed to give him strength, despite the wound in his side.

He took her upstairs and placed her on their bed, still wrapped in the blanket. Then, he went back downstairs and out to the carriage house, reeling like a drunken man as he did so. He paused just outside the carriage house and leaned against the wall for a moment in an attempt to regain some of his strength. It didn't really help.

He heard thumping and then a groan from inside the

building. The kidnapper was regaining consciousness again. This time, Conrad didn't intend to knock him out. Not until he had the answers he wanted.

He drew his gun and shoved the door open, then heeled it closed behind him as he went in. He had left a lantern burning, and in its flickering light, he saw the kidnapper looking around wildly and pulling against the rope that held him to the post. Conrad took a deep breath and forced his stride to be steady as he walked toward the man. He lifted the gun as he advanced, and the kidnapper grew wide-eyed and still as he stared down the barrel of the Colt.

Conrad stopped in front of the man and rasped, "What's your name?"

For a second, he thought the kidnapper was going to be stubborn and refuse to answer, but the sight of a gun muzzle only inches from his face was a powerful persuader.

"It's Winchell," the man said sullenly. "Jeff Winchell." He grimaced. "What'd you do to me? My head feels like it's about to fall plumb off."

"You're lucky you've still got a head," Conrad said. "What was your brother's name?" He didn't have to know that to carry out his plan of vengeance, since the kidnapper's brother was already dead, but for some reason he was curious.

"It was Hank. Hank Winchell, you murderin' son of a bitch."

"You're a fine one to talk," Conrad snapped. "After the way you killed my wife."

"I didn't have anything to do with that! I swear it, mister. That was all Lasswell's doin'. As far as any of the rest of us knew, we were gonna let her go as soon as we had that ransom money."

"Lasswell?"

"Clay Lasswell. Some old Texas gunfighter. He was the ramrod of the bunch. He's the one who wired Moss and had him get together some men."

Conrad nodded as he made a mental note of the man. So the ginger-bearded man was Clay Lasswell, and he was the leader of the kidnappers, just as Conrad had supposed. Winchell's frightened words confirmed Conrad's earlier speculation that Lasswell had crossed up his own men by shooting Rebel.

He didn't let any of that show on his face, though, as he went on, "Who's Moss?"

"Vernon Moss. He's the one who was waitin' in the trail for you. You broke both his legs when you run over him with that buggy, you know."

"Good," Conrad said. "He had it coming. What about the others? What are their names?"

Winchell's eyes narrowed. "I know what you're doin'," he said. "You're tryin' to get me to sell out my pards. Well, I won't do it, damn you. I won't!"

"I think you will," Conrad said. He eared back the Colt's hammer so that only the slightest pressure on the trigger would be needed to send a bullet into the kidnapper's brain. "If you won't tell me what I need to know, then you're no good to me."

Winchell stared at him. The kidnapper's face paled, and beads of sweat popped out on his forehead. "You . . . you can't kill me," he said. "You're a businessman. You own banks and mines and railroads. You don't go around shootin' people!"

"You know who my father is, don't you?"

Winchell didn't answer with words, but he bobbed his head up and down, then winced at the fresh pain the movement must have set off inside his skull.

"What do you think Frank Morgan would do if he were here right now?" Conrad asked softly. "Do you think he'd hesitate to pull this trigger?"

Actually, at this very moment, Conrad figured that he was closer to being able to commit cold-blooded murder than Frank would have been. Although exterminating this vermin hardly qualified as murder.

Winchell's resolve broke. He twisted his head to the side and closed his eyes. "Don't shoot me," he said. "Please, don't shoot. I'll tell you what you want to know."

"Everything," Conrad said. "I want to know everything."

Winchell looked at him again. "You gotta understand. I don't know all of it. Lasswell was the only one who did. He was the only one who'd talked to whoever the boss was."

"Lasswell didn't come up with the idea of kidnapping my wife?"

"I don't think so. I think he was just a hired hand, like the rest of us, only he knew who was really pullin' the strings."

"Keep talking," Conrad said.

Winchell did, details spilling from him, although the kidnapper really didn't know much beyond the things Conrad had already deduced for himself. He knew the names of all the other men involved, though, and Conrad was careful to memorize each one of them. In some cases, he had only one name—Buck, Carlson, and Rattigan—but that was better than nothing.

"The only other hombre I'm sure was in on it was that dude," Winchell finally said.

"What dude?"

"The one who was supposed to let us in the house after he knocked you out."

"Edwin Sinclair?" Conrad asked in a hoarse whisper.

"I never heard his name. All I know is that he worked for you, and Lasswell had Julio cut his throat once we had your wife."

A chill washed through Conrad. So Sinclair hadn't been trustworthy after all. He had plotted with the kidnappers, and then been done in by the treachery of his own allies. He hadn't been killed trying to save Rebel. Conrad wished briefly that the kidnappers hadn't killed Sinclair. He would have liked to have done that himself.

But that part was finished. He looked over the Colt's barrel at Winchell and said, "You're certain that's all you know?"

"That's it, Browning. Except . . ."

"Go on," Conrad grated.

"I don't know if it makes any difference or not, but nobody laid a finger on your wife except to bring her with us. She wasn't, uh, molested or anything like that. I give you my word on that."

"Why should I accept your word?"

"Because I'm tryin' to convince you not to shoot me! Some of the fellas wanted to, uh, you know . . . but Lasswell wouldn't let 'em. He made it clear that we had to leave Mrs. Browning alone. I reckon that must've been part of his orders, too."

Conrad couldn't see the logic in that, but as a matter of fact, he did believe Winchell. The man was too frightened not to be telling the truth. And even though the knowledge that Rebel hadn't been assaulted was scant comfort at a time like this, it was better than nothing. At least she hadn't spent her final hours in terror and pain, being brutalized.

A moment of silence stretched by, and then Winchell said, "I've told you everything I know. I swear it, Browning. What are you gonna do now?"

Conrad's lips drew back from his teeth in a grimace as he stared at the kidnapper. He said, "I know what I ought to do, what I want to do . . ."

Winchell swallowed hard.

Conrad tilted the Colt's barrel up and let down the hammer. He lowered the gun and slid it into its holster. Winchell sagged forward against the rope.

"I'm not going to kill you," Conrad said. "I'm going to turn you over to the police and let the law deal with you. You'll probably hang anyway, but I'm not going to be your executioner."

Winchell licked his lips. "I'm much obliged. I'm mighty sorry about what happened to your missus. I really am, Browning. I never wanted to hurt nobody." He began to sob. "I'm sorry, I'm so sorry . . ."

"Shut up," Conrad snapped. He turned away. His right arm was limp from holding up the gun as he interrogated Winchell, and his head was still spinning. He knew he needed medical attention. But not yet. First, he had to find someone to summon the police, so they could arrest Winchell, and then he had to deal with making the arrangements for Rebel's funeral.

He was stumbling toward the buggy when the buckskin horse suddenly threw his head up in alarm. Conrad started to turn, but before he could, something crashed into him from behind. He couldn't keep his feet. He went down hard, and Winchell landed on top of him. The belt Conrad had used to tie the man's wrists looped around his neck, and Conrad barely got a hand up in time to keep the belt from closing tightly on his neck. His fingers gave him a little room to breath, but Winchell planted a knee in the small of his back and heaved harder and harder, cutting off Conrad's air. The wound in his side had stopped bleeding earlier, but now he felt the hot, wet flow once again.

"Threaten me, will you?" Winchell rasped. "Kill my brother, shove a gun in my face, lord it over me . . . You'll pay for that, you son of a bitch!"

Conrad had no idea how the man had gotten loose, and it didn't matter. The only important thing at the moment was that Winchell was on the brink of strangling him to death. Conrad fought back desperately, driving the elbow of his free arm behind him, into Winchell's belly. That bought him a little respite. Conrad shoved hard with his knees and arched up off the floor. Winchell toppled off him and the belt around Conrad's neck came loose.

He wanted to stop and drag air into his lungs, but there was no time for that. Winchell came at him, flailing punches. Conrad lowered his head and bulled forward, tackling Winchell. They rolled across the floor, winding up almost under the buggy horse. The animal danced away skittishly as Conrad grappled with the kidnapper. Hatred mixed with desperation allowed him to find the last bits of strength remaining in his body, and he grabbed Winchell's shirt and heaved the man against one of the buggy wheels.

Winchell's feet slipped out from under him, and he went down. Conrad reached up and slapped the horse's rump. The buckskin leaped forward, and since he was still hitched to the buggy, the vehicle lurched ahead as well.

The iron-tired wheel rolled right over Winchell's throat, cutting short the terrified scream that had started to well from the kidnapper's mouth.

Conrad looked away as the wheel crushed the man's throat. The horse backed up, but the damage was done. Winchell thrashed wildly as he tried to get air into his lungs. His face turned purple, then blue. Then his spasms subsided and he lay still, except for a few twitches as his muscles caught up to the fact that he was dead. For the second time tonight, Conrad had used the buggy as a weapon, and this time it had been lethal.

He reached up, caught hold of the buckskin's harness, and pulled himself to his feet. Winchell had choked to death, he thought as he looked down at the body, but not at the end of a rope. Conrad didn't care. One more of the kidnappers was dead; that was all that mattered.

And as he gazed at the corpse, an idea began to form in his mind, an offshoot of things that had happened earlier. The remaining kidnappers might worry that he would come after them and try to avenge his wife, but they wouldn't think that if they believed he was dead. In fact, they might even let their guard down a little if they thought he was no longer a threat.

For the first time since this terrible night began, a smile touched Conrad's lips. An agonized, haunted smile, to be sure, but still . . .

He pulled Winchell's body clear of the buggy and then unhitched the horse and turned it into its stall. He picked up the rope he had used to tie Winchell to the post and saw that it was badly frayed. Running his fingers over the back of the post, Conrad found the rough spot where Winchell must have worked the rope back and forth until it parted. Even before that, he had worked his hands free from the belt. That had been going on all the time he was questioning the man, Conrad thought, and he hadn't even noticed because he was so light-headed from loss of blood and had been concentrating on what Winchell was telling him.

Weaving, Conrad walked back into the house and went to his study. He barely had the strength to pull out some paper and a pen, and the letters he scratched onto the paper wavered and blurred. That was all right; he wanted people to think that he had written the letter in a state of great emotional distress. Actually, he was cold inside just then, numb to everything except the need for vengeance.

Leaving the letter in the middle of his desk where someone was sure to find it, he went upstairs and stepped into the bedroom. He had to say good-bye to Rebel. For the next several minutes, he spoke from the heart, telling her how much he loved her and how sorry he was for everything that had happened, then finished by saying, "I promise you that they'll all pay for what they did. Each and every one of them." He knew that if the situation were reversed, she would have devoted the rest of her life to hunting down his killers. He could do no less for her, and he knew she would understand.

"I love you," he whispered one last time, and as he turned away, he thought he heard a whisper saying the same thing, brushing across him like a warm breeze.

Although not an overly religious man, Conrad prayed for strength to finish this as he went downstairs. He had a small supply of cash for emergencies in the desk. He stuffed the bills under his shirt, on the side that wasn't soaked with blood. He planned to take only one revolver and the Winchester with him, so he left the spare Colt on the desk, holding down the letter that explained how he couldn't go on living after what had happened to Rebel.

Dawn wasn't far off now. The eastern sky was gray as he walked behind the house to the carriage house, taking with him a jug of kerosene he'd picked up in the kitchen. He went inside and saddled the buckskin, then led the horse out and tied the reins to an iron bench that sat beside the path between the house and the carriage house.

"Be back in a minute, big fella," he whispered as he patted the horse's shoulder. He went inside and began splashing the kerosene around the interior of the carriage house. The building was far enough away from any other structures that Conrad was confident a fire wouldn't spread beyond it. When he was finished, he tossed the empty jug aside and walked over to Jeff Winchell's body.

Kneeling next to the dead kidnapper, Conrad slipped the Colt from its holster and pressed the muzzle to Winchell's right temple, the same place a man would hold a gun if he intended to blow his own brains out. He pulled the trigger.

Then he stood, holstered the gun, and took a match from his pocket. He went to the doorway, rasped the match alight against the jamb, and tossed it into a puddle of kerosene, which went up with a fierce *whoosh!*

Conrad turned his back and walked away. Now that Rebel was gone, his only living relative was Frank Morgan. He would have to stop somewhere and send a wire to Claudius Turnbuckle, advising the lawyer that he was really still alive and swearing him to secrecy. Conrad wanted Turnbuckle to let Frank know that he wasn't dead; he didn't want his father grieving over him. Let Frank grieve over Rebel. That was enough.

Conrad untied the buckskin's reins and climbed into the saddle. He knew he was on his last legs, but he wanted to get well away from Carson City before he stopped to seek medical attention. Maybe he could find a sawbones in some small settlement up in the mountains.

He didn't look back as he rode away, but he could hear the flames crackling behind him, consuming the body that everyone would believe was his. He wouldn't be here for Rebel's funeral, and he deeply regretted that, but he could come back some day and visit her grave. He would tell her that he had avenged her death, that everyone responsible for what happened to her was gone.

Everyone but him.

He forced that bitter thought out of his mind. As of tonight, Conrad Browning was dead, too, another victim of whatever he had become. Yeah, Conrad was dead, he told himself as he swayed in the saddle. Long live . . . long live . . .

Well, he would work on that. Later.

Chapter 9

Conrad didn't know where he was or how long he had been unconscious. He didn't even recall passing out. The last thing he remembered was riding alongside a tree-lined, sun-dappled creek in the foothills somewhere northwest of Carson City. It was the middle of the day. He had been riding for hours after leaving the city and the burning carriage house behind him, floating in and out of awareness and trusting that the buckskin would continue following the trail.

He didn't remember when he had last eaten, but he had no appetite. As he rode along beside the stream, though, he was suddenly achingly thirsty. The sight of the water dancing and bubbling along the rocky creek bed prompted him to dismount. The merry chuckling of the stream drew him like a siren's song. Conrad dropped to his knees at the edge of the water and leaned forward, longing to plunge his head into the crisp, cold stream.

That was the last thing he remembered until this very moment.

Slowly, he became aware of several things. He was

lying on something soft and comfortable, and when he moved his fingers, he felt a sheet under them. Another sheet covered him. Something tight around his midsection made it a little difficult to breathe. His eyes were closed, but he saw light through the lids. Light and shadow. Someone was moving around near him. He heard music, far enough away that it had to be coming from another room. Someone playing the piano?

And closer, someone humming softly, keeping time with the tune.

Conrad forced his eyes open. He winced against the glare of sunlight slanting in through a window with gauzy yellow curtains over it. A shape moved between him and the light. He squinted as his vision tried to adjust.

The other person in the room with him was a woman. A young woman, Conrad thought, although her back was to him and he couldn't see her face. The way she moved as she opened a drawer in a chest and placed some folded linen inside it seemed to indicate youth, though. So did the long, thick auburn hair that hung down her back. She was still humming along with the music as she closed the drawer and turned away from it, but the humming stopped abruptly as she saw him looking at her.

"You're awake," she said.

That seemed pretty obvious to Conrad. He started to say, *That's right,* but his voice didn't work very well. What came out of his mouth was more of an incoherent croak.

"Don't try to talk just yet," the woman said as she came toward the bed. "Let me get you some water."

He could tell for sure now that she was young, just

as he had thought, and the part of his brain that still recognized such things realized that she was pretty, a fair-skinned, green-eyed redhead with a faint dusting of freckles across her nose.

She picked up a pitcher and a glass from a table beside the bed. She poured a little water in the glass, then leaned over the bed and slipped her other hand behind Conrad's head, lifting it and supporting it as she brought the glass to his lips.

"Not too much now," she said. "As weak as you are, you don't want to rush anything."

He was weak, all right. Every muscle in his body was limp. He didn't think he could get out of this bed if it was on fire.

He drank eagerly, but she gave him only a little water, not enough to ease the parched condition of his mouth. After a moment, she let him take another sip. Then she carefully lowered his head to the pillow.

"That's enough for now," she said. "I'm going to go tell my father that you're awake."

This time when he tried to speak, he could form words in a husky whisper, but he barely had enough strength to get them out. "Wh . . . where . . . am . . ."

"Where are you? A little settlement called Saw-tooth."

"N-Nevada . . . ?"

She shook her head. "No, it's over the line in California. We're not far from Nevada, though."

Conrad managed to nod. With a sigh, he closed his eyes as the young woman hurried out of the room, but he didn't pass out again. So he had managed to ride across the border into California. That didn't surprise him all that much. He hadn't known where he was, and he had no specific destination in mind. He'd just wanted to get away from Carson City and the great tragedy he had left behind him.

Except he would never really leave it behind him, he realized as the image of Rebel's broken, wounded body filled his brain. He shuddered and felt like he ought to cry, but no tears came. Maybe the large amount of blood he'd lost had caused them to dry up.

Or maybe they were just frozen solid, like his heart.

The music in the other room had stopped while the young woman was giving him a drink, but now it started again. As Conrad listened to it, he realized that it wasn't coming from a piano. The notes had a slightly tinny quality to them. He decided that they came from a Gramophone cylinder. It was somewhat unusual to find one of the newfangled machines in some backwater frontier settlement, he thought, but he had heard them before and was convinced that was what it was.

Footsteps approaching the bed made him open his eyes again. He saw a gray-haired man in a rumpled shirt and vest, with a string tie around his neck, looking down at him. "So you're awake," the man said.

Whoever these people were, they sure had a grasp of the obvious, Conrad thought. He nodded and husked, "I could . . . use some more water."

The man gestured to the young woman, who had followed him into the room. "Go ahead and give him some, Eve," he said. "It's not going to hurt him. Burning up with fever like he is, he can use all the fluid he can get."

"All right, Pa." The glass on the table beside the bed still held some water. She supported Conrad's head again and helped him drink. Greedily, he sucked down the rest of the water in the glass.

His voice was a little stronger when he spoke again. "You say I've got fever?"

The man nodded. "That's right. The wound in your side had festered by the time you got here. I cleaned it up the best I could, but the infection had spread. You're still trying to fight it off, and I'll be honest with you, there's not much I can do to help you, other than keeping you comfortable and seeing that you get some nourishment. Your own body will have to do the rest."

Conrad didn't think his body was capable of doing much of anything right now. The effort of lifting his head a couple of times to drink had exhausted him. He wasn't sure he could move again.

"Are you . . . a doctor?"

The man nodded. "That's right, son. My name's Patrick McNally." He inclined his head toward the young woman. "My daughter Eve."

"Thank you . . . for helping me," Conrad said. "How long have I . . . been here?"

"Three days," McNally replied.

That answer surprised Conrad. He had supposed it was later in the same day on which he had passed out beside the creek. He was lucky he hadn't fallen into the stream and drowned.

"I've been . . . unconscious . . . for three days?"

"Oh, no," Eve McNally said. "You've come to several times. But you were never as clearheaded then as you seem to be now. That's a good sign, isn't it, Pa?"

McNally nodded. "A very good sign. When a man's mind starts working again, a lot of times his body follows along. You regained conscious-ness enough so that we could give you water and a little broth, but this is the first time you've talked. Coherently anyway."

A sudden worry struck Conrad. He wanted everyone to think that he was dead, but from the sound of it he'd been babbling away to the McNallys.

"What did I . . . say?"

Eve smiled. "You must be a student of history. You kept talking about the War Between the States."

"I . . . what?"

"You went on and on about the rebels."

A pang like a knife struck deep in Conrad's chest. He was glad they hadn't realized what he was really talking about, but the reminder of his loss was painful.

"You mentioned the name Lasswell, too," McNally added. "A lot of other names as well, but that was the one you talked about the most. Is that your name, son? Are you Lasswell?"

Conrad closed his eyes for a second and shook his head. "No," he whispered. "I'm not Lasswell."

"What is your name, then?"

He hesitated, then said the first thing he thought of. "It's Morgan."

"Is that your first name or your last name?"

"Just . . . Morgan."

Eve touched her father's sleeve. "Pa, you know it's not polite to pry too much into a man's business. Anyway, he needs more rest, doesn't he?"

"He does," McNally admitted with a nod. He leaned over the bed and rested his hand briefly on Conrad's forehead. "Still got fever."

"I'll get a cloth and bathe his face."

"That's a good idea. It'll help him rest."

Both of them went away. A few minutes later, Eve came back with a basin and a rag. She pulled up a chair beside the bed, dipped the rag in the water in the basin, wrung it out, then wiped the wet cloth over Conrad's face. It felt wonderfully cool and soothing. He closed his eyes and let himself concentrate on the sensations.

Somewhere along the way, the music had changed again. Conrad didn't recognize the song, but it held more than a hint of melancholy. "That music," he whispered without opening his eyes. "Where does it . . . come from?"

"Oh, that's just . . . my mother."

Conrad heard the slight hesitation in her answer, but he was too tired to ask her about it. And, he supposed, it was really none of his business.

He faded off to sleep without really being aware of it.

When he woke again, night had fallen. Or maybe it was several nights later, for all he knew. The sky outside the window, on the other side of the yellow curtains, was dark. The lamp on the table was turned so low that Conrad could barely see.

After looking around the room for a moment, though, he spotted Eve McNally sitting in a rocking chair in the corner. Her head was tilted back and her eyes were closed. She seemed to be asleep. Conrad watched her for a moment, then cleared his throat.

The swiftness with which she came alert in the chair told him that she was accustomed to sitting vigil with sick people. She had probably handled that duty for her father's patients many times. She stood up, came over to the bed, and rested her hand on Conrad's forehead.

"You still have fever," she told him. "You're burning up."

He knew that from the chills that ran through him, causing him to shudder. All his senses seemed a little distorted as well. "Water," he whispered.

Eve gave him a drink. As she lowered his head to the pillow, she said, "I should go get my father."

"Is he . . . asleep?"

"That's right, but I know he'd want me to wake him."

Conrad found the strength to give a tiny shake of his head. "No need. He said . . . there was nothing he could do . . . but what you're . . . already doing."

"Well . . . I suppose that's true." She pulled the straight chair closer to the bed and reached for the basin and the rag.

"Is it . . . the same day?"

Eve smiled. "You mean the same as when you were awake before? Well, technically, no, I suppose, since it's after midnight. But I know what you mean, and yes, it's only been about ten hours since you were awake."

"Have I . . . babbled any . . . since then?"

She shook her head as she started wiping his face with the wet cloth. "No, you just moaned every now and then. You haven't been trying to fight the Civil War over again." She paused, then went on. "Your father must have told you about the war. You're not old enough to have fought in it yourself."

As a matter of fact, Frank Morgan had been in the war. Conrad knew he'd fought for the Confederacy. But Frank had never really talked much about the experience, and Conrad hadn't pressed him for details.

He didn't confirm or deny Eve's speculation. After a moment, she said, "My father worked in a Union field hospital. He wasn't old enough then to be a doctor, so he was an orderly. All the terrible things he saw there were what convinced him to study medicine. He said there had to be something better that doctors could do."

Conrad felt too bad to really care that much about what Eve was saying, but the sound of her voice was soothing, like the wet rag on his heated face. He wanted to keep her talking, so he murmured, "How did you wind up . . . in Sawtooth?"

"Father practiced for a long time in Sacramento. That's where I was born and raised. But then my mother . . . got sick, and he wanted to go someplace where he wouldn't have as many patients or be as busy, so he could devote more time to taking care of her. My uncle owns the Sawtooth general store, so he suggested that we move out here. He said the town needed a doctor."

"It's a . . . mining town?"

"Mining and ranching," Eve said with a nod. "It's a nice place to live. Nothing like Sacramento, of course."

Conrad thought he heard a trace of wistfulness in her voice. That wasn't surprising. A young, vibrant woman, raised in a bustling city, was bound to find a little frontier settlement like this somewhat confining.

He wondered what was wrong with Eve's mother. Nothing that would keep her from playing a Gramophone, obviously. But he didn't think it would be courteous to ask, and old habits died hard.

"What about you, Mr. Morgan?" Eve asked. "Where are you from?"

Conrad smiled. "Thought you told your pa . . . it wasn't polite to pry."

"Yes, but turnabout is fair play, as the old saying goes."

"Boston," he said. "I was . . . raised in Boston."

Her eyebrows went up. "Really? I thought you didn't sound like you'd been a Westerner all your life."

"I've only lived out here . . . a short time."

"I hate to admit it, but the way you were dressed when Bearpaw brought you in, I thought you might be a desperado of some sort. Those black clothes and the guns, I mean."

"Bearpaw?" Conrad repeated with a frown.

Eve took the cloth and dipped it in the basin again. "Oh, that's right, you don't know how you got here, do you?" she asked as she wrung it out. "Phillip Bearpaw found you lying next to Sawtooth Creek, unconscious. He thought you were dead at first, but when he saw that you were still alive and had been wounded, he put you on your horse and brought you here. I'm sure he saved your life."

"I suppose he did. Phillip Bearpaw, eh?"

"That's right. He's a Paiute, but an educated one. He and my father are friends."

Conrad nodded. "I reckon I'm his friend now, too, since he saved my life. I'll have to thank him. And you and your father, too."

"No thanks are necessary. Pa's business is helping people after all."

That might well be true, Conrad thought, but as much money as he had, he could well afford to repay his debt to Dr. Patrick McNally—

That thought came to a sudden halt as he remembered that it was Conrad Browning who had all that money, and he was no longer Conrad Browning.

His name now was Morgan, and Morgan was a penniless drifter.

Well, maybe not penniless, he corrected himself. He had brought a few hundred dollars with him from the house in Carson City, although it was possible that money was now in the pockets of one Phillip Bearpaw—if the Paiute hadn't already spent it on liquor.

"You said Mr. Bearpaw brought my horse in, too?"

Eve nodded. "That's right. It's out back in our barn, along with Pa's buggy horse. I've been taking care of it. It seems like a fine horse."

"He is," Morgan agreed. "Seems like . . . you take care of a lot of things around here."

"I do my best. Pa has his hands full with . . . well, with his patients and all."

Morgan sensed that she meant something more than that. Something to do with her mother, more than likely, he guessed.

"I washed your shirt and got the blood out of it as best I could," she went on. "Luckily, you can't really see the stain on a black shirt like that. And I was able to mend the bullet hole."

"I'm obliged."

"It wasn't much trouble. Your gun and gunbelt are in one of the drawers, and your rifle is leaning in the corner. You won't need any weapons as long as you're here, of course. And if you're worried about the money that was inside your shirt, don't be. It's all safe."

Morgan didn't want to admit that he'd been wondering about that very thing a few moments earlier. He just nodded and said, "Thank you."

"You know," Eve said as she looked down at him,

"even though you're still running a fever, I think you're better tonight. You're more alert, and you're making more sense. If that fever would just break, I think you'll have turned the corner."

"Maybe it will."

"I'm sure it will. It's just a matter of time."

Unfortunately, time was something he didn't have a lot of, Morgan thought.

There were still a dozen men out there he had to kill, and chances were, they'd be getting farther away with each day that passed.

Chapter 10

Sometime during the night, the man who had been Conrad Browning dozed off again. When Morgan woke up, he was drenched with sweat. It must have run off him in rivers, because the bedclothes underneath him were soaked. They were cold and clammy and uncomfortable. He was going to call out, but then he heard a shuffling sound, as if someone were coming across the room toward him. He pried his eyes open, expecting to see Eve McNally, but in the dim light coming from the lamp, a totally different vision in a long, white nightgown presented itself to him.

The woman who leaned over him was much older than Eve, although her face was relatively unlined. White hair flew out wildly around her head. She looked down at Morgan out of wide, staring eyes but didn't say anything. Startled by her, he instinctively tried to jerk away, but he was so weak and the bandages around his midsection were so tight that he could barely move. He succeeded in causing fresh jolts of pain to shoot through his wounded side, however.

"Eve!" he called. "Eve!"

He must have frightened the old woman. Her eyes widened even more for a second, and then her face twisted as she started to cry. She blubbered like a child. Big tears rolled down her cheeks.

With a rush of footsteps, Eve hurried into the room. "Mama!" she said as she took the old woman's arm. "Mama, you shouldn't be up wandering around. You could hurt yourself!"

Mrs. McNally tried to pull away. Eve hung on to her arm, gently but firmly. The old woman lifted her other arm and pointed at Morgan in the bed.

"Joseph!" she said. "Joseph's come back!"

Eve slipped an arm around her shoulders and turned her away from the bed. "Mama, you know that's not Joe," she said. "I wish it was, but it's not. Joe's not here right now."

"But . . . but he's coming back sometime, isn't he?" Mrs. McNally asked between sobs.

"Of course he is. We just have to wait for him."

"I . . . I sit and wait for him all day."

"That's right. You sit and wait and play your Gramophone."

The old woman sniffled and said, "Joseph loved those old songs."

"We'll play all of them for him when he comes back," Eve promised.

Dr. McNally appeared in the doorway, wearing a nightshirt and a worried expression. "Dear Lord," he muttered. "I thought she was sound asleep."

Eve steered her mother across the room. "Mama, you go with Pa, all right? You need to get some rest."

"Will Joseph be back in the morning?" Mrs. McNally asked.

"I don't know," Eve said. "We'll have to wait and see."

The doctor took hold of his wife's other arm and led her from the room, glancing back at Eve as he did so and shaking his head sorrowfully. Eve sighed and eased the door closed behind them.

Then she turned to the bed and said, "I'm so sorry, Mr. Morgan. We try to keep a close eye on her. Sometimes at night, she gets up and roams around the house, looking for my brother."

"Joseph," Morgan guessed.

Eve nodded. "That's right. He . . . died a couple of years ago. That's what made my mother . . . like she is."

"I'm sorry," Morgan said, and meant it. These people had helped him, quite possibly saved his life. That meant that because of them, he was still alive to kill Clay Lasswell and the other men he intended to hunt down.

Eve sank down wearily on the straight-back chair near the bed. She wore a high-necked blue nightgown, and even though the part of Morgan that might have appreciated the fact she was an attractive young woman was numb with grief and loss, he still took note of it.

"For a while Pa hoped that she would come out of it," Eve said. "He thought that once the shock of losing Joe wore off, she would be herself again. But I guess it never has." She looked at Morgan with a sad smile, then suddenly exclaimed, "Oh, my Lord! Look at you. Your face is covered with sweat! Your fever's broken, hasn't it?"

"I reckon so," Morgan said in a husky voice.

"And here I was, babbling on." She stood up and leaned over the bed, cupping his face between her hands. "Yes, you're a lot cooler than you were. Thank God for that. You're going to be able to fight off the infection after all." She felt the bed around him. "These sheets are soaked. I'll need to change them. You'll need a fresh nightshirt, too."

Morgan felt a sudden and unexpected surge of embarrassment. "Don't you think you, uh, ought to get your father to do that?"

"Pa's going to have his hands full getting Mama settled down again. I can take care of this." She straightened and put her hands on her hips. "I've been working as my father's nurse for quite a while, Mr. Morgan. I don't think I'll be seeing anything I haven't seen before."

In general, maybe, Morgan thought, but not specifically. But he didn't argue. He was too tired and weak for that. He lay back, closed his eyes, and let Eve do what she needed to do. When she was finished, he had to admit that it felt a lot better lying on dry sheets and wearing a clean, dry nightshirt.

"With any luck, you'll be ready for some real food again tomorrow," she said. "We won't rush it, though. It'll take quite a while for you to regain your strength after what you've been through."

"How long?" Morgan asked.

She frowned at him. "How long what? Until you're up and around?"

"Yeah."

"I imagine it'll be a couple of weeks before you're able to get out of bed at least."

Morgan shook his head. "A week," he said.

"Don't be silly. You won't be strong enough by then."

"Yes, I will be."

"My, aren't you the stubborn one? Is there somewhere you have to be?"

"Yes," Morgan said. "And something I have to do, the sooner the better."

"Yes, well, if you rush it, you'll be taking a chance on having a relapse. You had a really close call, Mr. Morgan. You don't want to die now just because you insisted on doing something foolish."

Morgan heaved a sigh. "No," he whispered. "I don't want to die now."

But after Lasswell and the others were dead, it wouldn't really matter, now would it?

Morgan slept late the next morning. When he woke up, a man he had never seen before was sitting in the rocking chair, puffing on a pipe and watching him.

Even though the stranger was sitting down, Morgan could tell that he was big. The man wore a black hat with a rounded crown. A couple of eagle feathers were stuck in the band. He wore a blue shirt over fringed buckskin leggings, as well as high-topped moccasins. As if Morgan needed anything else to guess the identity of his visitor, the coppery shade of the man's skin was a dead giveaway.

"You're Bearpaw," Morgan said. "The man who saved my life."

The man took the pipe out of his mouth and said, "Phillip Bearpaw. You can call me Phillip."

Morgan nodded. "I'm pleased to meet you. And I'm mighty obliged to you for helping me. I'd likely have died out there if not for you."

Bearpaw grunted. "No likely about it. You would

have drowned. I heard the splash and came to see what happened. You were facedown in Sawtooth Creek."

"You were that close? I didn't see anybody around."

"People only see me when I want to be seen," Bearpaw said. He chuckled. "In this case, I was just around the next bend in the creek, fishing and reading John Milton's *Paradise Lost*. Ever read it?"

Morgan shook his head. "I'm afraid not. My father's an avid reader, though. He may have."

Bearpaw clamped his teeth on the pipe stem and gave a solemn nod. "You should try it sometime. It'll give you a new understanding of the condition of man's immortal soul."

Morgan frowned a little and said, "I haven't run into many Paiutes, but you're not like any of them."

"Bearpaw heap sorry. Ugh."

Morgan laughed out loud, then felt a sudden twinge of guilt. It had been less than a week since Rebel's murder. He shouldn't have ever laughed again, let alone this soon.

"Anyway, I'm grateful to you for saving my life, Phillip. I'd be glad to—"

Bearpaw frowned, and Morgan stopped short as he realized that the Paiute might take any offer of a reward as an insult. Instead, Morgan said, "If there's anything I can ever do for you, it would be my pleasure."

Bearpaw nodded. "I'll remember that." He took the pipe out of his mouth again. "How are you feeling this morning?"

"I reckon I'll live." Frank would have said something like that in a similar situation, and Morgan thought that if he was going to succeed in making everything think that Conrad Browning was dead, he would have to stop talking like him.

"Eve said your fever broke last night. That's good."

"Where is Eve?"

"Getting some rest."

"I'm glad," Morgan said. "She deserves it. I have a feeling she's been spending most of her time watching over me for the past few days."

Bearpaw nodded. "That girl's good at being a nurse, all right. She'd make a good doctor, too, one of these days, if that's what she wanted to do. She's too busy taking care of her folks, though, and helping out with Patrick's patients. You hungry?"

The sudden shift took Morgan a little by surprise. "Actually, I am. Starving, now that I think about it."

"Another good sign." Bearpaw stood. "I'll go get you something to eat."

He left the room, and came back a few minutes later with a plate and a cup of coffee. The plate had a couple of biscuits smeared with molasses on it. Bearpaw set the cup and plate on the table beside the bed and helped Morgan sit up, propping the pillow behind him. Moving like that caused pain to shoot through Morgan's side, and the room spun around him a little from his head being upright again. Both of those reactions settled down quickly, however, and he grasped the cup eagerly when Bearpaw handed it to him.

"Careful," the Paiute cautioned. "The coffee's hot."

Morgan took a sip. He couldn't remember the last time he'd tasted anything as good as the strong, black brew. Then he took a bite of biscuit, savoring the sweetness of the molasses, and that was even better.

"Don't wolf it down," Bearpaw cautioned. "Your stomach may not be used to solid food yet."

Morgan took it slow and easy, but he ate every bite and drained the cup of every last drop of coffee. His stomach protested a little, but overall he felt strength flowing back into his body from the food.

Drowsiness began overwhelming him even before he finished eating. As he polished off the last of the meal, he yawned prodigiously. Bearpaw took the plate and cup and set them aside, then said, "You'd better get some more sleep."

"I really ought to . . ."

Morgan's voice trailed off as he realized there really wasn't anything he *could* do right now. His only mission in life was to bring justice to the men responsible for Rebel's death. He didn't care about business anymore; Conrad Browning's lawyers were more than capable of keeping the various enterprises humming along smoothly. He was realistic enough to know that he was in no shape to face any of his enemies right now. Recovering from his injury was really the only job he had at the moment.

"All right," he said as he allowed Bearpaw to help him stretch out again. "I guess a nap wouldn't hurt anything."

"Someone will be here when you wake up," the Paiute promised.

That was the beginning of a long week for the man who now called himself Morgan. He slept and ate and gradually grew stronger. When he was awake, Eve McNally was usually there to bring him food and drink and make sure he was comfortable, although from time to time Bearpaw or Dr. McNally spelled her in those duties. Sometimes, Bearpaw sat in the rocker and read from his battered copy of *Paradise Lost,* his deep, resonant voice a perfect match for the English poet's high-flown words. At other times, Morgan just lay there and listened to the

Gramophone music coming from elsewhere in the house. As was often the case in frontier settlements, the doctor practiced medicine in the same house where he and his family lived. The bedroom where Morgan was recuperating was on the side of the house, close enough to the front so that occasionally he heard horses passing by on the road.

One afternoon when he was dozing, the sound of shots rang out somewhere not far away, coming in clearly through the open window. By now, Morgan was strong enough to sit up on his own, even though he hadn't tried to get out of bed and walk yet. When the gunshots startled him out of his half sleep, he bolted up in the bed and cried, "Rebel!"

No one else was in the room, but Eve hurried in a few seconds later. "Don't be alarmed, Mr. Morgan," she said as she came to the bedside. "There's no war. The rebels aren't attacking."

He fell back with a groan. She didn't understand, and he couldn't explain it to her without revealing who he really was. "Sorry," he said. "I didn't mean to yell."

"You must have been dreaming, and then when you heard those shots . . ." She made a face.

"Who was doing the shooting?"

Eve shook her head. "Just a couple of men riding by on the road. Troublemakers. They've been around town for the past few days. Trash like that drifts in from time to time and hangs around town for a while annoying everybody, but then they get bored and ride on. It's nothing to concern yourself with, Mr. Morgan."

Morgan wasn't concerned, now that he knew what was going on. For a moment, though, the sound of the shots had carried him back to that awful night full of blood and death that had stolen everything from him, even his own identity.

But losing his identity was his own idea, he reminded himself. He had given it up in hopes that would make it easier for him to deliver justice to Rebel's murderers. He didn't really mourn the loss of Conrad Browning, not for a second.

The next day, he said to Eve, "It's time for me to get up."

"I don't know about that," she replied with a frown. "You've only been here a week. I don't think you're strong enough yet."

"I'm getting up," Morgan said.

She held out a hand to stop him. "Let me at least go ask Pa what he thinks."

Morgan considered that, then nodded and leaned back against the pillow propped up behind him. "All right . . . but I'm getting up."

"You are the stubbornest man. Wait right there." She paused in the doorway to point a finger at him. "I mean it."

A couple of minutes later, Dr. McNally came in with Eve following him. "My daughter tells me you're ready to get up," the doctor said.

Morgan nodded. "It's time."

"You know, most people with a gunshot wound like that would be laid up for a couple of weeks, maybe even a month."

Most people couldn't have been shot like that and gone on to do everything he had afterward, Morgan thought. Thinking of his father, he said, "I come from good stock."

Eve crossed her arms and said, "I told him it was a bad idea."

McNally rubbed at his chin. "Oh, I don't know. He's young, and he was obviously in good health before he got shot. Plus he's been eating like a horse for days now."

That was true. Morgan's appetite had come back stronger than ever.

"I think it'll be all right to give it a try," McNally went on.

Morgan threw back the sheet and started to swing his legs out of the bed.

"Now, don't rush things," McNally said. He moved to Morgan's side and took hold of his right arm. "Eve, get his other arm. Take it slow and easy. Try standing up first, and see how that makes you feel."

With the two of them helping him, Morgan stood up. His legs were a little unsteady at first, but he was able to stiffen the muscles and straighten to his full height.

"I'm not dizzy," he said.

"That's a good sign," McNally agreed. "Take a step."

Morgan had a bad second or two when he thought his legs weren't going to obey his commands, but then he moved his right leg forward, braced himself, and took a step with the left. "I'm walking across the room," he said.

"Don't get in a hurry. Eve, hang on to him."

"I've got him," Eve said grimly.

With slow and methodical steps, Morgan walked across the room. Then he walked back to the bed, and by the time he got there, he was exhausted. As they helped him lie down, he sank gratefully onto the mattress.

"Guess I'm not . . . as strong as I thought I was," he said.

"Just stronger than most of the folks I've ever seen," McNally said with a smile. "You did just fine, Mr. Morgan. You'll be up and around in no time."

"I'll hold you to that," Morgan said.

By the time a couple of more days had gone by, McNally's prediction was proven true. Morgan could stand up by himself, walk around the room, and even venture out into the rest of the house. The first time he walked into the family's parlor, with Eve at his side, he saw where the music had been coming from.

Mrs. McNally sat in a rocking chair with a lace doily over the back of it. Her hair was neatly combed and braided now, and she wore a simple housedress. Next to the rocking chair was a table, also covered with a doily, and on the table sat the Gramophone, a polished wooden box with a crank handle on the side, a turntable for the shellac discs on which the music was recorded, and a needle arm connected to a large, brass, trumpet-shaped horn that angled into the air. The turntable was revolving at the moment, and as the needle followed the grooves etched into the disc, the vibrations were transmitted to a diaphragm in the base of the horn that converted them to music. Morgan had seen several of the machines before and was fascinated by the process.

Mrs. McNally looked up at him and exclaimed, "Joseph!"

"No, Mama," Eve said quickly, going to the chair to keep her mother from getting up. "This isn't Joseph. It's one of Pa's patients, Mr. Morgan."

"Oh." The old woman sat back in the chair and seemed to lose interest in Morgan. The Gramophone needle reached the end of the grooves. She moved it aside, took the disc off the turntable, and replaced it with another one she took from a box that sat on the table next to the Gramophone. She turned the crank on the side of the machine until the turntable was spinning smoothly, then placed the needle at its outer edge. Music filled the room again.

"She sits there and does that all day?" Morgan said under his breath as Eve came back to his side.

She nodded. "All day," she replied, and he plainly heard the sorrow in her voice. "But when people lose something so precious to them as Joe was to her, they do whatever they have to in order to keep going."

Morgan understood that all too well. Mrs. McNally clung to the hope that someday her lost boy would return.

Morgan's hope was that he would live long enough to see all the bastards who'd murdered Rebel die.

Chapter 11

The next afternoon, Morgan was sitting in the parlor with Bearpaw and Mrs. McNally when Eve came hurrying in from outside. Morgan knew she had walked down to the general store owned by her uncle to pick up a few supplies. She clutched a bundle in her arms, but as Morgan looked at her, he could tell that something was wrong. Her face was flushed and she was breathing heavily, as if she'd been running.

And she looked scared, too. Morgan recognized the expression right away.

He stood up and said, "What is it?" As long as he didn't try to move too quickly, he could get around fairly well now.

"Nothing," Eve said, but the answer came too fast. Morgan knew she was lying, and so did Bearpaw.

"Something is wrong," the Paiute said. "You might as well tell us, Eve."

She glanced at her mother and then inclined her head toward the door that led into the kitchen. "Not here," she said.

Morgan realized that she didn't want to explain in

front of Mrs. McNally. He nodded and followed her into the kitchen, along with Bearpaw.

Eve set the package of supplies on the table and turned to Morgan and Bearpaw. "There's no reason for either of you to get involved in this," she said. "It's over and done with, and nobody was hurt. You don't have to worry about me."

"Why don't you tell us what happened and let us be the judge of that?" Bearpaw said.

Eve grimaced. "All right. I was in Uncle Ned's store when those two troublemakers came in."

"Garrity and Jessup?" Bearpaw asked.

She nodded. "That's right." With a glance at Morgan, she added, "Those are the two men who've been hanging around town the past week or so, the ones who fired those shots yesterday."

"I figured as much," Morgan said.

"Anyway, they came up to me and started . . . saying things. Making rude comments. You know, the way some men do around women."

"A man who doesn't treat women with respect isn't worthy of the name," Morgan snapped. Another lesson he had learned from Frank.

"I can't argue with that," Eve said. "I tried to ignore them, but they wouldn't go away. Then Uncle Ned heard what was going on and got the shotgun he keeps under the counter. He told them to get out of his store and not set foot in there again."

"Did they leave?" Morgan asked.

"They did, but not before cursing Uncle Ned and telling him that he'd be sorry. That scared me even more than the things they'd been saying to me. But when they were gone, he told me not to worry about it. He said they were just full of hot air and bluster."

Morgan wasn't so sure about that. He had seen hardcases like those two before. Sometimes they'd back down if one of their victims stood up to them, but sometimes challenging them just made them more dangerous. You had to be prepared for whichever way it went.

"I went ahead and got the supplies and started to walk home," Eve continued, "but then I saw Garrity and Jessup following me on their horses."

Morgan stiffened with anger. "Did they bother you again?"

She shook her head. "No. They stayed back. But just seeing them following me like that, walking their horses along the road and grinning . . . well, it frightened me. I started running."

Bearpaw said, "That's probably all they wanted, just to scare you and upset you."

"Then they succeeded," Eve said. "I'm scared and upset. But like I said starting out, it's over now, and no harm was done."

"Let's hope that's right," Morgan said.

He wasn't convinced that Garrity and Jessup would give up that easily, though.

Bearpaw lived in a shack on Sawtooth Creek, about a mile from the settlement. He had gone home that evening, while Morgan sat in the parlor with the Mc-Nallys. Mrs. McNally played the Gramophone and rocked slowly back and forth. Dr. McNally dozed in a chair, the copy of the Sawtooth *Gazette* he had been reading spread out in his lap. Eve worked on some mending, while Morgan tried to read the copy of *Paradise Lost* that Bearpaw had loaned him. The words that had flowed so well off the Paiute's tongue weren't nearly as easy to read. Morgan couldn't get too interested in the poem's story either. He had already been to hell, and he had no real hope of heaven.

A knock on the door made McNally start up from his nap, sputtering and fumbling with the newspaper. "A doctor never gets to take it easy for very long," he said as he got to his feet. He went to the door and opened it.

The man who stood there didn't appear to need a doctor. He seemed to be hale and hearty. The badge pinned to his vest told Morgan that he was a lawman of some sort.

"Hello, Zeke," McNally said. "Is somebody sick at the jail?"

"No, but you better come downtown with me right away, Doc," the man said. "Somebody jumped your brother Ned while he was lockin' up his store and beat the hell out of him." The lawman glanced at Eve and Mrs. McNally and added, "Beg your pardon for the language, ladies."

Eve had cried out softly as the lawman broke the news. She put a hand to her mouth for a second, then stood up and said angrily, "It was those two drifters, Garrity and Jessup! It had to be, Marshal."

The man frowned at her. "Why's that, Eve?"

"Because Uncle Ned had trouble with them this afternoon." In a few hurried words, she told him about the encounter in the store. "They warned him he'd be sorry for pointing that shotgun at them. They came back and attacked him, Marshal. It had to be them!"

"Well, I haven't had a chance to ask Ned about it yet. Maybe he got a good look at them."

Dr. McNally had grabbed his hat, coat, and medical

bag. "I'm ready to go, Zeke," he said as he came back to the door. The two men hurried out.

Morgan felt the urge to go with them, but he knew there was nothing he could do to help. Also, even though he was a lot stronger than he had been, he wasn't up to a walk of several blocks.

Besides, he didn't think the two women ought to be left here alone.

"I'm sure your uncle will be all right," he told Eve. "Your pa's a mighty good doctor."

"Of course he is," Eve said. She clasped her hands together. "I'm just upset because this is all my fault."

Morgan stared at her. "How in the world do you figure that?" he asked. "You're not the one who jumped your uncle and beat him."

"No, but it's because of me that it happened. Uncle Ned wouldn't be hurt now if he hadn't been defending me from those two . . ."

"Varmints is a good word," Morgan suggested.

"I was thinking of something a little stronger," Eve said with a glance toward her mother, who was still rocking and playing the Gramophone, seemingly oblivious to what was going on.

Morgan stood up and went over to Eve. "Look," he said, "you're not to blame for any of this. The ones responsible are the ones who actually did it. Nobody else."

"I know that, but still—"

"No buts about it," Morgan said. "That's the way it is. Blaming yourself for something when it's not your fault isn't going to do anybody any good. Blaming yourself when it *is* your fault doesn't do any good either, unless you try to set things right."

He knew that from bitter experience.

"I suppose you're right," Eve said with a sigh. "I wonder if I should go down to the store."

"Might be better to stay here, in case your mother needs you." That was true enough. Morgan didn't particularly want to be left alone with Mrs. McNally either.

Eve paced worriedly until her father returned an hour later. "Ned's going to be all right," he said as soon as he came in. "They gave him a good thrashing, and he's got a broken rib and a busted nose. But he'll recover. We took him home and patched him up. Your Aunt Charlene will look after him."

"Thank God," Eve said. "It was Garrity and Jessup, wasn't it?"

McNally shrugged. "Ned couldn't say for sure. It was dark, and they jumped him from behind. He said he never got a good look at their faces."

"You *know* it had to be them," Eve insisted.

"I'm sure it was," her father agreed, "but knowing something and being able to prove it are two different things. Still, Marshal Chambliss said he was going to run Garrity and Jessup out of town anyway. They've stirred up enough trouble in other ways to justify that."

"I hope he's careful," Eve said. "Those two are loco. Crazy mean. You can tell it by looking in their eyes." She crossed her arms and shuddered.

A short time after that, when one of the Gramophone discs reached its end, Mrs. McNally said, "I'm tired. I'm going to bed. I want to be rested in the morning, because I think that's when Joseph will be back."

"You never can tell," McNally said, humoring her as he and Eve always did. He went to her and took her arm as she stood up from the rocking chair. "Come along, dear. I think I'll turn in, too."

They went into their bedroom, leaving Morgan and Eve alone in the parlor. Eve sat on the divan, Morgan in an armchair near the fireplace that was cold at this time of year.

"Another week or two and you'll be able to ride again," Eve said. "What will you do then, Mr. Morgan?"

"I'll have to be moving on. I told you, I have places to go and things to do." He didn't offer any details, and Eve didn't press him for them.

In fact, she said, "I'm not sure I want to know what sort of things you have to do. I have a feeling that they're not very pleasant."

Morgan shrugged. He didn't expect to get any pleasure out of killing Lasswell and the other kidnappers. It was just something he had to do, as he'd told Eve.

She stood up and said, "I'll help you get ready for bed."

"I can take care of myself," Morgan said. "Things are different now. I'm not helpless anymore."

"I suppose you're right about that. I'll say good night, then—"

Eve stopped short and Morgan's head lifted as the sound of shots drifted in from the night. These were farther away than the ones he'd heard yesterday, Morgan thought, but still close enough to be clearly audible.

"That came from downtown," Eve said as she stood up from the divan and turned anxiously toward the door.

Morgan got to his feet as well and said, "Hold on. You're not thinking about going down there, are you?"

"Someone could be hurt."

"Yeah, and maybe some drunk was just firing into the air, or somebody was blowing off steam like those two drifters yesterday. If anybody's wounded, I'm sure the marshal will come to fetch your father."

"Well . . . I suppose you're right. Still, I just hate to hear shots. I hope Mama didn't hear them. Things like that can really upset her."

The vehemence with which she spoke surprised Morgan a little, and he wondered if there was some special reason Eve didn't like the sound of gunshots.

"I'm not going to bed yet," she went on. "I'm going to wait up a little while and make sure nobody needs medical help before I turn in."

"I'll wait up with you," Morgan said.

"You need your rest—"

"I've been getting plenty of rest. Probably more than I ever have in my life."

That was true, Morgan thought, at least to a certain extent. Since he'd been an adult and been forced by his mother's death to take over the management of the Browning financial interests, he had worked long hours, and even when he was at home instead of the office, he spent too much time worrying about the business.

That was one thing about overpowering grief— it swept away all the other concerns and made a man realize just how petty so many of his worries really were. And getting shot and losing a lot of blood wore a man out to the point that he had no choice except to rest.

He and Eve sat down again. A couple of minutes

of awkward silence went by, and then both of them sat up straighter as they heard horses outside.

"Someone *was* hurt," Eve began. "I'll fetch Pa—"

"Hey!" a man shouted outside. "There in the house? Are you there, Red?"

Eve's hand went to her mouth. Her face paled in shock. "That's one of them!" she said to Morgan in a half whisper. "Garrity or Jessup! That's what they were calling me in Uncle Ned's store this afternoon."

The two troublemakers showing up at the McNally house so soon after those gunshots didn't bode well, Morgan thought. He got to his feet and blew out the lamp, then told Eve, "Don't answer them."

A second man shouted, "We know you're in there, Red! Blowin' out the lamp ain't gonna do you no good! C'mon out here and talk to us!"

The door to the elder McNallys' room opened. The doctor said, "Eve, what's going on? What's all that yelling?"

"It's Garrity and Jessup, Pa," she told him. Morgan heard her moving across the room toward her father. Eve knew the furnishings so well she didn't need any light in order to be able to get around.

"I thought I heard some gunshots a few minutes ago," McNally said worriedly. "Thank God your mother is already sound asleep."

"There were shots downtown," Morgan said. "Then those troublemakers showed up here."

"Oh, Lord," McNally mumbled. "I'd better see if I can find my gun—"

Morgan snapped, "Don't do it. You'd just be giving them an excuse to shoot you."

From outside, one of the men shouted, "You'd damn well better listen in there! We just shot your marshal! Ain't nobody comin' to help you! Send out that redheaded gal, or we'll torch the place!"

"Yeah!" the other hardcase agreed with glee in his voice. "We'll burn it to the ground!"

"What are we going to do?" Eve asked in a terrified whisper. "They've already murdered Marshal Chambliss!"

Morgan moved toward them in the darkness. He reached out, touched Eve's shoulder. She gasped and tried to pull away from him, but his fingers tightened on her.

"Listen to me," he said. "You and your father go back in your parents' room and stay there. I'll handle this."

"But you're wounded, son," McNally objected.

"I'm strong enough to deal with a couple of skunks like those two," Morgan declared. He hoped he was right about that. Otherwise, these people who had done so much to help him might be in bad trouble. He wasn't going to show them any doubts that he might have, though. Instead, he went on. "It'll be all right. You have my word on that."

Outside, one of the men howled, "Come on out, you redheaded bitch! If you're nice enough to us, maybe we'll let you and your folks live!"

"Why doesn't somebody come and help us?" Eve asked in an anguished voice.

"They gunned down the marshal," Morgan reminded her. "Before that, they attacked your uncle. Everybody in town probably knows that. They're scared. Garrity and Jessup have Sawtooth buffaloed."

McNally asked, "What are you going to do, son?"

A cold smile touched Morgan's lips in the darkness. "With any luck . . . buffalo them right back."

They had to be curious about what he meant by that, but he didn't explain as he hustled them into the bedroom and closed the door. Outside, the two hard-cases were still yelling at the house, their words growing angrier and more obscene as they went on. Morgan went back into the room where he'd been recuperating, and felt around until he found the chest of drawers where Eve had put his gunbelt.

He opened the top drawer, reached inside, and felt the smooth walnut grips of the Colt. He pulled out the belt and buckled it around his waist. He still wore the tight bandages around his midsection, which caused him to move a little stiffly, but he was able to reach down far enough to tie the holster's thong around his leg. Then he opened the Colt's cylinder and explored the chambers to see if the gun was still loaded.

Morgan grimaced as he felt the empty chambers. Eve must have unloaded it. He reached into the open drawer again and brushed his hand over the bottom. Cartridges rolled across the wood. Morgan gathered them up and thumbed them into the Colt. He had carried out this task enough times so that he could do it without any light, although it would have been easier if he could see what he was doing.

Then he closed the cylinder, slid the revolver back into the holster, and took a deep breath.

"I'm warnin' you, girl!" one of the men outside shouted as Morgan reached the front door. "If you don't come out now, we're gonna start shootin'! We'll ventilate that house and everybody in it!"

Morgan opened the door, stepped out onto the porch, and said, "You're not going to do anything except either get the hell out of here—or die!"

Chapter 12

His sudden appearance on the porch took them by surprise. Both men fell silent. Morgan could feel them staring at him.

After a couple of heartbeats, one of the troublemakers demanded in a loud, angry voice, "Who the hell are you?"

"The man telling you to leave these people alone."

"Do you know who we are?" the other man asked. "We just killed this town's marshal!"

"Do you know who *I* am?" Morgan shot back. If he was going to run a bluff, he knew it had to be a good one. Without waiting for them to answer, he went on, "They call me Kid Morgan."

"Never heard of you," one of the men said with a sneer in his voice.

"I'll bet you've heard of Wolf Dunston," Morgan said, plucking the name out of his memory. "I killed him last year in Santa Fe. And what about Linc Mc-Sween?" he hurried on, not giving Garrity and Jessup too much time to think. "He drew on me in Tucson, and he's dead now. Hardy Williams? Mart Dooley? Ed Cambridge? All notches on my gun, boys."

Every one of those names was fictional. Morgan had gotten them from dime novels he had read about his father. To Frank's great chagrin, he was the hero of dozens of those gaudy pamphlets, all of them featuring lurid stories made up by scribblers who probably kept bottles of whiskey on their desks so they could take slugs of hooch whenever what they were writing started to make too much sense. Although the man who used to be Conrad Browning probably wouldn't have admitted it, he'd read quite a few of those dime novels, and some of the names of the vicious outlaws and gunslingers who appeared in them had stuck with him.

Garrity and Jessup looked at each other. "You ever hear of any of those fellas?" one of them asked the other.

"Yeah, I think I have. They're supposed to be bad hombres."

Morgan heard a trace of nervousness edging into their voices. He added, "The last two men I killed were the Winchell brothers, Jeff and Hank." That much was true.

"I *know* I've heard of them. Damn it, Jessup, what the hell've you got us into?"

"I don't care who he is!" Jessup said. "There's two of us and one o' him! We can take him! You want to have some fun with that pretty little redheaded gal or not?"

"There were two of the Winchell brothers, too," Garrity pointed out, "and he killed them."

"So he says. All we got is his word for that!"

"It's true," Morgan said calmly. "Turn around and

ride away, or you can ask them about it yourselves, once you meet up with them in hell."

"You're a big damn talker."

That was true. Talk was Morgan's best weapon right now, because he had no idea whether or not he could beat these men to the draw. Considering that they outnumbered him two to one, it was mighty unlikely he could kill both of them before one of them got him.

But they had already gunned down Marshal Chambliss, he reminded himself. They had nothing to lose. If he didn't stop them somehow, they would carry off Eve McNally and do God knows what to her. He couldn't allow that to happen. If he could bluff them, make them ride off, that was his best chance. He didn't like the idea of letting them get away after they'd killed the marshal, but once they were gone from here, the law could go after them and deal with them. That wasn't his job.

"I'm done talking," he said now. "Anything else I've got to say, I'll let my gun do it."

For a second, he thought it was going to work. He really did. But then Jessup yelled at his companion, "Kill him!" and grabbed at the gun on his hip.

In that moment, Morgan became a creature of pure instinct. Without thinking about what he was doing, he reached for his gun, closed his hand around the grips, lifted the weapon from its holster, tipped up the barrel, and fired. The double-action Colt .45 was in excellent shape. Its mechanism worked smoothly. Morgan continued pulling the trigger as he raised the gun, extending his arm. Flame lanced from the muzzle again and again as the Colt bucked against his hand. Garrity and Jessup fired back at him from their saddles. What felt like a gust of hot wind fanned his face. The roar of gunshots was so loud and overpowering, Morgan felt like he was trapped in the center of the world's worst thunderstorm.

Approximately three seconds after Morgan drew his gun, the hammer fell on an empty chamber. He had turned sideways without even realizing it, making himself a smaller target, and now he stood there on the porch with his right arm held out straight from the shoulder, the empty revolver in his hand.

Garrity and Jessup were dark, motionless shapes on the ground. Their horses stampeded off down the road, the empty stirrups flapping as they ran.

A pounding roar still filled Morgan's head. After a moment, he realized it was the sound of his own pulse. Slowly, he lowered the gun.

He had fired all the rounds in the Colt, he told himself. The smart thing to do now would be to reload, as quickly as possible, just in case one or both of the gunmen weren't dead. Did he have any bullets? Or was the rest of his ammunition in the house?

The gunbelt had loops on it so that cartridges could be carried in them, he remembered. That was why some people called a belt like this a shell belt. He reached around to his back and felt of the loops. Sure enough, there were bullets in them, although at this moment he didn't recall putting them there. He pulled out five of them—the hammer always sits on an empty chamber, unless you're reloading in the middle of a fight, his father had taught him—and opened the cylinder to let the empties fall out. He thumbed the fresh rounds into the gun.

A dark figure loomed up beside him. Morgan snapped the cylinder closed and turned quickly. The figure stuck his arms into the air and said, "Whoa! Take it easy, Kid. It's just me, Phillip Bearpaw."

Morgan lowered the gun and heaved a sigh of relief. "Phillip," he said. "What are you doing here?"

"I heard there was trouble in town," the Paiute answered, "and came over in case Patrick needed anybody to stay with Lucinda. I figured he and Eve might be busy tending to the wounded."

"I think the only person who was shot was Marshal Chambliss." Morgan nodded toward Garrity and Jessup. "Except for those two."

"I saw the fight as I came up," Bearpaw said. "I heard some of what you told them, too, Kid. We'll have to talk about that . . . later."

Morgan frowned. What did Bearpaw mean by that?

"Right now," Bearpaw went on, "we'd better make sure those two miscreants are dead. I'll go inside and get a lantern."

The front door opened then, and Dr. McNally stepped out. "No need for that, Phillip," he said. "I've got one right here."

The doctor scratched a match into life and lit the lantern. As its glow washed over the porch, he went on. "Are you all right, Mr. Morgan?"

"I reckon." Morgan hadn't really thought about it, but now as he took inventory of himself, he realized that he hadn't been hit. Some of the bullets fired by Garrity and Jessup had come close to him, but not close enough to do any damage.

"What about that wound in your side? Does it feel like it's opened up again?"

Morgan shook his head. "I really think I'm fine."

The three men walked down the steps. McNally held the lantern high so that its light spread out over the bodies of the two gunmen. Bearpaw was carrying an old Sharps rifle, Morgan saw. The Paiute kept the weapon trained on Garrity and Jessup as he used a toe to roll them onto their backs.

Morgan felt a twinge of surprise as he saw the dark stain on the chest of each man's shirt. From the looks of it, he had hit them dead center.

"They won't bother any more young women or gun down any more marshals," he said.

"No, they won't," Bearpaw agreed. "They've gone west of the divide."

Morgan holstered the Colt. As he did so, he heard a rush of footsteps behind him. He turned, and Eve threw her arms around him.

"Are you all right, Mr. Morgan?" she asked as she hugged him tightly—tightly enough, in fact, to make a tiny twinge of pain go through his side.

"I'm, uh, fine," Morgan said. He lifted a hand and awkwardly patted her on the back. "Just fine."

He had been a widower for a little less than two weeks. He had no business having an attractive young woman in his arms, even one who was just hugging him out of gratitude. He put his hands on Eve's shoulders and gently moved her away from him. In the lantern light, he thought he saw a hurt expression flicker across her face.

"Doc! Doc McNally!"

The shout drew everyone's attention. They turned to see half a dozen townsmen hurrying toward them. As the men panted up and stopped, one of them went on. "Zeke Chambliss is hurt, Doc. He needs your help."

"Garrity and Jessup said they killed him," McNally exclaimed.

The townsman shook his head. "No, Zeke ain't

dead, but he's got a busted shoulder and a crease on his head that bled like a stuck pig. Can you come help him?"

"Of course I can. And thank God he's still alive," McNally added as he handed the lantern to Bearpaw. "Let me get my bag." As he started to turn toward the house, he paused and said to Morgan, "If you're sure you're all right . . . ?"

"I'm fine," Morgan said again. "Go tend to the marshal."

The townies were gawking at Garrity and Jessup. "Who killed these two?" one of the men asked.

Bearpaw nodded toward Morgan. "The Kid here did that. He's Kid Morgan, the famous gunfighter."

"Wait a minute—" Morgan began.

"Kid Morgan!" another of Sawtooth's citizens repeated. "I think I've heard of you. You're the fella Bearpaw found in the creek, all shot up."

"What happened?" a third man asked eagerly. "Did you get wounded in a gunfight, Kid?"

Morgan opened his mouth to explain that the whole thing was a pack of lies. His father was the famous gunfighter, not him. All he'd been doing was trying to scare off Garrity and Jessup so they'd leave the McNally family alone.

But then a realization struck him, and he stopped the explanation before he started it. He wanted everybody to believe that Conrad Browning was dead back in Carson City. The best way to insure that was to create a totally new identity for himself, and if these people wanted to believe some yarn he had made up that contained only a few shreds of truth, then so be it. Kid Morgan, he thought. It had a ring to it.

The townsmen were still clamoring for answers.

Morgan hooked the thumb of his right hand in his gunbelt and raised his left hand to silence them.

"I don't talk too much about what's happened in the past," he said. "That's sort of a rule of mine."

"We understand," Bearpaw said. "Let's leave him alone, fellas. He needs some rest. He's still recuperating."

One of the men laughed and jerked a thumb at Garrity and Jessup. "Looks to me like he's healed up just fine."

Dr. McNally emerged from the house with his medical bag. "Let's go," he said briskly. "Phillip, would you mind staying here to keep an eye on things? Not that it's really necessary, I guess, with Kid Morgan staying with us."

"Yeah, I can stick around," the Paiute replied with a nod.

"And I'll send the undertaker back for those bodies," McNally added over his shoulder as he hurried away.

Morgan turned wearily toward the house. He still had a little difficulty believing that he had actually killed those two men in a gunfight. Their bullet-riddled bodies were vivid proof of it, though.

He stopped in surprise as he saw the way Eve was looking at him. Her eyes were wide and staring, and from the expression on her face, she had just seen something ugly wiggle out from under a rotten log.

"Eve," Morgan said with a frown. "What's wrong?"

"Is it true?" she asked. "Are you a gunfighter?"

"Well . . ." It seemed like it was a little late to start denying it now.

Eve turned and ran back into the house without another word.

Morgan turned to look at Bearpaw. "What the hell was that all about?"

Bearpaw tucked the Sharps under the same arm he was using to hold the lantern, then clapped his other hand on Morgan's shoulder. "Maybe I'll tell you about it," he said, "but not until you've told me what all that Kid Morgan bullshit was about."

"So you knew I was making it all up?" Morgan asked a short time later as he and Bearpaw sat at the table in the kitchen of the McNally house. He kept his voice down so that they wouldn't be overheard.

"Yeah, I just played along until I got a chance to talk to you in private," Bearpaw said. "Your name may really be Morgan, for all I know, but like I told you, I got here in time to see that fracas, and I know you're not a professional gunfighter. I don't recall ever hearing about any gunslinger named Kid Morgan either, no matter what the other folks around here have talked themselves into believing. The only Morgan I know of who's a fast gun is Frank Morgan."

Since Bearpaw already knew some of the truth, Morgan figured the only thing to do was to tell him the whole story. The Paiute was too smart to be taken in by lies.

"I come by the name honestly. Frank Morgan is my father."

Bearpaw's eyebrows rose. "I never knew The Drifter had a kid."

"The fewer people who know about it, the better. I realize I already owe you my life, but now I have to ask you for another favor. I have to ask you not to tell anybody about this."

"I can't make a promise like that without knowing what the truth is," Bearpaw replied with a shrug. "But if you're not out to hurt the McNallys or any of my other friends, I don't suppose I'd have any reason to break your confidence."

Morgan clasped his hands together on the table in front of him. "All right," he said. "It's like this."

He spent the next fifteen minutes telling Bearpaw everything that had happened, from that interrupted picnic on the hillside above Carson City, to riding away from his old life while the carriage house burned behind him with Jeff Winchell's body in it. Bearpaw listened in silence for the most part, breaking in only to ask an occasional question.

When Morgan was finished, Bearpaw frowned across the table at him and said, "You never considered telling the McNallys the truth? Don't you think you owe them that much?"

"I thought about it," Morgan replied with a curt nod, "but I decided not to."

"Because you don't want anything to interfere with this vengeance quest of yours?"

"Don't you think I deserve some vengeance?" Morgan shot back. "Those men took away everything that was precious to me. They ripped my heart out and left me a walking dead man."

Bearpaw grunted. "A little melodramatic, don't you think?"

"No," Morgan said quietly. "I don't think so at all. Anyway, the reason I decided not to tell the Mc-Nallys the truth is that I thought it would be safer for them that way."

"Safer?" Bearpaw shook his head. "I don't understand."

"Think about it," Morgan said. "Lasswell's orders were to make me think that Rebel would be safe if I paid the ransom, then kill her right in front of my eyes. His job was to make me suffer as much emotional pain as possible. Someone gave him those orders, and whoever it was has one hell of a grudge against Conrad Browning."

Bearpaw thought it over and then nodded slowly. "So if word got around that Patrick and his family had helped Conrad Browning, then whoever was really behind the kidnapping might try to hurt them, too, just to get back at you."

"That's the way I figure it," Morgan said. "But nobody is going to connect Conrad to some obscure gunfighter called Kid Morgan. There'll be nothing to make anybody suspect that Conrad didn't die a suicide in that carriage house."

"You've got a tricky mind, Kid . . . but I think maybe you're right about this. It'll be safer for these folks if they don't know the truth."

"So I can count on you to keep my secret?"

Bearpaw nodded again. "Yes. I won't reveal what you just told me."

"Now," Morgan said, "you have to tell me how you knew I wasn't telling the truth out there. If I'm going to keep up this pose, it'll have to be as good as I can make it."

"First of all, tell me this. How do you intend to go about killing Lasswell and the other men who kidnapped your wife?"

Morgan frowned. "Well, I don't really know yet. I suppose I'll have to fight them . . ."

He stopped as Bearpaw solemnly shook his head.

"If you go up against anybody who's halfway decent with a gun, Kid, you'll just get yourself killed."

"I managed to take care of the Winchell brothers, and then Garrity and Jessup."

"You killed Hank Winchell by blowing his brains out when he was stunned," Bearpaw said with brutal honesty, "and it was a fluke that his brother fell so you could make the horse pull that buggy wheel over his neck. That was some fast thinking on your part, mind you, but you were still damned lucky."

"What about Garrity and Jessup? I outdrew them."

"Again, you were lucky. You came up against a couple of fellows who were slow as mud on the draw and terrible shots to boot. They thought they were dangerous gunmen, but they really weren't. I've seen some real gunfighters in my time, and those two weren't anywhere in the same league."

Morgan stared at the Paiute, dumbfounded. "But I hit them," he protested. "Shot them right out of the saddle."

"Yeah, each of them had one bullet wound to the chest. Not bad. But how many shots did you fire?"

Morgan recalled that he had emptied the Colt, and as he answered Bearpaw's question, he realized what the other man was talking about. "Five shots," he said. "Which means that three of them were clean misses."

"Sixty percent, to be mathematically precise. Hitting what you're shooting at less than half the time will get you killed in a hurry if you're going up against someone who's actually good with a gun. Maybe some of those kidnappers aren't any good. Maybe some of them aren't any better than Garrity and Jessup. But I'll bet some of them are. I *know* Clay Lasswell is a lot better. He'd kill you in the blink of an eye, Kid."

The bitter, sour taste of defeat and despair came up under Morgan's tongue. "Are you saying that I should just give up? That I shouldn't go after the men who are responsible for my wife's death?"

Bearpaw shook his head. "Not at all. I'm saying that you need to get a lot better before you face any of them."

"How am I going to do that?"

Bearpaw chuckled and leaned back in his chair. "Did you ever hear of a man called Preacher?"

"I don't think so," Morgan replied with a puzzled frown.

"How about Smoke Jensen?"

"Of course. He's as famous as Wild Bill Hickok or—"

"Or Frank Morgan?" Bearpaw finished. "It's a toss-up who was really faster in his prime, Smoke Jensen or your father, and I suppose it's a question that will never be settled. Preacher was an old mountain man who taught Smoke everything he knew about gun-fighting. Smoke had the natural ability, the vision and reflexes he was born with, and Preacher provided him with the know-how to use them. I knew Preacher, and he told me once that as soon as he saw Smoke handle a gun, he knew that the boy had the potential to be one of the best, if not *the* best." Bearpaw folded his arms across his chest. "I saw you draw on Garrity and Jessup tonight, and I tell you, Kid, I saw something similar to what Preacher must have seen with Smoke. You were born with a talent for gun-handling. I don't think you'll ever be at quite the same level as Smoke— or your father—but with practice and a good teacher, you could be better than just about anybody else."

"How much practice are you talking about?"

Bearpaw shrugged. "Months? Years? The really good ones never stop practicing."

"I don't have that long," Morgan declared with a shake of his head. "That gang has already had time to scatter to the four winds. The more time that goes by, the harder it'll be to track them all down."

"Maybe so, but you still can't afford to rush it."

"Anyway, where can I find a teacher like you were talking about?"

The Paiute glared at him and said, "White man heap hurt Bearpaw's feelings. Ugh."

"Stop that," Morgan snapped. "Are you talking about teaching me yourself? You're not a gunfighter."

"No, but I told you, I knew Preacher, and that old man liked to talk. He could go on for hours about all the things he taught Smoke Jensen. Didn't your father ever mention any of the little tricks he'd learned over the years?"

"As a matter of fact, he did," Morgan admitted. "I reckon I learned a few things without even being aware of it."

"I reckon you did, too. And I can teach you more. Most of it is really just common sense, and the first thing is, you have to hit what you shoot at. Being fast on the draw isn't worth a plugged nickel if you can't hit anything. That's why you work on accuracy first. The speed is already there. You were born with it. You just have to develop it once you've mastered the accuracy."

"Why would you want to take the time and trouble to help me?" Morgan asked.

"I pulled you out of that creek, didn't I? The way some cultures see it, once you've saved a man's life, you're responsible for him from then on. Anyway, you helped Patrick and his family, and since they're my friends, I figure I owe you. What do you say? Take a little time anyway to get better before you go after those men."

Morgan thought it over for a long moment, then nodded. "I reckon I can wait a little while. But not too long. If I don't catch up to those men fairly soon, someone else is liable to kill them first."

"Would that be so bad?" Bearpaw asked. "If they're dead, does it matter whether or not they died by your hand?"

"Yes," Morgan said. "It does."

Chapter 13

Marshal Zeke Chambliss came to the McNally house the next morning. The lawman's left shoulder was heavily bandaged, and that arm was in a sling. He had a bandage around his head as well, but he seemed fairly strong.

"Kid, I just wanted to thank you for what you did last night," Chambliss said as he shook hands with Morgan in the McNallys' parlor. "For all you knew when you braced those two hellions, they really had killed me."

"I'm glad they didn't," Morgan said with a faint smile.

"Oh, so am I!" Chambliss laughed. "Anyway, another reason I'm here is to make you a proposition. How'd you like to pin on the marshal's badge while I'm healin' up?"

"Wait a minute, Zeke," Dr. McNally protested. "Mr. Morgan's not yet fully recuperated from his own wound."

Morgan glanced at the doctor. "I thought you said when you changed the bandage this morning that the bullet hole looked like it was almost completely healed."

"Almost," McNally insisted. "I said *almost* completely healed."

"You said that after today, you didn't think I'd need to wear the bandage anymore."

McNally frowned. "You shouldn't use a man's own words against him."

"It doesn't matter," Morgan said, smiling again. He turned back to Chambliss. "Sorry, Marshal. I appreciate the offer, but I have to say no. I'm not cut out to be a lawman."

Chambliss looked disappointed. "Are you sure, Kid? I'm thinking that with a famous gunfighter wearing the badge, troublemakers will steer clear of Sawtooth."

The citizens of Buckskin had thought the same thing when they offered the marshal's job to Frank Morgan. But it hadn't really turned out that way, and as a result, Frank's relatively brief stint as a star packer was over.

Morgan shook his head and told Chambliss, "I've got business of my own elsewhere as soon as I'm fit to ride. And that's not going to be very long. I reckon your deputies will have to hold down the fort until you're better."

"Well, we'll muddle through, I guess," Chambliss said with a sigh. "If you change your mind, though . . ."

"No chance," Morgan said.

"In that case . . ." Chambliss put out his hand again. "I'll wish you good luck and say so long."

Morgan had noticed that Eve wouldn't meet his gaze this morning. When the marshal was gone, he waited until he got a chance to speak to her alone, then asked, "What's bothering you, Eve? Did I do something wrong?"

She shook her head, but again she wouldn't look at him. "No, of course not," she said. "You saved us from those two gunmen. There's no telling what they might have done if not for you, Mr. Morgan."

"Well, that's what I thought, but you seem like you're angry with me."

"I don't know what you're talking about," she insisted. "Now, if you'll excuse me, I have work to do."

Morgan could only stare after her as she bustled off to prepare her father's examination room for the day's patients.

Giving up any attempt to figure her out as a bad job, he stepped out onto the porch instead and looked down the road toward downtown. Sawtooth really wasn't a very big settlement, but this was his first good look at it. The road entered the town from the south. Dr. McNally's house was on the edge of the settlement. To the north, the road turned into a broad main street with businesses lining it for several blocks. Most of the residences were on the cross streets. The town was located in a valley between a line of wooded hills to the east and a range of more rugged mountains to the west. The mines were located in those mountains, Morgan knew, while beyond the eastern hills sprawled a vast plain cut up into large ranches. Sawtooth Creek twisted out of the mountains about a mile south of the settlement and provided water for those ranches.

Farther to the east lay the mostly arid Humboldt Basin, which wasn't good for much of anything, but this area around Sawtooth was nice country. A man could be happy here, Morgan thought as he leaned on the porch railing, especially if he had a woman like Eve McNally at his side.

He stiffened in surprise. Where had *that* come from? He had no feelings for Eve other than gratitude. He wasn't capable of anything else right now, and suspected that he never would be again. But that didn't stop him from recognizing that some other young man would be lucky to have Eve fall in love with him.

He hoped like hell that she hadn't fallen for him.

He went back inside and got his hat. As he settled it on his head, he paused to look into the mirror on the wall of his room. He hadn't really paid that much attention to the way he looked since he'd been here. He'd lost weight; his face was thinner than it had been before. Not surprisingly, his eyes had a solemn, almost haunted look to them. Eve had shaved him several times, but he thought that maybe he ought to let his beard grow. That would be one more thing to separate him from the clean-shaven Conrad Browning.

"Where are you going?" Dr. McNally asked as Morgan walked through the front room.

"I just want to get out and move around a little. I don't mean to sound ungrateful, Doc, but I've been cooped up here for long enough that I'm getting restless."

McNally chuckled. "I'm not so old that I don't remember that feeling, son. Go right ahead. Just don't overexert yourself. Remember, you don't have all your strength back yet."

Morgan left the house and walked down the road into the main part of the settlement. As he did, people on the street saw him and gave him friendly nods. Some of them spoke to him, shaking his hand and welcoming him to Sawtooth. Word had gotten around about what had happened with Garrity and Jessup.

But for that very reason, other citizens seemed leery of him, looking at him from the corners of their eyes and even crossing the street so they wouldn't have to greet him. They believed he was a famous gunfighter, Morgan realized, so they were afraid of him.

He had never really thought about it before, but now he realized that was the sort of thing his father had been forced to put up with for years and years, being admired and feared at the same time.

The blood on a man's hands was mighty hard to wash off.

Morgan didn't spend much time in town. He had nothing in common with these people. When he walked back to the McNally house, he found Phillip Bearpaw sitting in one of the rocking chairs on the front porch.

"How are you feeling this morning?" the Paiute asked.

"All right, I suppose," Morgan answered with a shrug.

"No lingering effects from that shoot-out last night, either physical or . . . ?"

"If you're asking if I lost any sleep over killing those two, the answer is no. I gave them a chance to ride away. It was their decision to go for their guns. But I don't take any real pleasure in killing them, any more than I would have if they'd been a couple of rabid skunks. It was just something that needed doing."

Bearpaw nodded. "That's a good attitude to take, I guess. It's the sort of thing that Preacher or Smoke Jensen would say. Don't look for trouble, but don't back down from it when it finds you. Don't brood about it either."

"Waste of time, as far as I'm concerned," Morgan said.

Bearpaw pushed himself to his feet. "Feel like taking a ride?"

"Actually, I do. And I'll bet my horse is even more anxious to stretch his legs. Where are we going?"

"I thought we'd go out to my cabin," Bearpaw said. "It's far enough away from town that the sound of gunshots shouldn't bother anybody. I picked up a box of cartridges at Ned's store. There's no time like the present to get started on that practice."

They walked around to the back of the house. Bearpaw's horse, a shaggy Appaloosa, was tied up at the shed where Morgan's buckskin and Dr. McNally's buggy horse were housed. Morgan started to get his saddle out of the shed and put it on the buckskin, but Bearpaw stopped him.

"Let me do that," the Paiute suggested. "If Patrick were to see you doing something like lifting a saddle, he wouldn't be happy. And Eve would be positively livid that you were risking opening up that wound again."

Morgan hesitated, then agreed. He didn't like having somebody taking care of a chore he could handle himself—just another example of how much he had changed since he was a young man—but he knew Bearpaw was right.

Eve must have heard them talking, because she appeared at the back door, looked at them for a second as Bearpaw saddled Morgan's horse, then came outside and strode toward them.

"Where do you think you're going, Mr. Morgan?" she asked.

"Out to Phillip's cabin," Morgan said with a nod toward Bearpaw. "He asked me to visit." He didn't see any need to explain that he was going out there to practice his gun-handling.

"Did you ask my father if it was all right for you to ride?"

"Well . . . no, I didn't. But it's not far—"

"Only about a mile," Bearpaw put in. "And we'll take it slow and easy, won't we, Kid?"

Morgan saw something flicker in Eve's eyes when Bearpaw called him "Kid." She said, "If you tear that wound open, you'll lose all the progress you've made since you've been here."

Morgan nodded in acknowledgment of the warning. "I know that. That's why I intend to be mighty careful."

Eve blew her breath out in an exasperated fashion and said, "All right. Go ahead. Just don't say I didn't tell you it was a mistake."

Carefully, Morgan put his left foot up in the stirrup and swung up onto the buckskin's back. It felt good to settle into the saddle. He smiled down at Eve and said, "So far, so good. That didn't hurt at all."

She said, "Hmmph," and turned to walk back to the house.

Bearpaw mounted up as well, and the two men rode slowly away from the house, following the trail to the south. When they were well out of earshot of the house, Morgan said, "You know, you never did tell me why Eve's so upset with me. I tried to convince myself it was just my imagination, but that's obviously not the case."

"It's not really my place to talk about Eve's feelings," Bearpaw said. "You should ask her yourself."

"I did. She insists that everything's fine."

Bearpaw shrugged. "It's her decision what she does . . . or doesn't . . . want to tell you."

"Yeah, I reckon you're right," Morgan admitted. That didn't mean he had to like it, though.

They reached Bearpaw's home, which was a sturdy-looking log cabin, a short time later. Morgan frowned at it, causing Bearpaw to chuckle and say, "What were you expecting, a wickiup or a tepee?"

"I thought the only Indians who lived in houses were the Cherokee and tribes like that back East."

"I happen to like an actual roof over my head, and a good solid wall between me and the cold wind in the winter. Plus I need better light to read by than a campfire. These eyes of mine aren't as young as they used to be."

"You're not like any other Indians I've run into."

"I never met a gunfighter with a Boston accent either," Bearpaw responded. "Although the accent does seem to be fading a little. You may never sound like a real Westerner, though."

"I'd better learn how to act like one."

"Amen to that." Bearpaw turned his horse. "Come on, let's go over by the creek."

They rode along the stream in which Morgan had almost drowned until they came to a large, open field bordered by a rocky bluff twenty feet high. Bearpaw reined in and told Morgan to dismount. They tied their horses to a couple of saplings. Then Bearpaw pointed to a large pine tree about twenty feet away, at the base of the bluff.

"Draw and fire at that tree," he said. "Hit it as many times as you can."

Morgan faced the pine and reached for the Colt, pulling the gun and bringing it up as fast as he could. He emptied all five rounds at the tree. The shots sounded like thunder as they rolled together, one after the other.

As Morgan lowered the gun, Bearpaw said, "Do you see any marks on the tree?"

Morgan gave a disappointed shake of his head. "No."

"How about on the bluff right behind it?"

A sigh came from Morgan as he counted. "I see five places where bullets hit the bluff. I missed with every shot."

"And that tree wasn't even shooting back at you like Garrity and Jessup were. You see, I told you you were lucky."

"You were right," Morgan admitted. "What did I do wrong?"

"You didn't listen. I told you to draw and fire at the tree. I didn't tell you to do it fast." The Paiute gestured toward the gun in Morgan's hand. "Reload and let's try it again."

This time Morgan understood what he was supposed to do. He holstered the revolver, faced the tree, and drew the gun again. He didn't waste any time about it, but he didn't rush either, as he lifted the gun and aimed at the pine. A second elapsed between each shot, giving him time to line his sights again.

This time chunks of bark and splinters flew in the air as the bullets chewed into the tree. Only one round missed and thudded into the bluff behind the pine.

"That's more like it," Bearpaw said.

"But way too slow to beat anybody to the draw," Morgan pointed out.

"What if the man you're facing is faster than you but a terrible shot? If he gets off three rounds and misses with all of them, and you just fire once but hit your target, you're going to win."

"And what happens if I face somebody who's faster than me and just as accurate?" Morgan wanted to know.

"Oh, well, in that case . . . you'll die."

Morgan laughed. He couldn't help it. As he shucked the empties from the Colt and started reloading, he said, "I'm going to try again."

"Of course you are. I didn't expect any less from you."

For the next hour, the two men stood beside the creek while Morgan practiced, pausing from time to time to let their ears have a break from the roar of gunshots. Morgan concentrated on hitting the tree, but even so, his draw became faster and smoother the more he repeated it. By the time Bearpaw said, "All right, I think we've burned enough powder for today," Morgan felt like he had made some real progress. It was just a start, of course, but still, he was pleased.

He was glad to stop, though, because his arm *was* getting tired. Drawing and firing a Colt .45 took quite a bit of effort. As Morgan reloaded for the final time, Bearpaw said, "Those arm muscles are probably going to be sore tomorrow."

"I can put up with it."

"How about your side? Any pain from that wound?"

"It aches," Morgan admitted. "Not so much that I can't stand it, though. I'm more interested in knowing how you thought I did today."

"Like I said, you have a considerable amount of natural talent. I didn't see anything today to make me doubt that."

"How long do you think it'll be before I'm ready to tackle Lasswell and the others?"

Bearpaw rubbed his chin and shook his head. "Now, that I couldn't tell you. You're not ready yet, I know that."

"You'll tell me when I am?"

"Sure, Kid."

Morgan wasn't sure whether to believe him. He wondered if Bearpaw would keep on insisting that he wasn't ready yet, in an effort to keep him safe. If that was the case, it wasn't going to work.

His shattered soul was still crying out for vengeance, and he could deny it for only so long before he had to answer its call.

Dr. McNally was waiting for them when they got back that afternoon. With a worried frown on his face, he said to Morgan, "I don't know if gallivanting around all over the country is good for you in your condition, son."

"We just rode down to Bearpaw's cabin," Morgan explained. "I told Eve that's where we were going."

"How's your side?"

"It's fine. A little achy, but not bad." Morgan didn't mention that his right arm ached a lot worse from the workout he had given it today.

"You youngsters are just too restless for your own good," McNally groused. "All I can do is tell you to be careful . . . and that I'm not going to be very happy with you if you undo all the hard work Eve and I have put in to get you healed up as much as you are."

"I'll be careful," Morgan promised.

Over the next two weeks, Morgan rode down to Bearpaw's cabin every day to practice with the Colt. Eve still seemed bothered by having him around, so he thought it was better to get away from the place for a while each day. Sometimes, Bearpaw came to the McNally house to get him; other times, Morgan just showed up at the Paiute's cabin, ready to do some shooting.

Nor was Bearpaw content just to help Morgan with the Colt. He wanted to see how the young man handled a Winchester, too. Morgan's sure eye and steady hand made him an excellent shot with the rifle.

One day, Bearpaw handed Morgan his old Sharps. "Try this buffalo gun," the Paiute suggested. "It's got a mighty powerful kick, though, so be ready for it."

"I can handle it," Morgan said confidently as he took the rifle.

"You're going to need something farther away than that tree to shoot at," Bearpaw mused. "A Sharps like that has quite a range. I've heard stories about how one of *your* people once used a Sharps to knock one of *my* people off his horse at distance of about a mile down in the Texas Panhandle." He squinted off across the field and then pointed. "See that white blaze on that pine yonder, where the bark's been peeled off? It's only about two hundred yards away, so I'm sure you can hit something that close."

"Close?" Morgan repeated. "I can barely see it, let alone hit it!"

"What happened to that confidence of yours? Give it a try. You might want to find a branch or something to rest the barrel on first, though. A Sharps is pretty heavy."

Morgan found a branch low enough on one of the pines to support the rifle barrel while he drew a bead on the distant target. He eared the Sharps's hammer back as Bearpaw instructed him, took a deep breath, lined up the sights, and gently squeezed the trigger.

What felt like the kick of a mule slammed against his shoulder and knocked him back a couple of steps.

"Son of a—" Morgan exclaimed.

Bearpaw grinned at him. "I told you it had a heck of a kick. I saw wood fly on that tree, though. Not bark. Wood."

"You mean I hit the mark?"

"You sure did."

Morgan felt a surge of pride. The marksmanship by itself meant nothing to him, but it was important because it might someday help him in his quest to avenge Rebel's death.

"A Winchester is a mighty fine gun," Bearpaw went on, "but when you need to make a long-range shot, nothing is better than a Sharps. You might want to think about getting one."

Morgan nodded. "I'll do that. Can I try again with this one?"

"If you think your shoulder can stand it. Here, let me show you how to reload . . ."

Late that afternoon, Morgan headed back to Sawtooth. The sun had dipped halfway behind the mountains to the west when he reached the McNally house. He started around the house, intending to put the buckskin in the shed and tend to the horse, when a rider moved out of some nearby trees and hailed him.

"Morgan? Kid Morgan?"

"That's right," Morgan replied as he reined in. A bad feeling caused his muscles to tense. "What can I do for you?"

"My name is Duke Garrity," the man said, "and that was my little brother you killed a couple of weeks ago. So you can fill your hand, you bastard, because you're about to die!"

Chapter 14

Garrity didn't give Morgan a chance to explain, or even to say a single word. He just reached for his gun, his hand moving to the Colt on his hip with blinding speed.

Morgan knew his life hung by a slender thread. Impulse cried out for him to rush his own draw, but the lessons hammered into his head by Phillip Bearpaw counteracted that urge. Even though he drew fast, he stayed under control. Garrity's gun roared first, but Morgan's blasted a fraction of a second behind it, the shots coming so close together that they were barely distinguishable from each other.

Garrity cried out and went backward out of the saddle to land on the ground with a heavy thud. His horse moved skittishly away from him.

Morgan threw his left leg over the buckskin's back and slid to the ground, coming to rest in a crouch with his gun still trained on Garrity. The man rolled onto his side and reached ahead of him, trying to get his hand on the Colt he had dropped when he toppled off his horse. His fingers fell short of the gun butt.

He struggled mightily to reach the weapon, but failed. With a gasp, he slumped face-first onto the ground. His outstretched fingers twitched a time or two and then were still.

Morgan moved forward and kicked Garrity's gun well out of reach. At that moment, the rear door of the McNally house burst open and the doctor rushed out, brandishing a shotgun. "What in blazes happened?" he demanded. "What were those shots?"

"That hombre rode out of the trees and threw down on me," Morgan explained with a nod toward Garrity's body as he replaced the spent shell in the Colt. "He was the older brother of that fella Garrity I had to kill a couple of weeks ago."

Eve had followed her father out of the house. She stopped behind McNally and listened to Morgan's explanation. Morgan holstered the Colt and moved toward her, saying, "It's all right, I'm not hurt—"

Without warning, she threw herself at him and started pounding his chest with her fists as she screamed, "Go away, go away, go away! We don't want you here! We don't want your kind around!"

Morgan stood there stunned, not even trying to stop her from hitting him. He knew she had seemed upset ever since the night of that first gunfight, but never in a million years would he have expected a reaction like this from her.

After a moment, Eve's fury seemed to run out of steam. She stumbled back a step, raised her trembling hands and covered her face with them, then said in a broken voice between sobs, "Please, just . . . just go away . . ."

Inside the house, Gramophone music played.

Morgan wasn't sure if Lucinda McNally had even heard the shots, lost as she was in her own world.

McNally lowered the shotgun and moved to his daughter's side. As he slid an arm around Eve's shoulders, he urged gently, "Come on back inside, honey. You don't need to be out here right now."

"M-make him go away, Pa," she said as she allowed him to turn her toward the house. "Make him understand we don't want him here."

After everything that had happened, Morgan would have thought that it impossible for his heart to harden any more, but at the sound of those anguished words, it did. He felt it happen, the chill stealing over him like frost creeping across the grass on a cold morning. "Eve, I'm sorry—" he began, but Dr. McNally looked back over his shoulder and shook his head, signaling for Morgan to leave it alone.

As father and daughter went inside, Morgan sighed heavily and caught up the reins of his horse. He collected the dead man's horse as well and led them both to the shed. By the time he got there, Marshal Zeke Chambliss arrived to check out the gunshots, accompanied by one of his deputies. The lawman still wore his left arm in a sling, but according to McNally, his injuries were healing well.

"What happened here, Kid?" Chambliss asked as he and his deputy stood there in the gathering dusk, looking down at the body of Duke Garrity.

Morgan explained about Garrity forcing the shootout. Chambliss scratched his jaw and said, "That name's familiar. I think I've seen a few reward dodgers on him come through. Didn't put the name together with that fella you ventilated a couple of weeks ago, though. This one's a bad hombre. Got three or four killin's to his credit, if I'm rememberin' right, as well as some holdups."

"He was fast," Morgan said with a nod. "Faster than his brother."

The deputy chuckled. "But not fast enough to beat Kid Morgan."

Morgan didn't say anything to that. The body on the ground spoke for itself.

But it didn't say as much as Eve had before her father took her in the house.

McNally came back out a short time later while Morgan was tending to the buckskin, giving the horse some grain and water. He had already unsaddled the buckskin and rubbed him down. Chambliss's deputy had led Duke Garrity's horse up the street to the livery stable, where it would be cared for for the time being. Garrity's body had been loaded into the back of the undertaker's wagon and carted off as well.

The doctor didn't have his shotgun with him this time. He stopped in front of the shed and jammed his hands in his pockets. Even in the gloom now that the sun was down, Morgan could see the unhappy expression on McNally's weathered face.

"I'm sorry about what happened, son," McNally said. "I've been afraid that Eve was building up to something like that ever since that other night."

"The night I saved her from those hardcases, you mean?" Morgan asked coolly.

"Don't think for a second that we're not grateful to you, Eve and me both. She was scared to death that night, especially when the shooting started, and she was mostly scared for you, I think. Her gratitude was real. But so was what she felt when she found out that you're a gunfighter."

"What's that got to do with anything?"

McNally sighed. "You know my son Joe died a couple of years ago."

"Of course," Morgan said with a nod. "I'm sorry."

McNally took one hand from his pocket and rubbed his jaw. "My wife's never recovered from what happened to that boy," he said. "You know that. You've seen it for yourself."

"I'm sorry about that, too," Morgan said quietly.

As if he hadn't heard, McNally went on. "But in her own way, Eve's never recovered either. She works so hard helping me and taking care of her mother so that she's too busy to think about what happened. That's what I believe anyway."

"I mean no offense, Doctor, but . . . what *did* happen?"

McNally looked squarely at Morgan and said, "My boy was killed in a fight. A gunfight."

A sort of understanding dawned inside Morgan. He couldn't have picked a worse identity to assume as far as Eve was concerned than that of a gunfighter. Having him around reminded her too much of what had happened to her brother.

McNally went on. "The thing of it is, Joe wasn't even involved in the trouble. He was just walking down the street in Sacramento when two men arguing about which one was faster on the draw decided to pull their guns and start blazing away at each other. They were both fatally wounded, but as one of them went down, he fired a final shot that missed the other man and hit Joe instead. Joe never had a chance to make it to cover when the shooting started. The bullet hit him in the head. Killed him instantly, I expect, like a bolt out of the blue."

"I'm sorry," Morgan said, and meant it. "No offense, Doctor, but that didn't have anything to do with me."

"Maybe not, but in Eve's mind, you're the same sort of man as the ones who killed her brother and caused her mother to be . . . the way she is. You can't expect her to forget. She sees too many reminders of what happened every day. Every time Lucinda plays that Gramophone . . ." McNally's voice trailed away as he shook his head. "I think she was afraid from the start that you'd turn out to be a gunman. It wasn't until she heard, though, that you're this notorious Kid Morgan that it got to be too much for her."

Morgan felt a strong impulse to tell the doctor that it was all a lie, that he wasn't really a gunfighter, just a businessman from back East named Conrad Browning. He wanted to tell Eve, so she would see that she was wrong about him.

And yet, doing that had the potential to ruin his plan. He wasn't even sure that it was true anymore either. Conrad Browning had killed the Winchell brothers, and maybe there had still been a little of Conrad left the night he faced down Garrity and Jessup.

But Conrad couldn't have killed Duke Garrity. The man was too slick with a gun for Conrad.

It had taken Kid Morgan to do that.

Knowing that it was too late for him to change the path he had chosen—or the path that had chosen him, some might say—he sighed and said, "I reckon the best thing for me to do is leave."

McNally shook his head. "I won't turn out an injured man. Never have and never will."

"I'm all right, Doctor," Morgan said. "Maybe not

at full strength yet, and maybe that wound hasn't completely healed, but I'm strong enough to travel."

"You know that a wound like that would put most men flat on their backs for at least a month. It hasn't even been three weeks."

"Long enough is long enough," Morgan said.

"But where will you go?"

Morgan peered off into the night. "Like I've told you, I have business to tend to. I don't know exactly where it will take me."

"At least wait until morning to leave," the doctor urged. "You can't ride off at night like this."

Morgan thought it over for a moment and then nodded. "I reckon I can do that. I'll try to stay out of Eve's way while I'm still here. I don't want to upset her any more than I already have."

McNally put a hand on Morgan's shoulder and squeezed. "You couldn't have known."

But he should have, Morgan thought. After all, didn't gunfighters always carry death and suffering with them, wherever they roamed?

Eve had gone to her room when she went inside the house, so Morgan didn't see her again that night. He slept fitfully and woke early. He thought it might be a good idea to get the buckskin ready to ride and leave before Eve had a chance to see him and get upset again.

She was in the kitchen when he walked in, though, already preparing breakfast even though dawn was still at least an hour away. "Good morning," she said without looking around at him as she stood at the stove putting biscuit dough in a pan. "Pa tells me you're leaving today."

"That's right," Morgan said. "I reckon it's time."

Eve didn't try to talk him out of it. She just said, "I hope you'll take care of yourself."

"I'll try," he said. If she wanted to act like her outburst the night before hadn't happened, that was all right with him. He wasn't comfortable talking about anybody's feelings. He never had been, even before the tragedy that had befallen him.

"I'll pour you a cup of coffee."

She handed him the coffee, still not meeting his eyes, and he sat down at the table to sip on the steaming brew while she went on getting ready for breakfast. After a few moments of silence, she surprised him by asking, "Where will you go?"

"I don't know yet."

That was true. He would have to pick up the trail of Lasswell and the other kidnappers, but he wasn't quite sure how to go about that. Frank would have known, he thought, and that reminded him that he'd never had a chance to send a telegram to Claudius Turnbuckle in San Francisco explaining the situation. It was possible that Frank had heard by now about what happened in Carson City. He might believe that his son was dead. The Kid hated that idea, but there was nothing he could do about it right now. Sawtooth didn't have a telegraph office, and he didn't know how long it would be before he came across one.

Dr. McNally came bustling into the kitchen and stopped short, seemingly a little surprised to see Morgan there. But he smiled and nodded and said, "Good morning," then went over to kiss Eve on the cheek. "Your mother is still sleeping soundly," he told her.

"That's good," she said. She turned and brought a

plate of biscuits and bacon over to the table and set it in front of Morgan. Now he understood. She was trying to get him out of here, and she thought that the sooner she fed him, the sooner he would be gone.

The back door opened while Morgan and the doctor were eating. Phillip Bearpaw came in, his Sharps rifle tucked under his arm. "Good morning, all," he said with a grin. He looked at Morgan. "You're up early, my friend."

"I'm riding on today," Morgan said.

A puzzled frown replaced Bearpaw's grin. "So soon? I thought you'd be around for a while yet."

"No, it's time for me to move on." Morgan glanced toward the stove. Eve stood there with her back toward him, but he could tell that she had stiffened as the conversation went on. He hoped Bearpaw wouldn't press him for details about why he was leaving now.

With the easy familiarity of a frequent visitor to the house, the Paiute poured himself a cup of coffee and then sat down at the table with Morgan and McNally. He looked like he was thinking something over, and after a moment, he said, "How would you like to have some company, Kid?"

Morgan's eyebrows rose. "You want to go with me?"

"I thought I might." Bearpaw looked over at McNally. "I'll miss you and your family, Patrick, but it's not like I'd be gone forever."

"What you do is your own business, Phillip. We'd miss you, of course, but you do whatever you think is best."

Bearpaw looked at Morgan again. "How about it, Kid?"

Morgan figured he had a pretty good idea what Bearpaw was thinking. Bearpaw thought Morgan wasn't ready to face down Lasswell and the others yet, and the Paiute was probably right about that. He wanted to keep on working with Morgan while they hunted down the kidnappers.

That wasn't a bad idea, Morgan realized. Bearpaw knew a lot more about surviving on the frontier than he did, although Morgan thought he was learning fairly rapidly. Bearpaw might be a big help in getting on the trail of his quarry, too, Morgan told himself. He wasn't even sure where to start, but he was willing to bet that Bearpaw would have some ideas.

One thing was certain, though. When it came time to face his enemies, Morgan intended to do that alone. He wasn't going to put Bearpaw in danger, although he had a hunch the Paiute would have been willing to back him up, no matter what the play.

They could hash that out later. For now, Morgan nodded and said, "I think I'd like that."

Eve turned and stalked out of the kitchen.

"Uh-oh," Bearpaw said when she was gone. "Why is she so upset this morning?"

"A man named Duke Garrity was waiting for me under the trees out back when I rode in yesterday evening," Morgan explained.

"Garrity," Bearpaw repeated. "Related to that fellow from a couple of weeks ago?"

"His brother."

"I take it there was gunplay?"

"They're supposed to bury Garrity this morning."

Bearpaw let out a tiny whistle. "How fast was he?"

"Pretty fast. Marshal Chambliss said that this Garrity had killed several men."

McNally said, "I guess all that practice down at Phillip's cabin paid off, Kid."

Morgan and Bearpaw both glanced at him in surprise.

"Did you think I didn't know what was going on?" McNally asked. "I have two eyes, and I'm pretty good at figuring things out. I know you've been working with the Kid here, Phillip. How's he doing?"

"Pretty good," Bearpaw admitted. "Good enough so that he's still alive this morning."

"But you don't think he's ready to go after the men he's looking for, especially not alone."

Bearpaw shrugged.

McNally looked at Morgan and asked, "Are they the ones who shot you, Kid?"

"They did a lot worse than that," Morgan said. "But it's not anything I want to go into right now."

"I suppose I can respect that." McNally picked up his coffee cup. "I think I can talk Eve into fixing up some supplies for the two of you."

"We'd appreciate that, Patrick," Bearpaw said. "Living off the fat of the land isn't as easy as it used to be when my ancestors roamed this land and game was abundant." He pushed his chair back and stood up. "I'll go get my gear together, and I'll be back here ready to ride in an hour, Kid. Will that be all right?"

"Sure," Morgan replied. "I'll be ready, too."

It wouldn't take him that long to get his things together, he thought. He didn't have all that much. The clothes on his back . . . and his guns.

Couldn't forget the guns.

Chapter 15

When it came time to ride away, Eve surprised Morgan by coming out of the house and putting her arms around him. "Take care of yourself, Mr. Morgan," she whispered as she hugged him. "I'd hate for anything bad to happen to you."

"Thanks, Eve. And thank you for everything you did to help me when I was hurt."

She stepped back and looked down at the ground. "I would have done as much for any of Pa's patients."

Somehow, Morgan didn't believe that. Even though a large part of him didn't want to admit it, he knew there had been a connection between the two of them that went beyond that of nurse and patient. If things had been different . . . if they had met at another place, in another time . . .

He shoved those thoughts out of his brain. They had no place in his head, not now, not ever.

Eve turned to Bearpaw and hugged him as well. "You be careful, too," she told him.

"Oh, I intend to," he said.

"And come back soon."

Dr. McNally and his wife came out of the house then, the doctor keeping a hand protectively on her arm. He offered his other hand to Morgan and said, "We'll be keeping you in our thoughts and prayers, son."

"Thanks," Morgan said. "I reckon I can use them."

Mrs. McNally turned to her husband and said, "Patrick, why is Joseph leaving again? He just got here."

McNally opened his mouth to try to explain, but before he could say anything, an impulse seized Morgan. He gave in to it, taking his hat off and stepping forward to put his arms around Mrs. McNally. He gave her a firm but gentle hug.

"Don't worry about me, Ma," he told her. "I'll be back soon."

She patted him on the back and then reached up to stroke his sandy hair, which had gotten fairly long. "Oh, Joseph," she said. "I'll miss you so much. I'll be waiting for you. I love you."

"I love you, too, Ma," Morgan said. "Listen, I really don't want you worrying about me, and you don't need to sit around all day waiting for me to get back either. You just go on living. Take care of Pa and Eve and yourself, and I'll see you when I see you. All right?"

She looked up him and nodded as he used his thumb to wipe a tear away from her cheek. "All right," she whispered. "If you say so, Joseph, that's what I'll do."

He nodded, stepped back, and put his hat on his head again. "So long, everybody," he said as he took hold of the buckskin's reins.

"Good-bye, son," McNally said. Tears glistened in his eyes, and in Eve's as well. "Take care. You, too, Phillip."

Morgan and Bearpaw swung up into their saddles. As they started to turn their horses, Eve stepped forward and put a hand on Morgan's leg. She looked up at him and mouthed the words *Thank you*.

Morgan nodded, then heeled the buckskin into a trot as Eve stepped back. Bearpaw rode alongside him on the Appaloosa.

"That was a mighty nice thing you did back there for those folks," the Paiute said quietly.

"No more than they deserve," Morgan said. "It was the least I could do."

The two men fell silent as they rode south, putting the settlement of Sawtooth behind them.

"How do you plan to go about finding the men you're looking for, Kid?" Bearpaw asked later.

"To tell you the truth, I don't know," Morgan answered. "I was hoping maybe you'd have some ideas."

Bearpaw chuckled. "It's a good thing I decided to come along, then. You said you know all their names?"

"That's right. At least, I know the names they were going by a few weeks ago. Some of them may be aliases."

"This may come as a shock to you, since you know me only as the educated, cultured individual that I am now, but there was a time when I . . . how shall I put this? . . . rode some rather dark and lonely trails."

Morgan looked over at him. "You were an outlaw?"

"Not to the extent that Lasswell and those others are," Bearpaw said quickly, "but from time to time some cattle or horses that didn't exactly belong to me may have wound up in my possession. As a result of that time in my life, I know some of the places frequented by men who have heard the owl hoot. We can start by asking questions in those places. We'll have to be careful how we go about it, though. We don't want it getting back to the men we're looking for that someone is on their trail."

That made sense to Morgan. He said, "I'll follow your lead."

"In that case, I think we should circle around Carson City—"

"That sounds good to me," Morgan declared. He had no desire to go back there now.

"And head for a trading post I know down where Nevada, Arizona, and Utah all come together," Bearpaw went on. "Chances are, the members of that gang scattered after what happened, rather than staying together. From what you told me, they didn't all ride together on a regular basis, but came together more for that one job."

It caused a twinge deep in the Kid's chest to hear Bearpaw talking so matter-of-factly about Rebel's kidnapping and murder, but he told himself that was how it had to be, not only for the Paiute, but for him, too. He couldn't allow his emotions to rule him. He remembered a quote—from Shakespeare, he thought—about revenge being a dish best served cold. Giving in to hot-blooded rage could lead a man into making mistakes, and those mistakes could doom his entire effort.

"Some of them may have headed for Mexico," Bearpaw continued, "and they may have stopped at this place I'm thinking of. If we can track down two or three of them, then maybe they can tell us where to find some of the others."

"So you're saying we'll find them two or three at a time."

Bearpaw nodded. "That's our best bet. The whole bunch isn't going to fall right into your lap, Kid."

"The problem will be convincing the ones we find to tell us where to look for the others."

"Oh, there are ways to persuade people to talk," Bearpaw said with a slight smile. "I *am* one of those dirty, torturin' redskins after all."

"At least you didn't say 'heap' and 'ugh' this time," the Kid said.

As Bearpaw suggested, they circled wide around Carson City and then headed southeast, keeping the various mountain ranges that ran along the Nevada-California border on their right hand. The Great Basin, broken up by a few smaller ranges, stretched out seemingly endlessly to their left. A couple of days into the journey, Morgan gazed off to the west and knew that the mining town of Buckskin lay in that direction. Conrad and Rebel had visited there while Frank Morgan was the marshal, and the Crown Royal Mine, owned by the Browning Mining Syndicate, still operated near Buckskin, although its output of silver ore had begun to dwindle, the Kid recalled.

All that was part of another life, he told himself. Someone else's life. He turned his face forward again and concentrated on the trail in front of them.

Bearpaw called a halt early enough every day so that they could make camp and then Morgan could practice with his gun for an hour or so. The muscles in his arm had strengthened so that drawing and firing the Colt time and time again no longer wore them out. Whenever he washed up in the icy streams that flowed down out of the mountains, he checked the scar on his side where the bullet had torn out a large chuck of flesh. The red, puckered scar was ugly, but the wound had healed cleanly and Morgan wasn't worried about it anymore. From time to time it ached a little, but nothing he couldn't handle. Dr. McNally had done a fine job of patching him up.

Dr. McNally—and Eve . . .

It took the two men a week to reach their destination, a week of riding through starkly beautiful, sparsely populated country. Arid desert flats alternated with rugged, rocky mountain ranges and the occasional grassy valley. Isolated ranches were located in those valleys. Bearpaw pointed out some of the squat, adobe ranch houses and said, "Twenty years ago, those folks had to worry all the time about my people, or the Apaches, attacking them and wiping them out. Now the Paiutes have made peace, and so have most of the Apaches. The few bands of renegades left have moved across the border into Mexico and never raid this far north anymore."

"Is that why you don't mind us having a campfire at night?" Morgan asked.

Bearpaw grinned. "That's right. It wasn't all that long ago that being so careless might have cost you your life. Now, the main thing the ranchers have to worry about is their herds dying of thirst. Same thing is true for pilgrims like us. You need to know where the water holes are when you travel through this part of the country. Lucky for you that I'm with you. I know where every spring and *tinaja* is."

"Is there anything you *don't* know?"

"Not much," Bearpaw said with a chuckle. "And if I don't know it, I'll probably lie about it and say that I do."

"Now you tell me how unreliable you are," the Kid drawled.

Late in the afternoon, they came to a place where two trails crossed. Several buildings were scattered around, the largest of them built partially of logs and partially of adobe. A long porch ran along the front of it. A latticework roof attached to the *vigas* that stuck out from the top of the wall provided shade. About a dozen horses were tied up at the hitch rails in front of the place. The other buildings were adobe shacks.

"A German named Immelmann owns the trading post," Bearpaw told Morgan as they approached. "The Mormons used to have a settlement here, thirty or forty years ago. They abandoned it, though, and all the buildings fell into ruin except that one. It was in pretty bad shape but still standing when Immelmann came along and fixed it up. A few wagon trains used to pass through, but those days are pretty well over. Now, most of his business comes from men like the ones we're looking for."

"Outlaws," the Kid said.

"Men who don't want to be found, for one reason or another," Bearpaw amended. "After Immelmann got the trading post going, a few other folks moved in. They've started calling the place Las Vegas. Some of them think there'll be a regular town here one of these days, but I doubt it. If Immelmann ever dies or leaves, the settlement will dry up and blow away without the trading post to keep it going."

Morgan didn't doubt that. He didn't care about the future of Las Vegas, though, only the present. And then only if he and Bearpaw could find a clue here to the men they were looking for.

They added their horses to the ones tied up at the hitch rails and stepped onto the porch. The shade, even though it was dappled by the sun coming through the latticework, was a welcome relief from the heat. Morgan thought it was considerably cooler on the porch.

The front and back doors stood open to let any stray breezes blow through the building. As Morgan and Bearpaw headed for the front door, three men started through it from inside, on their way out. The men stopped short as they saw the two newcomers.

"Oh, no, Injun," one of them said with a frown. "You ain't goin' in there where white men are drinkin' and playin' cards."

The Paiute looked down at the porch and shuffled his high-topped moccasins. "Bearpaw heap sorry," he said. "Injun mighty thirsty. Not cause trouble."

Morgan forced himself not to stare in disgust.

One of the other men laughed, a loud, braying hee-haw like a donkey. "The last thing a filthy ol' redskin like you needs is firewater," he said. "You get a snootful, and you'll be liable to go on the warpath. Where'll us poor white folks be then? You'll probably scalp us all!"

"Let us by," the Kid said tightly. "We're not looking for trouble."

"You travelin' with this redskin, mister? Hell, ain't you got no pride? Ain't you got nothin' better to do than hang around with a savage?"

Morgan thought about all the times Bearpaw had quoted Milton and Shakespeare and John Donne from memory, for hours at a time. Chances were, the Paiute knew more poetry by heart than these three louts had read in their entire lives combined.

But that wasn't the sort of thing that Kid Morgan would be thinking about, he reminded himself. Instead, he forced himself to stoop to their level and said, "Don't worry, I'll keep an eye on the redskin. I won't let him get into the whiskey, just regular water."

The first man sneered. "That's fine as far as it goes," he said, "but what about the stink?"

"Oh, I reckon he can put up with it. It ought to fade after a while anyway, since you fellas are leaving."

Bearpaw turned his head slowly and stared at Morgan.

He didn't know where the words had come from. Just a few seconds earlier, he'd been trying to be conciliatory. But then something had snapped inside him. He was tired of everybody's bullshit. Right now, Phillip Bearpaw was the best friend he had in the world, and he was damned if he was going to let these sorry-ass bastards talk about his friend that way.

The three men weren't quite as quick on the uptake as Bearpaw was, but it didn't take them long. Then Donkey-Laugh looked offended and exclaimed, "Hey! He's sayin' we stink worse'n an Injun!"

"You got a big mouth, boy," the first man growled.

"You can try to close it if you want," the Kid said.

Something about his stance and his cold, level eyes must have warned the men. None of them made a move toward a gun. But their leader, who was also the biggest of the trio, said, "You need a lesson in manners, you son of a bitch. And I'm just the man to give it to you!"

He lunged across the porch and swung a malletlike fist at Morgan's head. Morgan leaned quickly to the side. As long as he didn't let any punches land where that bullet had wounded him, he ought to be all right, he thought.

Of course, that might be easier said than done.

Morgan's swift move made the man's fist miss. As the man stumbled forward, off balance, Morgan grabbed the front of his shirt and heaved as he turned. The man flew past him and sailed off the shallow porch to go rolling and sprawling in the dust.

Donkey-Laugh yelled, "Hey!" again, and charged. Morgan met the attack by stepping in and hooking a hard left into the man's belly. Donkey-Laugh doubled over as the blow knocked the wind out of him. Morgan grabbed the back of his head and shoved it down as he brought his knee up. His knee cracked into Donkey-Laugh's jaw with stunning force. As the man crumpled, Morgan thought that he wouldn't be letting loose with any more of those braying laughs for a while. Not with a jaw that was either broken or was going to be pretty sore for a while at the very least.

That left the third man, but as Morgan turned toward him, he saw that the hombre was backing away, hands held at shoulder level. "Take it easy, amigo," the man said. "This ain't my fight. I *know* I stink."

A few feet away on the porch, Bearpaw suddenly lifted his Sharps and eared back the hammer. The Kid looked over his shoulder and saw that the first man was on his feet again. His hair and face and clothes were covered with dust. So was the hand that had started to reach for the gun on his hip. That hand had frozen where it was as the man found himself staring down the ominously large barrel of the Sharps.

"They say that discretion is the better part of valor, my friend," Bearpaw told the man. "You'd be wise to heed that advice."

The man gaped at Bearpaw and muttered, "What the hell—?" But he slowly moved his hand away from the butt of his gun.

"I told you we weren't looking for trouble," Morgan said. "We still aren't. Why don't the two of you pick up your friend and head on to wherever you were going when you stopped to harass us?"

"You're lucky you got that redskin watchin' your back, mister," the man said between clenched teeth. "I was about to blow a hole in you."

"You were about to try," Bearpaw said. "The way I see it, I just saved your life. You were going to draw on Kid Morgan."

"Who?" the man asked with a frown.

"Kid Morgan. The man who killed the Winchell brothers and Duke Garrity, not to mention Garrity's little brother and a man called Jessup."

The third man put in, "Say, I've heard of Duke Garrity. He's pretty fast."

"*Was* pretty fast," Bearpaw said.

Morgan saw the nervousness in the first man's eyes now. He was starting to realize that he might have bitten off too big a chunk. He said, "Look, Kid, let's just let this go, all right?"

Morgan nodded. "Fine by me."

The man motioned to his companion, and together they picked up the half-conscious Donkey-Laugh, who started moaning as they helped him to his horse. They got him into the saddle and then mounted up themselves. Flanking their injured pard, they rode off. Morgan and Bearpaw watched them go, just to make sure the men didn't try to double back and attack again.

"Was ist los?" a voice asked from the doorway. "What is this disturbance on my porch?"

They turned to see a tall, gaunt man with a white spade beard. The man's lean, leathery face creased in a sudden grin as he recognized the Paiute.

"Bearpaw!" the man said. "I thought I recognized your voice. If you had started spouting poetry, I would have known for sure, *ja*."

Bearpaw shook hands with the man. "It's good to see you, too, you old Dutchman. How long has it been, seven or eight years?"

"Ja, about that. Who is your friend?"

"This is Kid Morgan."

The Kid nodded and said, *"Guten tag, Herr Immelmann."*

"Ah! Sprechen sie Deutche?"

"Ein bischen." Morgan hoped he hadn't make a mistake by greeting the trading post's proprietor in German. He had about exhausted his knowledge of the language when he told Immelmann he spoke only a little.

"Come in, come in," Immelmann urged them. He waved a knobby-knuckled hand toward the retreating riders. "Don't worry about those three. They think they are tough hombres, but they are really not."

As Morgan and Bearpaw stepped into the trading post, which was even cooler because of its thick log and adobe walls, the German went on. "You must tell me what brings you here, if such a question will not be considered impolite."

"Things got a mite too warm for us where we were," Bearpaw said.

Immelmann let out a laugh that sounded too hearty for his slender frame. "The more things change, the

more they stay the same, eh, my old friend? Come.
The beer is cold, and the women are warm! What
more does a man need?"

Vengeance, the Kid thought. That was what some
men needed—and he was one of them.

Chapter 16

Immelmann had a Mexican bartender working for him, so he was able to sit with Morgan and Bearpaw at a round table in the rear of the big, shadowy barroom half of the trading post instead of serving drinks. The three men nursed beers. Bearpaw explained to Morgan that while he couldn't handle whiskey, like most of his people, beer never muddled his mind.

Immelmann said, "The two of you are on the dodge, *ja*?"

"Not exactly," Bearpaw said. "I don't think there's any paper out on us, so you don't have to worry about any bounty hunters showing up to look for us. We'd just as soon avoid any lawmen, though, just to be on the safe side."

Immelmann nodded sagely. "I understand."

The German thought he understood anyway, the Kid mused. That was what he and Bearpaw wanted.

"Have you seen an hombre called Moss pass through these parts lately?" Bearpaw went on. "We heard that he's looking for some men for some sort of job up north, and we thought we might try to sign on with him." He and Morgan had decided that would be a safe enough question to ask, grounded in truth as it was.

"Do you mean Vernon Moss?"

"Yeah, that's the fellow's name."

Immelmann gave a solemn shake of his head. "Have you not heard what happened to him?"

Bearpaw leaned forward and frowned. "No. He get shot up or something?"

"Both of his legs were crushed in an accident. I'm told that he will be a cripple for the rest of his life. And this happened while he and some other men were engaged in that job you mentioned."

"You mean we missed out on it?"

A sour look appeared on Immelmann's face. "You would not have wanted to be part of this, old friend. It was an ugly business, nothing like rustling or stealing horses. Moss and some other men kidnapped a woman."

"Yeah, that's pretty bad," Bearpaw agreed with a frown.

"It was even worse than you think. They held the woman for ransom, and even though her husband agreed to pay, they murdered the poor woman. Clay Lasswell shot her. Do you know Lasswell?"

Bearpaw shook his head. Across the table, the Kid kept a stony expression on his face, but it took an effort to do so.

"I thought better of Lasswell, to tell you the truth," Immelmann went on. "He has killed a number of men in gunfights, true, and I suspect he may have shot a few in the back from long range while he was working as a regulator in Wyoming, but I would not have guessed that he would murder a woman in cold blood." The German shrugged. "I suppose as we get older and more tired, the list of things we will not do for money grows shorter and shorter."

"How do you know about all this?" Bearpaw asked, still making it sound like he was only idly curious.

"Julio Esquivel told me. You remember Julio? Short, has a beard, very good with a knife?"

Bearpaw shook his head. "I don't think I ever crossed his trail. How about you, Kid?"

Morgan said, "Nope."

"Well, Julio stopped here about a week ago with a couple of other men." Immelmann made a face. "One of them was a huge brute who treated one of my whores badly. I was glad to see them go."

Morgan remembered Esquivel and the big, moon-faced man from that awful night. Trying not to sound like he was prying, he said, "Who was the third man?"

"I hadn't seen him before," Immelmann replied. "They called him Buck."

So Buck, Esquivel, and the giant Carlson had ridden through here a week earlier, Morgan thought. "Did they say where they were headed?" he asked.

Immelmann frowned, and the Kid saw a warning look flash in Bearpaw's dark eyes. He might have pushed things too far by asking such a direct question. But after a moment, Immelmann shrugged and said, "I might not tell you if that monster had not been so rough on my girl, but when they left here they were riding east. I heard them say something about going over to the Four Corners."

"We're obliged," Bearpaw said.

Immelmann looked back and forth between Morgan and the Paiute. "You had no interest in joining up with

Moss," he said coldly. "You're looking for him and the men who rode with him on that job." It wasn't a question.

"You and I go way back, my friend," Bearpaw said. "I know we can count on your discretion."

An angry frown creased the German's face. "You used me," he accused. "Played on our friendship."

"As you said, those men did a very bad thing."

"I think perhaps you two are the bounty hunters now. Such men are not welcome at my trading post."

"I'm sorry you feel that way," Bearpaw said. "But you won't mention to anybody that we were here, will you?"

"Doing so might make people suspect that I gave you information." Immelmann shook his head. "I will say nothing. But I would ask you to leave now."

Morgan and Bearpaw started to get to their feet. The Paiute paused and said, "For what it's worth, if anything, there's no blood money involved in this hunt, Immelmann. It's personal."

Immelmann held up a hand to stop him. "I don't wish to hear any more. Anyway, any time you set out to kill a man, it is personal, is it not? How can it be any other way when you end another life and risk your own?"

Those were good questions, the Kid thought. And from the way Immelmann was looking at him, he wondered just what the German was thinking. He would have been willing to bet, though, that Immelmann didn't suspect Conrad Browning and Kid Morgan were one and the same.

As he and Bearpaw rode away from the trading post a short time later, Morgan said, "Sorry. I know I pushed too hard back there. I should have waited and let you get the information out of him at your own pace."

Bearpaw shrugged. "It doesn't matter. We found out what we needed to know."

"Can we trust Immelmann?"

"Maybe. I think so. Like he said, he can't tell anybody too much about us without making them suspect that he gave us the information we were looking for. He's better off keeping his mouth shut, like he would have if it had been anybody but me asking. He owed me a favor."

"And now I've ruined your friendship," Morgan said.

"Justice doesn't come without a price."

"This isn't your fight, you know," Morgan pointed out.

"Maybe it didn't start out that way, but after everything you did for the McNallys, and the way you stood up for me back there . . . I reckon I've made it my fight."

The silence that fell between them was awkward, since neither was the sort of man who expressed emotion all that well. After a moment, the Kid asked, "What's the Four Corners?"

"That's the area where Colorado, Utah, Arizona, and New Mexico all come together," Bearpaw explained. "Some of the most desolate country you'll ever see. A fitting place for the sort of men we're after."

"We've got some ground to make up on them," Morgan said. He heeled the buckskin into a faster pace. Bearpaw followed suit, and soon the trading post at Las Vegas fell far behind them.

* * *

Bearpaw had warned him that they were heading into some desolate country, and the Paiute was right. As they traveled almost due east over the next two weeks, Morgan didn't know if they were in northern Arizona or southern Utah. It didn't really matter, Bearpaw told him. One was just about as ugly as the other, seemingly never-ending wastelands of dirt, sand, and rock.

And yet, here and there, great beauty existed, such as the long line of sandstone cliffs that shone a brilliant red in the sunlight. Wherever there was water, grass grew and flowers bloomed, little bits of paradise among the desert vastness.

They came to such an oasis a couple of days after leaving Las Vegas, late in the afternoon, and when Morgan spotted an adobe ranch house among the cottonwoods that lined a small creek, he was eager to ride on in and find out if the people who lived on this isolated ranch had seen the three men they were after.

But as Morgan lifted the reins and started to heel his horse into a trot, Bearpaw reached over and grasped his arm, stopping him.

"Take it easy, Kid," the Paiute said. "Something's wrong up there."

"What do you mean?" Morgan asked. Then, black shapes circling in the sky caught his eye, and he answered his own question. "Damn. Those are vultures, aren't they?"

"Buzzards, some call them. They're bad news, regardless of the name." Bearpaw pulled the Sharps from the saddle sheath in which he carried it. "Unlimber that Winchester of yours. We'll ride in, but we're going to be careful about it. Slow and easy."

That was how they approached the ranch, which

consisted of the adobe house, an adobe barn, and a pole corral. The lack of a bunkhouse meant the family that owned this place worked it by themselves, without any hired hands. As Morgan and Bearpaw drew closer, Morgan expected at least one dog to come running out to meet them, barking its head off. Instead, an ominous silence hung over the sun-blasted day.

"If this was twenty years ago, I'd say the Apaches had been here," Bearpaw commented quietly. "I don't know what to make of this yet, except that it can't be good."

The Kid spotted a dark shape on the ground inside the corral. "Is that a horse?" he asked, pointing toward it with the barrel of his Winchester.

"No. Milk cow more than likely. Another bad sign."

"Bad how?"

"A ranch with a milk cow usually has kids around."

Morgan grimaced. He hadn't thought about that.

"In the door," Bearpaw said a moment later. His voice was bleak, and his face looked like it had been carved out of the same red sandstone that had formed those cliffs a ways back.

Morgan saw the body lying across the threshold of the ranch house door. The man lay facedown, a large black stain on the back of his shirt. That stain shifted as the riders drew closer, and Morgan heard a loud buzzing. His stomach twisted in sick revulsion.

"Those are flies," he said.

Bearpaw nodded. "That's right. They're after the blood on the man's shirt. Quite a feast in surroundings like this."

Another huddled shape between the house and the barn turned out to be the family dog. Morgan averted his eyes, thinking of the big cur that traveled with his father. He had a soft spot for dogs. He was sure he and Rebel would have gotten one sooner or later if . . .

Those thoughts wouldn't do any good. The Kid forced them out of his head.

"So we've got a man, a dog, and a cow," he said. "Where is everyone else?"

"Inside, I suppose." Bearpaw reined to a stop in front of the house. "Why don't you stay out here, Kid? I'll have a look."

"I can stand it," Morgan said. "I've already seen things worse than any man should ever have to see."

"I reckon you have, at that." Bearpaw nodded. "Come on then, if you're sure."

Both men dismounted. Holding their rifles at the ready, in the unlikely event that any danger still lurked inside the ranch house, they stepped over the body of the man who sprawled in the doorway. Morgan felt sick as he heard flies buzzing again. It took a moment for his eyes to adjust to the dimness inside the house— and when they did, he almost wished that they hadn't.

A boy about eight or nine lay on his back on the hard-packed dirt floor, staring sightlessly at the ceiling. He appeared to have been shot once in the chest. The flies had been at him, too.

"Baby's over there in the crib," Bearpaw said, gesturing toward a little bed on curved rockers that sat in one corner. "Don't look, Kid."

This time, Morgan followed the advice.

"Where's the mother?" he asked.

Bearpaw nodded toward a doorway leading into another room. "She'll be in there, I expect. That's probably the bedroom."

He was right on both counts. The woman lay naked on the bed, arms and legs spraddled out, the sheets around her head dark with dried blood from the hideous wound in her neck. Someone had cut her throat almost from ear to ear.

"Esquivel," the Kid breathed.

"That Mexican traveling with Buck and Carlson?"

The Kid nodded. "He cut Edwin Sinclair's throat the same way."

"I don't see how you could really tell something like that . . . but I'm sure you're right, Kid." Bearpaw stepped over to the bed and reached down to close the woman's staring eyes. She had been pretty, with short blond hair that curled around her head, until her face had frozen in lines of agony and torment.

Bearpaw jerked his head toward the door. "I need some air," he said.

Morgan knew just what the Paiute meant. He felt the same way himself.

They had to step over the dead man in the doorway again, but once they did, they were back in the open air, with the hot sun blazing down on them. Morgan said, "Maybe we can find a shovel around the place so we can bury them."

"Yeah, there's bound to be one. Come on. I want to have a look at the corral."

The Paiute opened the gate and walked into the corral, circling around the bloated corpse of the milk cow. Numerous piles of horse droppings littered the dirt. Bearpaw hunkered on his heels next to one of them and studied it for a moment, then reached out to pick up some of it and rub it between his fingers.

"This isn't more than seven or eight hours old," he said.

Morgan frowned. "What does that mean?"

Bearpaw wiped his fingers in the dirt. "Those

three left Immelmann's place a week ahead of us. Even given the fact that we've been pushing our horses and they probably weren't, they must have arrived here at least four days ago. And they only left this morning."

Morgan frowned and shook his head. "I still don't understand."

Squinting against the sun, Bearpaw nodded toward the ranch house. "The man's been dead the longest. Three days, maybe a little more. But the woman and the kids were killed a lot later, maybe as late as this morning."

Morgan tried to figure out what that meant, and as he did so, he felt horror growing inside him. "Those three we're after rode in here, and the family offered them food and water for their horses and a place to spend the night," he said, putting it together in his head.

Bearpaw nodded. "Yes, and then they got up the next morning and murdered the man. They probably told the woman that if she cooperated, they would spare her and the children. She had to know that was unlikely, but she had to try to save her kids any way she could. So she went along with whatever they wanted."

Morgan took a deep breath. He knew that Buck, Carlson, and Esquivel must have put that poor woman through three days of hell and degradation. They had assaulted her in her own bed, again and again, with her children in the next room and her husband's body lying only yards away.

And then, when the bastards were tired of their sport, they had brutally slaughtered all three members of the family and ridden away as if the whole blood-drenched business meant nothing. Morgan hoped that Esquivel had slashed the woman's throat before her children were killed, so she hadn't had to hear the shots that ended their lives. But he wouldn't have wanted to bet on that. That would have been one last bit of torture to end things on.

He forced his mind on to more practical considerations. "They're less than a day ahead of us now. If we push on, we'll be able to catch up to them tomorrow for sure."

Bearpaw came out of the corral and closed the gate behind him, even though there was nothing alive in there to get out. "What about the burying?" he asked. "If we do that, it's going to be so late that we can't push on today. We'll have to wait until tomorrow."

A part of Morgan didn't want to accept any delay. The need for vengeance was stronger than ever in him after seeing what had happened here.

But he knew he couldn't just ride away and leave these poor people as bait for the scavengers. "We'll bury them," he said, "and we'll let our horses get a little extra rest while we're doing it. Because tomorrow . . . we're going to ride like hell."

Chapter 17

The sun was almost down before Morgan and Bearpaw finished scraping out a single grave big enough for all four members of the luckless ranching family as well as their dog. There was nothing they could do about the milk cow. The two men took turns using a shovel they found in the barn. Digging in the hard ground was backbreaking work, and neither of them could do it for very long at a time.

Morgan's side ached quite a bit when they were finished. If Eve had been here, she would have warned him that he was going to damage that wound and undo all the healing he'd done, he thought with a grim smile. He knew he was all right, though. He just needed some rest.

He would get that rest once they were done. They wrapped each body in a blanket and carried them out one by one, placing them carefully in the grave. Then they had to cover it up again. The sun was down and night was falling when they finished that. A dwindling arc of orange and gold light remained in the western sky as Morgan tamped down the mounded dirt.

They had removed their hats and shirts while they were digging. Now, the breeze that sprang up felt chilly on the Kid's bare, sweat-soaked torso. He drew his shirt back on and buttoned it up, then stood by the grave with his hat in his hand. Bearpaw followed suit.

"Are you saying the words, Kid, or am I?" the Paiute asked.

"You know better words than I do, Phillip. You should do it."

Bearpaw nodded solemnly. He held his black hat over his heart and intoned, "The Lord is my shepherd; I shall not want." Morgan closed his eyes, and as he listened to Bearpaw continue with the Twenty-third Psalm, he wondered what words had been said at Rebel's funeral.

It didn't matter, he told himself. No words on earth held the power to bring her back, and that was all he would have wanted if he had been there.

"Surely goodness and mercy shall follow me all the days of my life," Bearpaw concluded, "and I will dwell in the house of the Lord forever. Amen."

"Amen," Morgan murmured. He hoped these poor people were at peace now.

They didn't spend the night at the ranch. It was too ghost-haunted a place for that. Instead, they followed the creek for about half a mile and found a good place to camp. That night, as they sat by the embers of the fire, Bearpaw asked, "What are we going to do when we catch up to them, Kid? That's going to be tomorrow or the next day, if I don't miss my guess."

"*We're* not going to do anything," Morgan said. "I'm going to confront them."

"I don't know if you're ready for that," Bearpaw replied with a frown.

"You've been working with me for more than a month now. How much more do you have to teach me?"

"A man never stops learning, not if he's wise," Bearpaw said.

"But you know I'm fast," Morgan insisted. "And I hit nearly everything I aim at."

"*Nearly* can get you killed."

"So can getting up in the morning."

The Paiute shrugged. "I suppose you can look at it that way. What you're asking me, Kid, is if you're good enough to face three hardened killers. And what I'm telling you is . . . I don't know. But between the two of us—"

"No," Morgan said.

"Listen, Kid, be reasonable. Three against two is better odds than three against one. I can hold my own in a fight."

"You said yourself that you're not a gunfighter," Morgan pointed out. "I won't have your blood on my conscience, too, Phillip. When I face them, it'll be alone."

"Then you're a damned fool," Bearpaw said hotly.

Morgan shrugged. "I've been called worse. I've called myself worse."

With a surly expression on his face, Bearpaw said, "We'll talk about this in the morning. I'm turning in."

"Fine. But things won't be any different in the morning."

As a matter of fact, though, things were different, because Morgan and Bearpaw had visitors in the morning. The sun wasn't up yet when they heard a dog barking, and then a moment later, bells ringing.

Morgan rolled quickly out of his blankets and snatched up the Winchester from the ground beside him, but Bearpaw said, "Take it easy. I've heard sounds like that before. Listen closer."

Morgan frowned as he heard some sort of bleating. "What *is* that?"

"Sheep," Bearpaw said. "Some sheepherder is bringing his flock down to the creek to give them water before he turns them out on their graze."

The sheep came in sight a few minutes later, fifty or sixty of the woollies being herded along by an old Mexican man in a sombrero and serape, aided by a long-haired, black-and-white dog that dashed back and forth with seemingly endless energy, keeping the sheep bunched up.

The Mexican stopped short at the sight of Morgan, Bearpaw, and their horses. A worried look stole over his face, which was as brown and wrinkled as a walnut. Bearpaw greeted him in Spanish, though, and although Morgan wasn't fluent in the language, he was pretty sure the Paiute was telling the sheepherder not to worry, that they meant him no harm and had simply camped here for the night.

"Ask him if he's seen the men we're looking for," Morgan suggested.

For the next few minutes, Spanish flew back and forth between Bearpaw and the Mexican, the conversation going too fast for the Kid to keep up with it. Then Bearpaw turned to him, nodded, and said, "He saw them yesterday, over east of here. He moves the sheep around every day, bedding them down in a different place along the creek each night so they'll have fresh grass. Sheep are hell on the grass."

"What about those three bastards?" Morgan prodded.

"Emiliano—that's this fellow here—says they were headed toward Gomez's place. According to him, that's a cantina in a village about twenty miles east of here. I hadn't heard of it before, but evidently it's the same sort of place as Immelmann's trading post, where a man can get what he wants without too many questions being asked."

"How does he know that's where they were going?" Morgan asked.

"He overheard them talking about it. He savvies some English, even though he doesn't speak it very well. He was afraid when he saw them coming, so he took his dog and hid in an arroyo until they had ridden past. He was lucky; they didn't notice his sheep."

Morgan nodded as he thought about the information Emiliano had given them. "They'll probably stay for a while at Gomez's," he said. "A few hours anyway."

"They'll stay the night more than likely."

"That should give us plenty of time to get there today."

"And what are you going to do then, eh?" Bearpaw asked.

Morgan gave him an honest answer. "I don't know yet," he said. "But I know I won't ride away from there until I've dealt with them . . . and found out where we need to go next."

* * *

And that was the way it had played out, the Kid thought now as he rode away from what had been Gomez's cantina.

Bearpaw had continued to argue fervently that Morgan ought to let him come along, but in the end he had sighed and agreed to stay out of the fight.

"I'm warning you, though," he had told Morgan, "if you make me go back to Sawtooth and tell Eve McNally that you're dead, I'll find you in the happy hunting ground one of these days and make you wish you had listened to me."

"The happy hunting ground?" Morgan had said with a raised eyebrow.

"Ugh," Bearpaw had said.

As Morgan rode back toward the spot where he had left the Paiute, he raised his right hand and looked at it. He saw it tremble, just slightly. He had felt no fear when he faced the three killers, only a cold desire to see justice done. Now, however, a little reaction was setting in. A tiny case of nerves. He would have to work on that. One of these days, he hoped, he would ask his father if he felt the same way after a gunfight.

Luck had been with him today. Skill, too, of course, but no man survived such a battle without at least a smidgen of luck on his side. And there was more at stake than just survival. He really *had* been a damned fool, just as Bearpaw had warned him. He had come within a whisker of killing all three of his enemies without finding out where any of the other kidnappers had gone. If Julio Esquivel hadn't clung stubbornly to life for a few minutes, until Morgan realized his mistake . . .

But despite everything, Esquivel had lived long

enough to tell him that Clem Baggott and Spence Hooper had been headed for Gallup, New Mexico Territory. According to the Mexican knife artist, Baggott's sister ran a whorehouse there, and the two men planned to stay with her for a while, until they decided what they wanted to rob next.

Bearpaw must have been watching for Morgan. The Paiute came galloping out of the little canyon where he had stayed while Morgan rode into the village. "Kid!" Bearpaw greeted him anxiously. "Are you all right? I heard the shots from down there."

"I'm fine," Morgan assured him. "They came close . . . but not close enough."

"They're dead?"

Morgan nodded.

"All three of them?"

"That's right. But before he died, Esquivel told me that two of the others were on their way to Gallup."

Bearpaw heaved a sigh of relief. "I was afraid you might forget we needed to question one of them."

"When they started shooting at me, I almost did forget," Morgan admitted with a slight smile. "Lucky for me, I didn't kill Esquivel right off."

. Bearpaw's shaggy black brows drew down in a frown. "How'd you get him to talk? I thought I was supposed to be the one in charge of torture."

"I had something he wanted," the Kid said. "A quicker death than a bullet in the gut."

Bearpaw let out a little whistle. "Yeah, that would loosen a man's tongue, all right. You'll have to tell me all about it."

"On the way to Gallup," Morgan said. "And that is . . . which direction?"

Bearpaw pointed south.

* * *

Gallup was a railroad town, and in less than ten years of existence, it had become noted for two things. One was its high Indian population, which was no surprise because it was located in the middle of several reservations. The other was that it was rough as hell, also no surprise, because most settlements that sprang to life along the railroads were that way. The term "Hell on Wheels" had originated with the railroad towns, and Gallup certainly fit the description. It had a multitude of saloons, gambling dens, and whorehouses.

One of those whorehouses was called Rosa's, and according to what Julio Esquivel had said, Rosa was Clem Baggott's sister. The first thing Morgan and Bearpaw did when they rode down out of the mountains north of the settlement was to stop a man walking along the street and ask him if he knew where the brothel was located.

The hombre frowned indignantly and demanded, "Do I look like the sort of man who would know anything about a house of ill repute?"

As a matter of fact, the man had been weaving slightly as he made his way down the street, and his nose was red from drink. So yeah, the Kid thought, he looked exactly like the sort of man who might know such a thing.

But the Kid just said, "Sorry, mister, didn't mean any offense. I just thought I might stand you to the price of a drink if you could help us out."

"Oh." The man hiccupped softly. "Well, in that case . . . you go down this street a couple of blocks, then turn right just past the railroad tracks. Rosa's will be on the left, four blocks down."

Morgan dug a coin out of his pocket and flipped it to the drunk. "Much obliged."

"They may not let the Injun in, though," the man warned. "Depends on what kind of mood Rosa's in."

"Bearpaw take his chances," the Paiute intoned.

As they rode away, Morgan said, "You like doing that, don't you?"

"People expect it. If you give people what they expect, then they don't get suspicious. And if a fellow thinks that I don't speak much English, he's not going to be as careful about what he says around me."

That made sense, the Kid thought. It had been a lucky day for him in more ways than one when Bearpaw heard that splash and came along to pull him out of the creek.

Rosa's was a large, two-story clapboard building across the street from the railroad tracks and down a ways from the depot. A balcony ran along the front of the building so that the soiled doves who worked there could stand outside in their skimpies and wave to passengers as eastbound trains pulled in. The hope was that some of those passengers would disembark from the trains and hurry back up the street to take advantage of the local hospitality. It probably worked, at least some of the time.

A corral stood next to the whorehouse. Morgan and Bearpaw led the buckskin and the Appaloosa into it, unsaddled the horses, and placed the saddles on the corral fence along with seven or eight others. Morgan wondered which of the other horses in the corral belonged to Baggott and Hooper, if indeed any of them did. Since the two outlaws were staying a while, they might have stabled their mounts somewhere else.

It didn't matter, Morgan told himself. Baggott and Hooper weren't going to have any need of horses for much longer.

They went up the steps onto the porch underneath the balcony. A large black man sat in a wicker chair next to the door. He wore a derby hat and a dusty black suit over a collarless white shirt. "Afternoon to you, sir," he said to Morgan. He looked at Bearpaw and added a noncommittal grunt, then went on. "Lookin' for some fine ladies, are you?"

"That's right," Morgan said.

"You can go right on in, and welcome. The Injun's got to stay out here, though."

"But he's my friend," Morgan objected.

The black man shook his head. "Don't matter. Miss Rosa says no Injuns today, and what Miss Rosa says goes."

Bearpaw thumped himself lightly on the chest with a fist and said, "No worry 'bout Bearpaw, friend Morgan. Bearpaw sit on step, wait for friend."

"No, you can't sit there either," the black man said. "Mosey on down to the train station, why don't you? There'll be a westbound in soon; you can probably cadge some money for firewater."

Bearpaw nodded. "Bearpaw do like dark man say." He turned away, and one eye opened and closed quickly in a wink that Morgan could see, even though the bouncer couldn't.

The Paiute shuffled off down the street while Morgan stepped inside the whorehouse. As a younger man, well before his marriage to Rebel, he had been inside a few such establishments in Boston, but those had been high-class enterprises, nothing like this shabby, squalid brothel. The rug on the floor in the parlor was threadbare, and some of the overstuffed furniture around the room was losing its stuffing.

The same was true of most of the women waiting in the parlor for customers. They were getting on in years, blowsy in soiled shifts, and more than one smile was missing some teeth as they grinned at Morgan in what was supposed to be an enticing manner. He didn't feel the least bit tempted. He couldn't imagine any circumstances in which he would. Maybe if he hadn't actually *seen* a woman for fifteen or twenty years . . .

One of the whores caught his eye, though. She was younger than the others, around twenty years old, and even though her skin lacked any reddish hue, her raven hair and high cheekbones testified to at least some Indian blood in her. She was even slightly pretty, in a coarse way.

A woman in a crimson gown, with graying blond hair piled high on her head, came into the parlor through another door. She had a cup of coffee in one hand, and Morgan guessed she had been out in the kitchen heating up the brew. She stopped short at the sight of Morgan and said, "Howdy, mister. I didn't know anybody had come in."

"He's a pretty one, ain't he, Rosa?" one of the whores purred.

The madam moved toward Morgan. "You looking for some female companionship, cowboy?"

Morgan hesitated. He was going to have to spend some time here, more than likely, until he got a line on Baggott and Hooper. He wasn't sure how to go about this, but he knew that he couldn't stay if he didn't act like he wanted to partake of the dubious pleasures offered by the house.

"That one," he said as he pointed to the youngest whore, the one with Indian blood.

The other soiled doves looked disappointed. Rosa smiled and said, "Good choice. Tasmin, take our guest upstairs and show him a fine old time."

The young woman stood up from the divan, sidled over to Morgan, and took hold of his arm with both of her hands, pressing herself against him so that he felt the warm mound of her breast prodding his side.

"You come with me, mister," she said as she smiled up at him. "I promise, you won't ever be sorry that you picked me."

Morgan felt a surge of panic inside him. He didn't want this woman. He didn't want any woman— except the one he could no longer have.

At that moment, the door from the parlor to the kitchen opened again, and a man came into the room. Morgan glanced at him, saw a middle-aged hombre with a battered Stetson shoved back on his head and a close-cropped, salt-and-pepper beard. He said, "Rosa, how's about frontin' me some more money? There's a poker game down at the saloon tonight, and I reckon I can clean up in it."

The young whore started tugging Morgan toward the stairs. Rosa turned to the man who had just come into the room and snapped, "Damn it, Clem, I've told you not to bother me while I'm working."

Clem Baggott. The name rang in Morgan's mind. This was one of the men he and Bearpaw had come here looking for. Morgan turned his head to look closer at the man, and recognized him from that awful night in Black Rock Canyon, even though he had only seen Baggott for a moment by the glaring light of those torches alongside the trail.

Morgan wasn't the only one who recognized somebody, though. Even though Morgan looked quite a bit different now, Baggott's eyes bulged out in shock. He yelled, "Son of a bitch! You're that bastard from Carson City!"

Then he reached for the Colt on his hip, even as the whore called Tasmin screamed and tightened her two-handed grip on Morgan's gun arm.

Chapter 18

Morgan knew he had only an instant to act. He reached over with his left hand, grabbed Tasmin's shift, and hauled hard on it. The garment tore a little, but held enough together enough to pull her away from him. He swung her around and slung her right into Rosa. The two women collided with startled yells and fell to the floor, out of the line of fire.

At the same time, Morgan lunged the other way. Baggott's gun blasted, flame licking from the muzzle. Morgan couldn't hear the whine of the bullet past his head because all the women in the room were screaming by now, but he felt the hot wind-rip of its passage.

His Colt had flickered into his hand. It roared and bucked as he squeezed the trigger. Baggott grunted in pain and spun halfway around. He tried to catch himself on the back of a divan, but his groping hand missed. He pitched to the floor, dropping his gun as he did so.

Morgan had time to hope that Baggott wasn't fatally wounded, since he didn't know yet where Hooper was, and then the front door crashed open and the huge black bouncer came into the room like an avalanche, bellowing angrily.

"Get him, Hyde!" Rosa screamed from the floor. "He killed Clem!"

Morgan hoped again that wasn't the case, that Baggott wasn't dead. Then the bouncer called Hyde was on him, reaching for him with long, tree-trunk-like arms.

Morgan could have shot the man, but as far as he could tell, Hyde was unarmed. Anyway, he wasn't sure bullets would stop the charging behemoth. Morgan tried to twist away, knowing that if those arms ever trapped him in their circle, he would be in for some rib-crushing.

He managed to avoid the bear hug, but Hyde grabbed the back of his shirt and threw him at the wall. The planking vibrated as Morgan's right shoulder slammed into it. He cried out in pain as that arm went numb. A thud sounded as the gun slipped from his fingers and fell to the floor.

He had been hoping to wallop Hyde over the head a few times with the Colt and maybe slow him down that way. Now he was unarmed, and definitely out of his class as far as weight, reach, and rough-and-tumble ability were concerned. As Hyde charged him again, he dropped into a crouch and threw himself at the big man's knees, hoping to chop Hyde's legs out from under him.

The maneuver was only partially successful. Morgan hit Hyde low, and the bouncer fell. But he landed on top of Morgan, who was pinned to the floor by Hyde's weight. Hyde got one hand on Morgan's throat and closed it, cutting off his air. Morgan's vision started to blur as he tried to gasp, but he could still see Hyde looming above him, raising a giant fist and getting ready to bring it down like a sledgehammer into the middle of Morgan's face.

Even over the roaring of blood in his ears, Morgan heard a solid thump. Hyde's eyes rolled up in his head until only the whites showed; then he pitched forward senselessly. He was still on top of Morgan, though, so all the Kid could do was stare over Hyde's shoulder at Bearpaw, who stood there with the Sharps clutched in his hands. Morgan figured it was the butt of the rifle he had heard connecting solidly with the back of Hyde's skull.

"Get him . . . off me!" Morgan managed to croak.

Bearpaw looked like he wanted to laugh, but he kept a straight face as he bent down and grasped the collar of Hyde's coat. "You'll have to help me," he said. "I'm not sure I can budge this big fellow by myself."

Morgan got his hands against Hyde's shoulders and shoved while Bearpaw heaved. After a moment of grunting struggle, they were able to roll the big man off Morgan.

"Check on . . . Baggott," Morgan said as he sat up and tried to catch his breath. "I had to . . . shoot him . . ."

Bearpaw turned toward Baggott, and as he did so, Morgan heard a small popping sound. Bearpaw grunted again and took a sudden step back.

"I'm shot," he said.

Morgan surged to his feet and saw Rosa swinging an over-and-under derringer toward him. "You son of a bitch!" she screamed. "You killed my brother!"

Morgan leaped and swatted the little pistol aside just as it popped again. That emptied it, but he closed his hand over it and twisted it out of Rosa's fingers anyway, so she couldn't reload and try again to shoot him. He was worried about Bearpaw, so he gave the madam a shove that sent her stumbling backward to sit down hard on her ample rump.

Morgan swung around and saw that Bearpaw had sunk onto the arm of a ratty divan. The whores had all scurried away and vanished except for Tasmin, who stood huddled in fear against one of the walls.

Bearpaw slipped a hand inside his shirt, pulled it out, and looked at the crimson stains on his fingertips. "Yeah, I'm shot, all right," he said.

Then he toppled over backward onto the divan.

Morgan started toward him, but he had taken only a single step when another gun blasted from somewhere above him. The slug whipped past him. He looked up and saw a man standing at the top of the stairs, smoke curling from the barrel of the gun in his fist.

Morgan recognized this man from Black Rock Canyon, too, and knew he had to be Spence Hooper. As Hooper fired again, Morgan launched himself in a dive toward the Colt he had dropped a few moments earlier while battling with Hyde. The feeling had returned to Morgan's arm, so he was able to snatch up the gun as he slid across the threadbare rug. He came to a stop at the bottom of the stairs and fired up at Hooper.

Hooper screamed and listed sideways as blood and bone exploded from his left kneecap. He pitched forward, squeezing off another shot as he did so. The bullet chewed splinters from the stairs halfway down. Still screaming from the pain of his shattered knee, Hooper tumbled on down the stairs, coming to a stop just a few steps up from Morgan.

The Kid scrambled to his feet. Hooper had dropped his gun, and Morgan didn't see any other weapons. He turned so that he could cover Hooper while checking on Rosa, Tasmin, and Hyde. Rosa had crawled over to her brother, and now lay half on top of him, sobbing and wailing. Baggott hadn't moved since he went down, so Morgan thought there was a good chance he really was dead. Tasmin still stood against the wall, watching wide-eyed.

Bearpaw rolled onto his side and started trying to struggle to his feet. "I'm all right," he said as Morgan hurried over to help him. "That bullet just nicked me. Keep an eye on the other one."

Morgan ignored what Bearpaw said, got an arm around the Paiute, and helped him stand up. Morgan looked at Tasmin and asked, "How quick will the law get here?"

"Wh-what?"

"The law," Morgan repeated. "The local sheriff, police, whatever they have here. How long?"

She shook her head. "I don't know. They leave this end of town alone mostly. But with that many shots, they'll have to come see what it's about. Five or ten minutes maybe?"

Morgan hoped that would be long enough. "Hooper's still alive," he said to Bearpaw. "We need to question him."

Bearpaw nodded. "Help me over there, then stand back and keep an eye out for trouble."

The two men went to the foot of the stairs. Hooper lay there whimpering. Bearpaw reached down, rested a hand on the outlaw's thigh just above the shattered knee, and pushed hard.

Hooper shrieked.

"That was just to get your attention," Bearpaw said as the cry died away. "Where are the others?"

"Wh-what . . . others?" Hooper gasped.

"The other men who rode with you when you kidnapped Conrad Browning's wife."

Hooper blinked up at the Paiute. "I . . . I don't know what . . . you're talkin' about . . . I never kidnapped no woman—"

Bearpaw didn't let him go on. Instead, he pushed on Hooper's leg again. Hooper gobbled in pain.

But when the agony eased a little, words began to spill from Hooper's mouth. "I don't know where they all went, but Rattigan and that breed, White Rock, were gonna do some prospectin' in Colorado! Rattigan said he knew a place up in the Sangre de Cristos where he thought there might be some gold! I think it was called Blue Creek, or something like that. God, don't do that again, redskin. I can't stand it."

"What about the others?" Bearpaw insisted.

"I don't know! I swear! Vernon used to talk about someplace down on the border, but I don't know any more than that. And nobody else told me anything about where they were goin' when we split up." Hooper sobbed. "You gotta get me to a sawbones. I'm hurt bad."

"You're sure you don't know where we can find any of the others?"

"No, I swear! That's all I know."

"Then you don't have to worry about a sawbones," Bearpaw said. His arm and shoulder moved.

Morgan saw Hooper give a little jerk. The man's eyes widened. Morgan looked down in time to see Bearpaw let go of a knife with a staghorn handle that protruded from Hooper's chest. The thrust must have gone right into the outlaw's heart. Hooper opened his mouth, but no more words came out before his head fell back on the steps. He kept staring as the life faded from his eyes.

On the other side of the parlor, Hyde groaned as he began to stir.

"Help me up," Bearpaw said. "We'd better get out of here."

It was too late for that. Heavy footsteps sounded on the porch, and three men crowded into the room, each of them carrying a shotgun. Morgan started to lift his gun, then stopped as he spotted the badges the men wore pinned to their coats.

"Arrest them, Marshal!" Rosa screamed. "String 'em up! They murdered my brother!"

The lawmen leveled their Greeners at Morgan and Bearpaw. "Shuck your irons, boys," one of the men growled. "We got some sortin' out to do here."

"I hope that telegram you sent does some good, Kid," Bearpaw said an hour later as the two of them sat on an iron cot in a cell in the Gallup city jail. "Otherwise, things don't look too promising for us. 'Therefore never send to ask for whom the bell tolls,' John Donne said. 'It tolls for thee.'"

"And just what does that mean?"

"It means that if you hear them hammering together a gallows, it's probably going to be for us."

Morgan took a deep breath. It had taken a lot of talking to convince Marshal Davis to let him send a telegram to Claudius Turnbuckle in San Francisco. The message had been a short one.

STILL ALIVE STOP NEED LEGAL HELP GALLUP
NMT STOP CONRAD

Rosa had insisted, tearfully and at the top of her lungs, that Morgan and Bearpaw had burst into the whorehouse and started shooting for no reason. They had gunned down her brother, and then they had shot Spence Hooper and caused him to fall on his own knife. That was the only explanation that made any sense to the marshal, since the knife in Hooper's chest belonged to him. Even Rosa admitted that. She had been too busy grieving over her brother—who was indeed dead, shot cleanly through the heart—to realize that that version of events didn't make complete sense. Hooper wouldn't have lived long enough for Bearpaw to question him if that had been the case.

But they already had one murder charge hanging over their heads, Morgan thought, so why complicate matters even more?

"You didn't have to kill him," Morgan whispered now as he sat beside Bearpaw. "I would have done it, once we found out everything we could from him."

"You mean you would have shot him in cold blood?" the Paiute asked.

"That's the way I killed Hank Winchell."

"There was nothing cold-blooded about that night," Bearpaw said with a shake of his head. "You had just seen your wife murdered. You were in a state of shock. Pulling the trigger on a man weeks later is different."

"I shot Esquivel."

"You put him out of his misery. He would have died anyway from that bullet in his guts, and he would have suffered a lot more. You were merciful to him, Kid. That wasn't murder. Me, I've already got plenty of bad things on my conscience. Taking care of one outlaw who needed killing won't cause me to lose any sleep."

Morgan didn't say anything. Despite the hatred

and the need for vengeance that had consumed him since leaving Carson City, he was coming to realize that there was a difference between killing a man in a fair fight and snuffing out the life of someone who couldn't fight back.

After a few minutes, Morgan asked, "How's your shoulder?"

Bearpaw started to shrug, then stopped as the motion caused him to grimace in pain. "It hurts like the devil," he said, "but I'll live. That little popgun of Rosa's didn't have much punch. The bullet wasn't more than a couple of inches under the skin."

A doctor had come to the jail after Morgan and Bearpaw were locked up and tended to the Paiute's wound, which was messy but not life-threatening. A bulky bandage showed now as a lump under Bearpaw's shirt.

"Kid, I'm sorry things got out of hand," he went on. "I never figured on Baggott recognizing you like that."

"Neither did I," Morgan said. "I guess he's got a good eye for faces, because I've changed a lot since that night. We just didn't have any luck."

"A man's always got luck. It's just that sometimes it's good . . . and sometimes it's bad. Mostly, it's some of both. We're still alive, aren't we?"

"For now," Morgan said. He had visions of a trial, and a judge passing sentence, and a long walk up thirteen steps to the gallows . . .

The door into the cell block opened, and Marshal Davis came in with another man, a tall, imposing, white-haired gent in an expensive suit and Stetson. Morgan and Bearpaw were the only prisoners at the moment, other than a couple of drunken Navajos sleeping off a bender, but the marshal pointed at them anyway and said, "There they are, Colonel."

"Thank you, Marshal," the man said in deep, powerful tones. Morgan had heard voices like that before, and they were nearly always in courtrooms. He got to his feet and went over to grasp the iron bars in the door as Marshal Davis went back into the jail office and the stranger came over to the cell.

"Did Turnbuckle send you?" Morgan asked tensely.

The man smiled and said, "Colonel Theodore Binswanger at your service, sir. My old friend from law school, the esteemed Claudius Turnbuckle, did indeed communicate urgently with me this afternoon via the telegraphic wires. He asked that I render any possible aid to you, and, I suppose by extension, to your ruddy companion there. It's quite fortunate for you that Claudius is acquainted with someone who practices law here. Marshal Davis tells me that the charge will be quite serious when you're arraigned. Murder."

"It wasn't murder," Morgan snapped. "Baggott fired first, and so did Hooper. It was self-defense in both cases."

"The story told by the proprietress of the establishment varies considerably from that version, Mr. . . . Morgan, is it?"

"That's right." Morgan didn't know how much Turnbuckle might have told Colonel Binswanger in his telegram, so for now he was going to keep his connection with Conrad Browning to himself.

"Oh, by the way," Binswanger said as he reached into his coat, "Claudius sent a private wire for you as well." He held out a folded, sealed paper. "I've honored the sanctity of your communication."

"Obliged," Morgan said as he took the telegram and tore it open to read the words printed on it.

WHAT IN THE BLAZES STOP THOUGHT YOU WERE
DEAD STOP WILL TRY LOCATE FRANK AND TELL
HIM STOP TRUST BINSWANGER STOP FULL OF HOT
AIR BUT HONEST STOP

Morgan folded the message and slipped it into the pocket of his black shirt. He was glad he had finally gotten in touch with Turnbuckle. At least, he had started the process of letting his father know that he was still alive. It had taken a lot longer than Morgan had intended.

"Now, what can you tell me about the fatal incident?" Binswanger asked.

Morgan rubbed his jaw. He had been thinking about how to play this.

"Bearpaw and I just stopped at the whorehouse for . . . well, you know."

The lawyer sniffed. "I am aware of the establishment's unsavory reputation naturally, though I have no, ah, personal knowledge of what goes on there."

"Bearpaw was outside, and I was just standing there in the parlor when that first fella came in, yelled something about Carson City, and started blazing away at me. All I can figure is that he thought I was somebody else, somebody he had a grudge against."

"Have you ever been to Carson City?"

"Yeah, but I never saw that hombre before," Morgan lied. "He didn't have any reason to throw down on me."

"What happened then?"

Morgan told the rest of the story just the way it had

happened, leaving out only the part about Bearpaw questioning Spence Hooper—and then putting Hooper's own knife in the outlaw's chest.

Binswanger nodded and said, "That does indeed sound like classic, clear-cut cases of self-defense. Unfortunately, it's your word against that of this . . . Rosa. And I'm relatively certain that the, ah, ladies in her employ will corroborate her testimony." The lawyer lowered his voice. "However, I happen to know that there's a move afoot among the city fathers to clean up some of the more unsavory sections of town. I have a feeling that if there was even one witness to support your claims, the judge could be persuaded to drop the charges against you before the case proceeds any further . . . on the condition, of course, that the two of you depart from our fair city posthaste."

"We'd be glad to," Morgan said, thinking of what Hooper had told them about Rattigan and White Rock prospecting in the Sangre de Cristos up in Colorado, "if the marshal would just let us out."

Binswanger sighed. "I'll see what I can find in the way of a witness," he said. "But to be honest with you, sir, I don't hold out much hope of success."

Neither did Morgan. He knew that the soiled doves who worked for Rosa weren't going to contradict her story.

Binswanger left the jail, and Morgan sat down on the cot next to Bearpaw again. He picked up his hat, which was lying on the cot next to him, and looked at it idly. After a moment, he said, "Well, damn."

"What is it?" Bearpaw asked.

Morgan held up the hat and poked his finger through a hole in the crown. "There's a matching one on the other side," he said. "My hat fell off when I was tussling with Hyde, and then when Hooper took that shot at me, the bullet must have hit the hat while it was lying on the floor."

"Pure luck once again. Good luck, in this case."

"How can you say that? I've got a hole in my hat!"

"Better than a hole in your head," Bearpaw said.

Morgan laughed. "You're right about that."

They watched the light fade in the cell's single, barred window. It faced west, so they could see a slice of sky as it turned orange and crimson from the setting sun. Some of those brilliant hues still remained in the sky when Colonel Binswanger appeared again, bustling into the cell block when the marshal unlocked the door. A smile wreathed the old attorney's face.

"Superlative news," Binswanger said as he came up to the cell door, followed by the marshal, who was jingling a ring of keys. "A witness came forward to support your story. I didn't even have to locate her. She came to me when she heard that I was representing the two of you."

"She?" Morgan repeated.

Binswanger waved off the question as Davis unlocked the cell door and swung it open. "Judge Applewhite has dismissed the charges."

"We weren't even arraigned yet," Morgan said, not wanting to look a gift horse in the mouth, but puzzled by the turn of events.

"You were arraigned in absentia, and then the charges were dismissed. Simple really. Informal, but effective. The only caveat, as I said, is that the two of you are now expected to depart as soon as possible. You are henceforth persona non grata in Gallup."

"He means light a shuck outta here," Marshal Davis growled.

"We intend to," Morgan said as he retrieved his Stetson from the cot. "Just as soon as I buy a new hat."

"Make it quick," the marshal warned. "Rosa's gonna pitch a fit when she hears about this. And she's still got some influential friends in this town. Men who use the back door when they visit her place, if you know what I mean."

Morgan did. He wasn't surprised to hear that some of Gallup's leading citizens were also secret patrons of the whorehouse.

He and Bearpaw followed Binswanger out of the cell block, with the marshal bringing up the rear. Binswanger led them through the jail office. They stepped out onto the porch, and Morgan was surprised to see the young whore Tasmin standing there, wearing a simple brown dress.

"You?" he said. "You're the one who told the law what really happened?"

She nodded. "That's right. I couldn't let you and your friend be railroaded for something you didn't do."

She stood there while Binswanger shook hands with Morgan and nodded civilly to Bearpaw. "I'll bid you gentlemen farewell. Claudius instructed me to submit the bill for my services to Turnbuckle and Stafford, and he would see to taking care of it."

"Thanks," Morgan said. "You were a big help, Colonel."

Binswanger shook his head. "I didn't do all that much." He gestured toward Tasmin. "It was mostly this young lady here."

He tipped his hat to her and then walked away.

"You know you're not going to be able to work for Rosa anymore after this," Morgan told her. "I don't know how we can thank you for what you've done."

"I do," Tasmin said. "I heard what that bastard Hooper told you." The loathing in her voice told Morgan that she'd probably had a few unpleasant experiences with Hooper while he and Baggott were staying at Rosa's. "You're going to Colorado to look for those two men he was talking about, aren't you?"

Morgan glanced at Bearpaw, who inclined his head as if to say that it was pretty obvious they were, but he was leaving the decision of what to tell Tasmin to Morgan.

"That's right," Morgan said to her. "I reckon we are."

"Then if you want to pay me back for helping you . . . take me with you."

Chapter 19

Morgan and Bearpaw both stared at the young soiled dove. "Take you with us?" Morgan repeated after a moment, thinking about the danger he and the Paiute would be riding into for the foreseeable future. "We can't do that."

"Well, I can't stay here in Gallup," Tasmin said. "Do you think Rosa's going to let me get away with helping you? At the very least, she'll have Hyde beat me. She might even order him to kill me." She shook her head. "No, I've got to get out of town, and since I got in trouble helping the two of you . . ."

"She has a point, Kid," Bearpaw said.

Morgan struggled with the decision facing him. When he rode away from Carson City, he'd had in mind tracking down the kidnappers on his own, so that no one else would be endangered. Then he had wound up traveling with Bearpaw. That had worked out all right so far, other than the fact that the Paiute had been wounded. Now this young woman—little more than a girl actually—was asking to join them on their journey as well.

Tasmin seemed somehow different now that she was out of the whorehouse. She had scrubbed the paint off her face and was dressed more modestly, of course, but she also sounded more intelligent when she spoke. Morgan supposed that most men didn't go to a place like Rosa's for the conversation . . .

His thoughts were straying, and Tasmin still stood there on the jail porch waiting for an answer. Morgan took a deep breath. Considering what she had done for him and Bearpaw, he didn't see how he could deny her request. All she wanted was a chance to be safe from Rosa's revenge.

"All right," he said. "You can come with us . . . for now. But if we find a good place for you to stay, that's it. You'll need a horse, too—"

"I have one. How do you think I got here to Gallup?"

"I don't have any idea. And don't take that as a request to tell me your life story." Morgan knew he was being a little rude, but he didn't like being forced into things. "We'll be leaving in about ten minutes. Can you be ready to ride?"

"I can," she replied without hesitation. "I don't have much in the way of belongings, and I brought it all with me when I slipped out of Rosa's and went to look for Colonel Binswanger. My bag is down at the livery stable with my horse."

"All right. We'll meet you there in ten minutes."

"Thank you. You won't be sorry, Mr. Morgan."

She had said something similar when she was about to take him upstairs in the whorehouse, but it sounded entirely different now.

Tasmin hurried off, while Morgan and Bearpaw angled across the street toward a general store so that Morgan could buy a new hat. He still had quite a bit of the money he had brought with him from Carson City. As plentiful as game was, they hadn't had to spend much on supplies.

The store didn't have a black hat like the one Morgan had been wearing. He settled on a brown one instead, with a lighter brown band. The crown was slightly higher than his old hat, but still flat.

"Looks good on you," Bearpaw said. "Why don't you get that buckskin jacket there to go with it?"

Morgan frowned as he looked at the jacket Bearpaw indicated. It was the sort that pulled over the head, with a neck opening that laced up with a rawhide thong. Fringe decorated the shoulders and arms of the garment.

"Sort of gaudy, isn't it?" he asked. "And this weather's too hot for a jacket."

"Sure, it's hot now," Bearpaw admitted, "but it won't be long before the northers start blowing down through these parts. You can be sweating at noon and shivering by the time the sun goes down. Besides, that rawhide fringe comes in mighty handy for mending saddles or harness."

Morgan thought it over for a moment, then shrugged and nodded. "All right, you've talked me into it. I don't reckon it would hurt to be prepared for cooler weather."

He paid the storekeeper for the purchases, then walked out wearing the brown hat, with the buckskin jacket thrown over his left arm. He still thought it was a little gaudy—but he had to admit it was the sort of thing a notorious gunfighter might wear, at least in dime-novel illustrations. And since Morgan had been basing a lot of his new personality on those very dime novels, he supposed he ought to dress the part.

Give people what they expected to see, Bearpaw had said. Morgan was willing to do that.

Their horses were still in the corral next to Rosa's. Morgan kept a wary eye on the place as they retrieved the buckskin and the Appaloosa, in case Rosa spotted them and sent Hyde after them. The door was closed and the shades were pulled on the windows, though. It looked like the house was closed down, maybe because Rosa was mourning her brother.

Tasmin was waiting in front of the livery stable when they walked up, leading their horses. She had changed into a man's work shirt with the sleeves rolled up a couple of turns on her forearms, as well as a pair of denim trousers.

Morgan glanced at her saddle and asked, "You're going to ride astride?"

Her chin lifted defiantly. "I reckon you already know that I'm not exactly a lady. I never cared for a sidesaddle."

"That's fine with me," Morgan said. A faint smile touched his lips as he recalled all the times he had seen Rebel riding that way. She didn't have any use for a sidesaddle either.

The three of them mounted up. Tasmin had a canvas bag tied to her saddle horn. She reached inside it and brought out an old hat with a floppy brim. She jammed it down on her head and heeled her horse into motion. Morgan and Bearpaw exchanged quick grins as they let her take the lead.

"Where exactly are we going?" Morgan called after her as they reached the edge of town.

"Colorado, right? Somewhere in the Sangre de Cristos?"

"You know how to get there?"

Tasmin slowed her horse and looked back at the two men. "Well . . . no," she admitted. "I just wanted to get out of Gallup as quickly as I could." She gave Morgan a challenging look as she went on. "Do *you* know how to get there?"

"Just a general idea. I reckon Bearpaw does, though."

"Heap right," Bearpaw said. "Know-um way to mountains."

Tasmin's expression was withering as she said, "You've forgotten that I heard you talking back at Rosa's place. Don't try to pull that on me."

Bearpaw chuckled. "Sorry. You get in the habit of doing something and it's hard to stop."

"Not me," Tasmin said as she faced forward again. "I'd just as soon break all of my habits, and the sooner the better."

Bearpaw was right about the weather. As they traveled eastward across the rugged New Mexico landscape, the first couple of days remained warm, even hot, but then on the third morning, a strong wind started blowing out of the north. It carried more than a hint of a chill in it.

"I told you," Bearpaw said as they got ready to break camp. "Tonight, it'll be cold enough to make your breath fog."

Morgan wondered what that would mean for the sleeping arrangements. The first two nights, there had been a minimum of awkwardness because Tasmin took her bedroll and carried it a good distance away from the men before she spread it out. Tonight, she would probably want to be closer to the fire.

By noon, he had taken the buckskin jacket out of his saddlebags and slipped it on to help shield him from the chilly wind. Tasmin wore a flannel coat, and Bearpaw had a small buffalo robe draped around his shoulders. The sky was clear, but the Paiute frowned as he squinted up at it.

"Snow in less than a week," he announced with serene confidence.

"How can you tell that?" Morgan asked.

"My people live in harmony with nature. We know these things."

Tasmin laughed. "One of my grandfathers was a Hopi medicine man. He always said things like that."

"And he was right, wasn't he?" Bearpaw asked.

"Usually," Tasmin admitted with a shrug.

That night, the air was frigid. As Morgan expected, Tasmin spread her blankets near the fire. He made sure there was a little distance between them when he laid out his own bedroll. He went to sleep with the sound of the north wind howling in his ears.

When his eyes snapped open sometime later, the wind had died down. Unsure what had woken him, he gazed up into a crystal-clear sky in which the stars seemed like they were about to tumble down around him.

Then, something moved against his back. His muscles tensed. His hand moved toward the Winchester that lay on the ground beside him.

"It's just me," Tasmin said in a sleepy voice as she snuggled closer to him. "I got cold, so I moved my blankets over next to yours. All right?"

Morgan grunted, then said, "Fine. I wouldn't want you to freeze. Go back to sleep."

She didn't, though, and neither did he. After a few minutes, she said in a small, tentative voice, "Kid?"

"What?"

"The other day at Rosa's place, when you picked me to take upstairs . . . you didn't really want to go up there with me, did you? You were just looking for Baggott and Hooper, right?"

"That's right," Morgan said. He tried not to be curt or cruel about it, but he wasn't going to lie to her.

"And you don't want me now either, do you?"

Morgan hesitated, not because he was unsure of the answer, but rather because he didn't want to hurt her feelings. Finally, he said, "It's not that I don't want you, Tasmin. I don't want any woman right now. I have other things I have to deal with first before I can even think about anything like that."

She squeezed his shoulder. "You have so much sadness in you, Kid. I'm sorry for whatever caused it. If there's anything I can do to help . . ."

"Just stay out of the way if there's trouble."

That came out more abruptly than he'd intended. He felt her flinch as if she'd been struck. But she said, "Fine. I won't be a bother."

Then she turned over and pressed her back against his, rather than spooning with him. That was probably better, he thought.

Craggy peaks, lushly timbered valleys, arid wastelands all passed under their horses' hooves as they continued eastward, angling somewhat to the north toward Colorado as they did so. The cold weather passed by, the wind turned out of the south again, and the temperatures warmed. This was a volatile time of year, though, Bearpaw pointed out. There might be another blue norther at any time, and he hadn't backed off on his prediction of snow.

They avoided large towns, traveling north of Albuquerque and south of Taos and Santa Fe, then turned in a more northerly direction to follow the mountains. The Sangre de Cristos were in the northeastern corner of the territory, running north and south from New Mexico into southern Colorado. Raton Pass was on the border between the two. Bearpaw explained all this to Morgan and Tasmin, and since he seemed to know where he was going, they were content to let him take the lead.

"Is there anywhere west of the Mississippi you *haven't* been?" Morgan asked as they approached the towering pass.

"I'm sure there is," Bearpaw replied with a grin, "but I can't think of any place right now."

"How did you wind up in Sawtooth?"

The Paiute could shrug now because the minor bullet wound in his shoulder was almost healed up. He did so and said, "Everybody's got to be somewhere. I'd lived a pretty eventful life, and Sawtooth seemed like a nice quiet place to settle down and live out the rest of my years in peace. It was, too . . . until Kid Morgan showed up."

Tasmin looked over at Morgan. "I know you're supposed to be a famous gunfighter," she said, "but I don't think I'd ever heard of you."

"You just don't travel in the right circles," Bearpaw told her. "The Kid's famous, all right."

She looked like she wasn't sure whether she believed him or not. Morgan didn't say anything. He still felt a little uncomfortable about the whole business of pretending to be somebody else, somebody who didn't really exist.

Although Kid Morgan was becoming more and more real with every gunfight, he realized.

The view from the top of the pass was one of the most spectacular they had seen so far, with majestic mountains rising on either side of them, and behind them plains stretching away for scores of miles to the south and east. Up ahead, in Colorado, the mountains continued, although they were higher and more rugged to the west, falling off into rolling hills to the east.

The climb to the pass was steep, so Bearpaw reined in to rest his mount when they reached the top, and the Kid and Tasmin followed suit. They swung down from their saddles and stood there for long minutes, looking out over the impressive landscape.

"This is a lot prettier than the pueblo where I grew up," Tasmin commented.

"You said you're Hopi?" Morgan asked.

"Only a fourth. My other grandparents were white." Her mouth quirked in a bitter smile. "Missionaries, in fact, who came out here from the East to save the heathen savages. They must not have done a very good job of it, considering the way I turned out."

"I'm not sure I'd go that far," Morgan told her.

"You don't know just how heathen I am." She gave a defiant toss of her head. "And you never will, Mr. Kid Morgan. All that is behind me now."

That was fine with him, he thought.

Bearpaw's attention was focused on their backtrail, and when Tasmin went off into the brush to take care of some personal business, he motioned Morgan over to him and said quietly, "I think somebody's following us, Kid."

Morgan's eyes narrowed as he scanned the landscape below the pass. He didn't see anything moving except a couple of hawks soaring on the wind currents, but he trusted Bearpaw.

"How many?"

"Three, I think. They're a long way back, and I can't even see them right now. But I've caught several glimpses of them today, and I'm pretty sure they're back there."

"How do you know they're actually following us?"

"I don't, of course," Bearpaw admitted. "They could be pilgrims who just happen to be going the same direction we are. A lot of people use this pass. But I slowed down, and they slowed down. I pushed a little harder, and they pushed a little harder."

Instinctively, Morgan's hand dropped to the butt of his gun. "Who'd have a reason to follow us?"

"That madam back in Gallup could have hired some gun-wolves to come after us and settle the score for her brother," Bearpaw suggested.

Morgan nodded. That was a possibility, all right. But it didn't seem likely to him. "We'll keep our eyes open. If they're following us, when do you think they'll make their move?"

"No telling. They're close enough they can catch up to us tonight, if they want to."

Tasmin was coming back. Morgan glanced at her and said, "I wish we'd found a place to leave her."

"I'm not sure she would have stayed. That girl's got ideas in her head about you, whether she'll admit it or not . . . and whether you like it or not."

That was one of the last things Morgan wanted to hear, but he was afraid Bearpaw might be right.

"If there's trouble, I'm counting on you to keep her safe," he told the Paiute.

"What are you going to be doing?"

"Killing whoever's giving us that trouble," Morgan said.

Chapter 20

Later that afternoon, Bearpaw pointed to a dark blue line on the northern horizon and said, "That's a storm coming. Remember that snow I told you about?" He nodded toward the distant clouds. "It's up there. We'll need to find a good place to camp where we can get out of the weather."

"Maybe we should make for the nearest town," Morgan suggested.

Bearpaw squinted at the sky. "That'd be Trinidad. But I'm not sure we've got time to make it that far before nightfall." He hitched the Appaloosa into a faster pace. "We'll give it a try."

The horses were tired after a long day on the trail, though, so Morgan and his friends could only push them so hard. The dark blue line on the horizon seemed to rush southward toward them, and it wasn't long before it turned into looming, bluish-gray clouds. The wind picked up, and the chill was back.

"If you see a good place to camp," Morgan called to Bearpaw, "we'll go ahead and stop."

The Paiute nodded. It was hard to tell because his

face was usually impassive anyway, but Morgan thought he looked more concerned than usual. Between the weather and those three riders following them, this might turn out to be a long, dangerous night.

A short time later, Bearpaw pointed to a ridge to the left of the trail and said, "I think we'd better go over there and see if we can find somewhere to hunker down. A nice overhang would give us a place to get out of the weather."

Morgan nodded. "Lead the way. We'll be right behind you."

It took about half an hour for them to locate a suitable place. A granite bluff jutted into the air and sloped inward to a cavelike area at its base. It would provide shelter from the north wind and block at least some of the snow, if Bearpaw was right about that being on the way as well.

Morgan and Bearpaw tended to the horses while Tasmin gathered wood and built a fire. Ever since they had left Gallup, she had been good about helping out around camp and had done her share of the work without any complaints. She soon had a nice little fire blazing away merrily, the smoke rising to spread out against the overhanging rock and then disperse.

By now, the sky was completely overcast. Dark gray clouds scudded swiftly overhead. The temperature dropped steadily. As Morgan and Bearpaw hunkered next to the fire, Morgan said, "It looks like you were right, Phillip."

Bearpaw grunted. "I just hope we're not in for a full-fledged blizzard. We may be stuck here for several days if the snow gets too deep."

"Do you expect that to happen?"

"Not really," Bearpaw replied with a shake of his

head. "It's too early in the season for that. But when you're talking about the weather, Kid, you can't really take anything for granted. It does what it wants to do, and there's not a blessed things we humans can do about it except try to adapt."

They had some dried venison plus the makings for biscuits. Bearpaw prepared supper, and the three of them sat by the fire and ate the meager meal. While they were eating, Morgan saw snowflakes begin to fall, whipped along by the wind.

"There's your snow," he told Bearpaw with a grin. "I guess you knew what you were talking about after all."

"I told you. Never argue with a redskin about the weather."

The light had begun to fade. Morgan went to the front of the cavelike area underneath the overhanging bluff and looked out across the hills he could see from there. He was especially watchful for any signs of motion, but didn't see any. Maybe the riders who had been behind them earlier had sought shelter from the storm, too. If they had any sense, that's what they had done, whether they were following Morgan and his companions or not.

Morgan turned and went back to the fire. Behind him, the snowfall grew thicker.

If the circumstances had been different, they would have put out the fire so that anyone tracking them wouldn't be able to see it. As it was, though, without the fire it would get mighty cold before morning. They would let it burn down to embers, but wouldn't extinguish it completely.

During the time they had been traveling together, Morgan had gotten a little more comfortable having Tasmin around. She didn't make any pretense of separating her bedroll from his anymore. She was huddled against him for warmth as the flames died down. During a brief, private conversation earlier in the evening, Morgan and Bearpaw had agreed to take turns standing watch tonight, just in case anything happened. Bearpaw took the first turn.

Morgan dozed off, feeling a chill seeping into his bones from the rocky ground despite the blankets underneath him. Outside their little sanctuary, the wind howled and the snow blew almost horizontal to the ground.

"Wake up, Kid."

The voice penetrated Morgan's sleep-fogged brain. It took a second before he realized that it didn't belong to Bearpaw. Nor was it Tasmin's voice. The tones were male, harsh and angry.

Morgan lunged up from his blankets and reached for the gun on his hip.

Something crashed into his face and sent him sprawling onto his back before he could grab the Colt. A second later, there was another jarring impact, this time on his left side. Somebody was kicking him, he realized.

The faint glow from the embers, reflected back from the overhanging bluff, showed him a dark shape looming above him. He rolled away as the man tried to kick him again. That took him past the Winchester he had placed beside his blankets when he turned in. He snatched up the rifle and started swinging the barrel around to bear on his attacker.

"Hold it, Kid, or I'll blow the whore's brains out!"

Morgan froze, and not from the frigid chill in the

air. Somebody snapped a match into life, and its harsh glare revealed a shocking scene. Bearpaw lay huddled near the horses while the man with the match stood over him, holding a gun on him. Another man had jerked Tasmin to her feet and had an arm looped around her throat while his other hand pressed the barrel of a revolver to her head. The third man, the one who had been trying to stomp the Kid to death, was Hyde, the giant black bouncer from Rosa's place in Gallup. He pushed some fresh wood into the fire, and after a moment it caught and grew brighter.

Hyde wasn't the only one of the trio Morgan recognized. The other two hombres had been members of the gang that had kidnapped Rebel. He hadn't seen them since that night in Black Rock Canyon, but their images were still fresh in his mind, preserved perfectly by the hatred he felt.

"Put the rifle down, Kid," warned the man holding Tasmin. "I ain't gonna tell you again."

Morgan grimaced and tossed the Winchester aside. On the other side of the fire, Bearpaw moaned and stirred. The bastards must have snuck up on him under the cover of the storm and knocked him out, Morgan thought.

"Reach over with your left hand and take the Colt out," the man holding Tasmin ordered.

"Once he's unarmed, I'm gonna bust him into little pieces," Hyde rumbled.

"Not until we have a talk with him," the other man said. "Do what I told you, Kid. Shuck that iron."

Carefully, Morgan reached over with his left hand and slipped the Colt out of its holster. He wondered for a second just how good a shot he was with that hand

Not good enough, he decided. He bent over and placed the revolver on the ground next to the Winchester.

"Now back away from them."

Morgan did so reluctantly. Tasmin was watching him with a fearful expression on her face. He knew from some of the things she had said during the trip that she was terrified of Hyde. Rosa had run the house with an iron fist, and Hyde was her enforcer. The beatings he doled out on Rosa's command had seriously injured some of the soiled doves.

"I guess Rosa sent you after us to settle the score for her brother," Morgan said. He didn't say anything about recognizing the other two men from Black Rock Canyon. He didn't want them to know about that just yet.

"We got scores of our own to settle," the man said. "Clem Baggott and Spence Hooper were friends of ours. We came to see them and found out they'd been shot dead by some fancy gunslinger. Clem's sister was glad to send this big darkie with us to help track you down."

Even after splitting up, most of the gang seemed to have converged on Gallup, Morgan thought. He supposed that wasn't so surprising. Baggott's sister ran a whorehouse after all. These hardcases probably had thought they could lie low there as well as anywhere else.

"What's your game, mister?" the man went on. "Why'd you come gunning for Clem and Spence?"

"We weren't gunning for them," Morgan said. "I explained it all back in Gallup. I just stopped off at Rosa's for a little slap-and-tickle, and that fella Baggott came into the parlor and started shooting at me."

The man shook his head. "Clem was a pretty level-headed sort. He wouldn't have blazed away like that and put his sister in danger without a good reason. He recognized you."

Morgan shook his head. "He mistook me for somebody else, if anything. I never saw him before."

The man sneered and pressed the gun barrel against Tasmin's head hard enough to make her cry out softly in pain and fear. "I don't believe you," he said.

"It's the truth," Morgan insisted. He was looking desperately for some way to turn the tables on these men, but so far he hadn't found any.

The other man, the one guarding Bearpaw, frowned as he stared at Morgan. "Abel, there's somethin' familiar about this hombre," he said suddenly. "I'd swear I've seen him before."

Abel . . . That had to be Abel Dean. Morgan plucked the name out of his memory. Dean squinted at him and said, "Yeah, Jim, I think maybe you're right. He looks familiar to us, and Clem recognized him . . . Who the hell can he *be*?"

"All I know is he's Kid Morgan," Hyde said, "and I'm gonna kill him."

Jim Fowler—that was the other man's name, Morgan recalled—took a step forward. "Maybe I'm goin' loco," he said, "but I'd swear this fella looks like the one from Carson City. The one whose wife we took out to that canyon—"

"Son of a bitch!" Dean exclaimed. "It *is* him!" He jerked the gun away from Tasmin's head. "Kill him!"

Before either of the kidnappers could fire, Bearpaw suddenly lunged hard against Fowler's legs. The Paiute had regained more of his senses than he had let on. Fowler stumbled to the side as he pulled the trigger.

The blast was deafeningly loud as it echoed back from the overhanging bluff.

At the same time, Tasmin turned her head and sank her teeth into Dean's throat under the shelf of his jutting jaw. His yell was one more of surprise than pain, but she kept him from firing at Morgan while he tried to knock her loose.

Morgan dived for the Colt on the ground. Hyde moved with surprising speed for such a big man and rammed into him, knocking him away from the gun. Blood streamed down the side of Hyde's face from his ear, and Morgan realized that the wild shot fired by Fowler must have clipped him. Hyde swung a sweeping backhand at him. Morgan ducked under it.

He wasn't going to make the mistake of trying to tackle Hyde again. That hadn't worked too well the first time. Instead, he lunged behind the horses, using the animals to shield him from Hyde's charge and from Dean's and Fowler's guns. The shot had spooked the horses, so they were dancing back and forth.

Morgan tore the buckskin's picket rope loose and leaped onto the horse's back. He banged his boots against the horse's flanks and sent him leaping forward. The buckskin's shoulder collided with Hyde. The big man had more than met his match. He went sailing off his feet from the impact.

Morgan leaped off the buckskin and tackled Dean, knocking him away from Tasmin. Both of them went down hard. Morgan crashed a fist into the outlaw's face and used his other hand to grab the wrist of Dean's gun hand. He slammed that hand against the rocky ground a couple of times, and the second time, the gun came loose. Morgan hit him again.

He didn't have time to do anything else before Hyde

grabbed him from behind, lifted him into the air, and threw him against the bluff. Pain shot through Morgan as he crashed into the unyielding surface. Hyde came at him again.

Shots began to roar. Hyde's eyes widened as bullets punched into his back. He stumbled forward, reaching behind him and trying to paw at the wounds like a maddened beast. The shots continued until the hammer fell on an empty cylinder. Hyde lost his footing and fell to his knees, then pitched forward on his face, revealing Tasmin standing behind him, both hands wrapped around the butt of Morgan's Colt as smoke curled from the muzzle.

"Kid, watch out!" Bearpaw yelled.

Morgan whirled around and saw that Fowler had broken away from the Paiute, who had been wrestling with him while Morgan had his hands full with Dean and Hyde. Fowler snapped a shot at him. The bullet whined off the rock as Morgan dove and rolled, grabbing the Winchester as he did so. He came up on one knee and fired the rifle from the hip. Flame lanced from the barrel. Fowler jerked backward as the bullet drove into his chest. Morgan worked the Winchester's lever and cranked off two more shots. The impact of the slugs sent Fowler stumbling away from the fire. The wind whipped snow around him, hiding him from sight.

Morgan sprang to his feet and grabbed Tasmin's arm. "Are you all right?" he asked. When she nodded, he shoved her toward the horses. "Get behind them and stay there!"

He stepped over to Bearpaw and bent down to help the Paiute to his feet. "How about you? Are you hurt?"

Bearpaw shook his head. "No, this old skull of

mine is too hard for it to be dented easily. Better keep an eye on that one," he added, nodding toward Dean.

"What about the one I shot?"

"You put three rifle slugs in his chest, Kid. I don't think we need to worry too much about him."

Morgan hoped Bearpaw was right about that. He wasn't going to venture out into the storm to look for Fowler, though.

Dean was still only half conscious. Morgan made sure he was disarmed, then tied his hands behind his back.

Hyde was dead. Even as big as he was, five .45 slugs in his back had been enough to put him down for good. As Morgan checked him to be sure, Tasmin asked from behind the horses, "Did I kill him?"

"You sure did."

A couple of seconds of silence passed. Then she said, "Good. He had it coming to him. You don't know all the things he did back there at Rosa's."

Bearpaw built the fire up. As its flickering light filled the area under the bluff, Morgan knelt in front of Dean and lightly cuffed the man back to consciousness. Dean groaned and then lifted his head, staring at Morgan with pure hatred. His lips were bloody and swollen from Morgan's punches.

"You're him, aren't you?" Dean said thickly. "Browning."

"I don't know what you're talking about. My name is Kid Morgan."

Dean shook his head. "I don't care what you call yourself. You're him."

Morgan had reloaded and holstered his Colt after taking it back from Tasmin. He slipped it out now and placed the barrel under Dean's jaw. He eared back the hammer and said in a quiet, dangerous tone, "If you believe that, then you know you'd better tell me what I want to know."

Dean looked like he wanted to tell Morgan to go to hell. Defiance burned in his eyes. But that defiance faded under the steady, level gaze of the Kid, and finally he swallowed hard and said, "What is it you want?"

"Rattigan and White Rock are supposed to be prospecting somewhere up here at a place called Blue Creek. Is that true?"

Dean managed to nod. "As far as I know, it is. I remember them talking about it."

"Do you know where Blue Creek is?"

"From the way Rattigan talked, it's about fifteen miles west of Trinidad."

"All right. Where are Clay Lasswell, Ezra Harker, and Vernon Moss?"

Dean's mouth twisted bitterly. "You crippled Moss. He'll never walk on those legs again. Lasswell and Harker got a wagon and put him in it. They were gonna take him back where he came from, somewhere down in Texas. Some little town called Diablito."

"Little Devil," Bearpaw translated.

Morgan nodded. He understood that much Spanish. He asked Dean, "You know where to find that town?"

The outlaw shook his head. "Not really. I just know that it's somewhere on the Rio Grande, right across the river from Mexico."

The Texas-Mexico border was pretty long, Morgan recalled, but he would travel every mile of it if he had to in order to find Lasswell, Harker, and Moss. He didn't care if Moss was crippled. The man hadn't yet paid the price for the crime he'd helped commit. Not by a long shot.

As Morgan took the gun barrel away from Dean's neck, the man looked around and said, "Where's Fowler? Where'd he go?"

"He stumbled out into the storm after I shot him," said Morgan.

"Damn it! You're gonna leave a wounded man out there in that blizzard?"

"I'm not going to go out there looking for him if that's what you mean."

"You can't just leave him to die!"

"He's probably dead already," Bearpaw put in. "The Kid hit him three times in the chest with that Winchester."

Dean closed his eyes and began to curse in a low, bitter voice. Morgan ignored him, stood up, and went over to Tasmin. "You'd better crawl back in your bedroll and try to get some more sleep," he suggested.

"What about you?" she asked.

"I'll turn in after a while."

"What are you gonna do with me?" Dean demanded in a shaky voice. "Are you gonna kill me, too?"

Bearpaw hunkered beside him and grinned evilly at him. "I'd say you've got it comin' for what you did, mister."

"It wasn't my idea," Dead protested. "Lasswell and Moss were the ones behind it. The rest of us were just hired hands."

Lasswell and Moss had been hired hands, too, Morgan thought. For the first time in a while, he pondered the question of who had hired Lasswell and given him his orders.

But the snowy night held no answers.

Chapter 21

The storm blew itself out during the night. The sky was still overcast the next morning, but the wind had died down and no more snow fell. During the blizzard, the wind had scoured the flatter terrain so that only an inch or two of snow remained on it. The white stuff had piled up in deep drifts, though, against rocks and other barriers.

It had drifted against Jim Fowler's body during the night and eventually spilled over it, so that now the corpse appeared to be a long, white, low mound about fifty feet from the camp. Fowler had made it that far before collapsing.

Morgan went out and brought in the body, dragging it by its heels. Abel Dean glared at him in hatred as he left Fowler's body sprawled under the bluff next to Hyde's corpse.

"Damn it, at least you could bury them!"

"Or you can, if you want to try to dig a grave in this cold ground with your fingers," Morgan said. "We didn't bring along a shovel."

Dean frowned. "Well, it just don't seem right to leave them for the wolves."

Bearpaw said, "Wolves have to eat, too. And it may be a long, hungry winter."

Dean shuddered, but didn't say anything for a moment. Then he asked, "What are you gonna do with me?"

"I guess we'll have to take you with us," Morgan replied. "You'll have to walk, though, unless we happen to find the horses the three of you were riding. I'm hoping they pulled loose from wherever you tied them up last night and found someplace to get in out of the storm. Hate to think about good horseflesh freezing to death for no good reason."

"But you left Jim out there to freeze," Dean snapped. "He was a human being, not an animal."

"That's debatable," Bearpaw said.

They got ready to ride. Morgan tied a length of rope from Dean's bound wrists to his saddle horn. "We'll turn you over to the law in Trinidad," he said. "To tell you the truth, I planned to kill you, but I reckon I'm not as cold-blooded as I thought I was."

"You mean you don't have the guts."

Morgan turned and looked at Dean, who paled at what he saw in the younger man's eyes. Dean didn't say anything else.

As long as they avoided the drifts, the going wasn't too hard. The horses had no trouble with a couple of inches of snow. There was no sign of the other horses, so Dean had to stumble along behind Morgan's horse. It would be a long walk to Trinidad for him, but it wouldn't kill him.

Bearpaw found the trail that ran between Raton, New Mexico, and Trinidad, and the four of them headed north again. They would reach the settlement before the day was over, Bearpaw said.

"When we get there, it'll be time for us to say so long," Morgan told Tasmin. "You can't go with us after that."

"I've held up my own end so far, haven't I?" she shot back at him. "I'm the one who killed Hyde when he was about to beat you to a pulp."

"And I appreciate that. But we weren't planning on those three jumping us like that. We *know* that once we leave Trinidad we'll be riding into trouble."

She looked over at him. "I heard enough, last night and back in Gallup, too, to know that you're hunting down a group of men. What did they do to you, Kid?"

Morgan shook his head. "It wouldn't change anything for you to know."

"Dean called you Browning. Is that your real name?"

"I'm just Kid Morgan. That's all."

Tasmin blew out her breath in frustration. It fogged in the chilly air in front of her face. "You're the stubbornest man I ever did see."

"You'll be staying in Trinidad," Morgan said again. That ended the discussion.

They stopped at midday to gnaw on some leftover biscuits and to let the horses rest. Morgan didn't untie Dean. The man sat on a log and glared at his captors as he ate.

When they were almost ready to go, Morgan walked over to the buckskin. Suddenly, Tasmin cried out behind him, a cry that was choked off abruptly. When he spun around, he saw that Dean had lunged up from the deadfall, gotten some slack in the rope that connected him to Morgan's saddle, and whipped that slack around Tasmin's neck from behind. She must have strayed too close to him. Morgan had warned her to keep her distance from the prisoner, but obviously she hadn't been careful enough about following that order.

"Drop your guns!" Dean shouted at Morgan and Bearpaw. "Drop 'em now or I'll choke her to death, I swear I will!"

"Take it easy," Morgan urged. He didn't want the commotion to spook his horse. If the buckskin got nervous and bolted, even for a short distance, it would tighten that rope and squeeze the life out of Tasmin in a matter of seconds.

"Drop your guns and back away from them!" Dean screamed.

Bearpaw looked at Morgan, who nodded grimly. "I guess we'd better do what he says."

He eased his Colt from its holster and bent to place it on the snowy ground. A few yards away, Bearpaw did the same with the Sharps. The Paiute didn't carry a handgun.

"The knife, too, redskin!" Dean ordered.

Bearpaw took his knife from its sheath and tossed it on the ground next to the Sharps. He and Morgan backed away from the weapons.

Dean forced Tasmin forward. Morgan knew that if Dean ever got his hands on a gun, the three of them were dead.

The outlaw grinned and said to Tasmin, "You're not gonna bite me this time, you little bitch. I'll be lucky if I don't come down with hydrophobia, bein' bit by a slut like you."

They reached Bearpaw's rifle and knife. Dean paused and bent down, trying to pick up the knife and keep the pressure on the rope around Tasmin's neck at the same time. Morgan guessed he wanted to cut the rope so he'd be free from the horse.

That was fine with Morgan. Dean might not realize it, but once he cut the rope, Tasmin would be in less danger. Maybe then one of them could make a move.

Morgan and Bearpaw stood there tensely while Dean sawed on the rope. As soon as it parted, Dean dropped the knife and shoved Tasmin toward the revolver. As she stumbled forward, she seemed to accidentally thrust a leg behind her, so that it went between his legs. Suddenly, their feet were tangled, and Dean let out an angry curse. He threw Tasmin aside and lunged for the gun.

Morgan knew he couldn't beat the outlaw to the Colt. But the knife was closer, so he made a dive for it. His fingers wrapped around the handle just as Dean snatched up the gun. Dean wheeled around as Morgan scrambled to his feet. They were still too far apart. Morgan couldn't reach him with the knife.

Bearpaw leaped between them as flame gouted from the muzzle of the gun. The bullet struck the Paiute in the body and spun him around. He had occupied Dean's attention for only a second, but that second was long enough for Morgan to leap forward and slam the blade into Dean's chest. With his other hand, he knocked the gun aside as Dean fired again.

Dean took a step back and fumbled at the handle of the knife protruding from his chest. Morgan hit him hard with a right to the jaw. Dean went down, and the gun flew out of his hand. He spasmed as he tried to pull the blade out of his body, but then he went limp, his hands falling away from the knife. Blood welled from his mouth as he kicked a final time.

Seeing that Dean was dead, Morgan whirled around

and ran to Bearpaw's side. The Paiute had fallen on the snowy ground, which was now speckled with crimson droplets in places. Morgan went to a knee and lifted Bearpaw's head.

"How bad is it?"

"Bad enough to . . . hurt like blazes."

"You'll be fine," Morgan said. "We'll get you to a doctor. It can't be much farther to Trinidad." He fumbled with the buffalo robe and the shirt underneath it, finally pulling them aside so that he could see the wound. The bullet had ripped into Bearpaw's side and then torn out his back. Blood was everywhere. Morgan wasn't sure how serious the wound was. He told himself that Bearpaw would be all right. He had to be.

Tasmin knelt on Bearpaw's other side. She had removed the rope from her neck and seemed to be fine, except for a welt where the rope had scratched her skin. "How bad is it?" she asked.

"I don't know." Morgan answered honestly because Bearpaw had passed out. "Help me get something tied around these wounds."

They labored frantically for the next few minutes, tearing strips from a blanket and winding them tightly around Bearpaw's midsection after Morgan pressed more wads of cloth into the wounds to try to stop the bleeding. Then they lifted him into his saddle. Thankfully, Bearpaw roused enough to grab hold of the saddle horn with both hands and help keep himself mounted.

Then Morgan and Tasmin swung up into their saddles as well and set off for Trinidad with Bearpaw riding between them. None of them looked back at Abel Dean, who lay motionless in the snow behind them.

* * *

The doctor, a tall, balding, rawboned man, came out of his surgery rubbing his bloody hands on a rag. He gave an anxious Morgan and Tasmin a nod and said, "It looks like you got him here in time. I got the bleeding stopped, cleaned out the wounds, and stitched them up. He's got a good chance to pull through, but he'll be laid up for quite a while. A month maybe."

Morgan thought back to what Dr. Patrick McNally had said about him, which was pretty much the same thing. He had beaten that prediction because he had the need for revenge driving him. Bearpaw didn't have to do that. The Paiute had helped Morgan this far.

From here on out, the Kid would go it alone.

He turned to Tasmin and said, "You'll stay here in Trinidad and make sure that he gets better."

"But, Kid—" she began with a frown.

Morgan shook his head. "I owe my life to Phillip."

"Then why don't *you* stay here and take care of him?"

"Because there arc still things I have to do, things that won't wait." He looked in her eyes and went on. "Tasmin, I need you to do this. For him . . . and for me. I need to know that both of you are safe."

"While you're off risking your life on some sort of . . . of vengeance quest?" she whispered.

"Don't mind me," the doctor said behind them. "I think I'll go have a cup of coffee. The two of you can hash out whatever you need to. Just remember there'll be a bill for my services."

"You'll get your money," Morgan said. "I'll see to that."

The doctor nodded and went out, leaving Morgan

and Tasmin looking squarely at each other. After a moment, Tasmin sighed and said, "I'm not going to be able to budge you, am I?"

Morgan shook his head. "I'm afraid not."

"You know, most of the time men do whatever I want. It's not fair that you're not like them. Who was she?"

Tightly, Morgan asked, "What do you mean?"

"The woman who left you in such pain."

"She didn't leave me," he said. "She was *taken* from me."

"By the men you're hunting down?"

Morgan shrugged.

Tasmin reached out, rested a hand on the chest of the buckskin jacket Morgan wore. "I'll take care of Bearpaw," she promised. "I'll see to it that the doctor does everything that needs to be done. What are you going to do?"

Morgan glanced at the window. Night had fallen outside. It had taken them most of the rest of the day to reach Trinidad, which at the moment was a picturesque little settlement with snow on the roofs of its buildings and the mountains looming up in the west.

"It's too late to leave now. In the morning, I reckon I'll head for Blue Creek."

"Where there are two more men you need to kill."

Morgan shrugged again. There was no need to put it into words.

The doctor came back into the room, carrying a cup of coffee. He said, "I had to give Mr. Bearpaw some laudanum, so he'll probably sleep the rest of the night. I'll keep an eye on him. You don't have to worry. You can both go have something to eat and then get some rest. The Trinidad Hotel ought to have a room for you."

Neither Morgan nor Tasmin corrected the doctor's assumption that they would just need one room. Tasmin said, "I'll be back in the morning to check on him and help out any way I can."

"Is there a Western Union office in town?" Morgan asked.

The doctor nodded. "Two blocks down the street on the left."

"Much obliged for everything."

They left the doctor's house, stepping out into another frigid night. Morgan spotted a café, so he and Tasmin stopped and had an actual meal, which tasted good after long days of making do on the trail. Then they went to the Trinidad Hotel, where Morgan rented two rooms and used most of the rest of his money to pay for a couple of weeks in advance on Tasmin's room.

"I'll see you later," he told her. "Go on up and get some rest."

"Where are you going?"

"I need to send a wire."

He found the Western Union office and sent another telegram to Claudius Turnbuckle, asking that the lawyer arrange to pay for the doctor and any other expenses Tasmin and Bearpaw might have. He wanted both of them to have money in the bank in Trinidad to take care of any emergencies, too.

With that taken care of, he returned to the hotel and stopped at the desk to get the key to Room Seven. Tasmin was across the hall in Room Eight.

The clerk gave Morgan a puzzled frown. "The young lady already took the key to your room, sir. She said she would take care of both of them."

Morgan hadn't told her to do that, but he supposed

that no harm was done. He nodded his thanks and went upstairs. Pausing in front of Tasmin's door, he knocked softly on it, intending to ask her for the key to his room.

There was no answer.

Morgan knocked again and called, "Tasmin?" Maybe she was already so sound asleep that she couldn't hear him, he thought. He turned and stepped across the hall to try the door to his room, hoping that she had unlocked it before turning in.

The knob twisted easily in his hand. He swung the door open, and saw that the lamp on the table next to the bed was already burning with its flame turned low.

The bed was occupied, too. Tasmin sat there with her back against a pillow propped between her and the headboard. She wore a simple white nightgown, and her dark hair was loose and flowing around her shoulders.

"Oh, no," Morgan said as he began to shake his head.

"Why not?" she asked. "It doesn't have to mean anything. I *am* just a whore after all."

Tears shone in her eyes as she spoke.

Morgan stepped into the room and eased the door closed behind him. "I never thought you ought to . . . I mean, you don't have to feel any obligation to . . . I never expected—"

"Shut up," she whispered. "We both need this."

Morgan shook his head. Maybe someday, but not now. Not yet.

"I can't."

Her hands clenched into fists. "I'll bet you can. You just won't."

"That's not true. I just can't be with any woman right now."

"Until you've finished killing the men who took the last woman from you?"

Morgan dragged a deep, ragged breath into his body. "If you must know," he said, "that's right. And maybe not even then. Maybe not ever."

She leaned forward in the bed. "Then for God's sake, at least *tell* me about it. Tell me the truth for a change, Kid. If you don't, then I'll think it's just because I'm a cheap whore."

"That's not true," Morgan insisted. "I swear, Tasmin, ever since I've gotten to know you, I never think of you that way. That's all in the past."

Her lips curved in a thin smile. "So, you can put what I used to be behind you without any trouble, but you can't put your own past behind you, too?"

Morgan just stared at her, unsure what to say. He didn't think anything would make a difference.

"Did you ever stop to think that if you talked about it, it might be easier to let go?"

"I don't want to let go. Not yet." He struggled with the thoughts that filled his head. "I . . . I need to hang on to the pain for now. It keeps me going. When I'm done with . . . what I have to do . . . maybe then things will be different. Maybe I can start looking ahead again, instead of looking back."

Tasmin looked at him for a long moment, then sighed and shook her head. "You might as well go across the hall and get some sleep," she said.

Relieved, he turned and reached for the doorknob.

"You'll need to be well rested to do all that killing," she said to his back.

Chapter 22

The log cabin sat against the snowy, timbered slope of a hill. The little stream known as Blue Creek twisted along at the base of the hill. Morgan supposed that was where the two men who occupied the cabin did their panning for gold. He saw an old-fashioned sluice box at the edge of the creek. The odds of them finding much dust like that, in this day and age when modern mining methods had replaced those old ways, was mighty slim, Morgan thought as he hunkered behind a boulder on the opposite slope and watched the place. A die-hard prospector always had hope, though, even when he didn't have much of anything else.

Smoke curled from the cabin's stone chimney. Both men were in there, Morgan knew. He had seen them moving around a short time earlier, right after he got here. They had tended to the horses in the little corral and shed out back, then gone into the cabin. It was late in the afternoon. They might not emerge again until the next morning.

Morgan didn't intend to wait that long.

It had taken him most of the day to get here from

Trinidad. The clouds had finally broken up during the day, so the sun was shining brightly now as it dipped toward the peaks behind the cabin. With the weather clearing like that and the wind dying down, the night would be really cold. Morgan's eyes narrowed as he looked at the stack of firewood beside the cabin.

Could be that one of the men would decide to bring in some more wood before nightfall, just so they'd have plenty. He began working his way toward the cabin, circling so that he could come in from that direction. If neither of them came out to fetch wood, he'd have to think of some other way to lure them out.

He crossed the creek upstream, leaping from rock to rock in order to do so, then headed for the cabin. It didn't have any windows on this side, but Morgan used the trees for cover anyway. When he reached the cabin, he pressed his back to its rear wall, just around the corner from the stack of firewood.

He could hear Rattigan and White Rock moving around inside and talking, and the knowledge that he was this close to two more of the men responsible for Rebel's death gnawed at his guts. He wanted to go around to the front of the cabin, kick the door open, and go in shooting. If it came down to it, that was exactly what he would do. But he hoped there would be a better way.

The sun had touched the mountains to the west and shadows had begun to gather when Morgan heard the cabin door open. He slipped the Colt from its holster and waited.

Booted feet crunched in the snow as one of the men came around the cabin to the stack of firewood. Morgan heard him muttering to himself. He waited until the man had gathered up several pieces of wood

and turned back toward the front of the cabin before
he sprang out of concealment and brought the Colt
crashing down on the man's head.

The man dropped the firewood and toppled forward. From inside the cabin, a voice yelled, "White
Rock? What was that racket? You all right out there?"

White Rock wasn't going to answer. He was out
cold. Morgan moved quickly past the unconscious
half-breed. He reached the front corner of the cabin
just as Rattigan came out the door, gun in hand.

Morgan hesitated for a second as he saw how old
Rattigan was. The man's face was lined and leathery,
and the beard stubble dotting his angular jaw was
pure white. For that second, Morgan was reminded
of his grandfather, and his finger froze on the trigger.

Then Rattigan's face twisted in an evil grimace, and
flame erupted from the barrel of the gun in his hand.
Morgan felt a tremendous impact on his left hip that
slewed him around. Rattigan fired again. This slug
burned past Morgan's ear, and he didn't waste any
more time thinking about Rattigan's age. Old or not,
the outlaw was as vicious and evil as any of the others
Morgan had faced. Maybe more so, because he'd had
more time to practice. Morgan snapped his gun up and
triggered it as his left leg folded up beneath him.

Because he was falling, his aim was a little off. His
bullet caught Rattigan in the left shoulder and knocked
the old man back a step. Rattigan kept his feet and
hung onto his gun, though. He threw a third shot at
Morgan. The bullet plowed into the snow-covered
ground only inches away. The Colt bucked in Morgan's hand for a second time. This bullet punched into
Rattigan's chest and knocked him down. When he
tried to raise his gun, Morgan shot him again. Rattigan

went over onto his back, the revolver slipping from his fingers as he slumped.

Boots crunched in the snow. Morgan rolled over and saw that White Rock had regained consciousness and was coming at him, a piece of firewood held high over his head. The breed's face was contorted with hate as he yelled, "You son of a bitch!"

Morgan knew that White Rock intended to crush his skull with that firewood. He tipped up the barrel of the Colt and fired. The bullet struck White Rock in the throat and ripped through at an upward angle into his brain. Blood fountained as he stumbled forward another step. The firewood slipped from his fingers and fell to the ground as White Rock pitched forward, landing on the crimson spray that had come from his ruined throat and stained the snow.

Unable to stand because his left leg was still numb, Morgan scooted backward so that he could cover both men. He was pretty sure that Rattigan and White Rock were both dead, but injured as he was, he didn't want to take any chances.

Neither man moved. Morgan could tell they weren't breathing anymore. He reached for the loops on his gunbelt, intending to take some cartridges from them and reload.

The belt was surprisingly loose around his hips, he discovered. He moved his hand to the place where he'd been hit, and found that the thick leather was torn almost completely apart. He didn't feel any blood, though, and after a second, he realized that Rattigan's bullet had hit the gunbelt and glanced off, ruining the belt but failing to penetrate Morgan's body. His leg had gone numb from the impact; that was all.

Relief washed through him. He had worried that

he might bleed to death out here, far from town. Now he knew that the numbness in his leg ought to wear off after a while. He'd be bruised and sore, but if the bullet hadn't broken any bones, he would be able to get back to Trinidad.

Morgan reloaded the Colt, then untied the holster thong from his leg and took off the ruined gunbelt. He tossed it aside and crawled over to the cabin, dragging his injured leg behind him. When he made it to the wall, he reached up with his free hand and found a good grip between a couple of the logs. He was able to pull himself up and lean against the cabin.

As he did that, feeling began to come back into his leg. He waited until he trusted his muscles to obey him, then limped toward the door, which stood open. Rattigan hadn't closed it behind him before he started shooting. By the time Morgan made it to the door, he was confident that the bullet hadn't broken his hip. Everything seemed to be working, albeit painfully.

He stepped inside and shoved the door closed to trap the heat from the fireplace. As he warmed up, the stiffness in his leg eased even more, although the place where the bullet had struck the gunbelt was still very tender to the touch. A coffeepot was on the stove. Morgan found a cup on a crude shelf and filled it with the strong black brew, then sat down in a rough-hewn chair at an equally rough table to sip from the cup and rest his leg.

After a while, he felt strong enough to limp outside and drag the bodies of Rattigan and White Rock around to the back of the cabin. He left them there and crossed the creek to head back up the hill to the place where he'd left his horse. The buckskin was still there. He tossed his head, obviously glad to see Morgan.

"Sorry," the Kid muttered. "Let's get you down to that shed."

By the time he'd finished tending to the horse, night had fallen. Morgan went inside, taking some firewood with him, and built up the blaze in the fireplace. The two outlaws had enough supplies on hand so that he was able to scrape together some supper without much trouble. Not wanting to use either of the bunks in the cabin where Rattigan and White Rock had slept, he had brought in his bedroll. He spread it out in front of the fireplace and crawled into the blankets to sleep, using his saddle as a pillow.

But between his painful hip and the knowledge that two dead men lay on the cold ground just on the other side of those logs, Morgan was a long time dozing off.

He wouldn't have been surprised if wolves had dragged off the corpses during the night, but Rattigan and White Rock were still there the next morning. Morgan's hip and leg were pretty sore, but he was able to get around fairly well. He hauled both bodies into the cabin, one at a time, and dumped them on the bunks. He planned to leave them there, a mystery for whoever stumbled on this cabin next.

Although he didn't like stealing from the dead, he needed a new gunbelt, and Rattigan wore one with a brown, buscadero-cut holster attached to it. Morgan took it off the body and tried it on. It fit fairly well around his lean hips. He slipped the Colt into the holster, worked it up and down a few times, and nodded in satisfaction. The belt and holster would do.

He left the corral gate open as he rode away. The outlaws' horses would have to fend for themselves.

If he showed up in Trinidad with a couple of extra horses, the law might start asking too many questions.

It was late afternoon by the time he reached the settlement. He went straight to the doctor's house and tied the buckskin outside. When he limped into the front room, he found it empty, but voices came from the room where he had left Bearpaw the day before.

The Paiute was propped up in bed when Morgan came in. He grinned and said, "Kid!"

Tasmin sat in a straight chair beside the bed. She looked at Morgan and smiled in relief, but didn't say anything.

"Are you all right?" Bearpaw went on. His grin disappeared and was replaced by a frown as Morgan limped across the room to get another chair and pull it up beside the bed.

"I'm fine," Morgan said. "A little gimpy, that's all."

"That's a new gunbelt you're wearing. A different one anyway."

"My old one got ruined."

"By a bullet?" Bearpaw didn't wait for Morgan to answer. He continued. "What about Rattigan and White Rock?"

"We don't have to worry about them anymore."

Bearpaw heaved a sigh of relief and nodded. "Good. That just leaves the three down in Texas. As soon as I'm able to travel, we'll head down that way—"

"I'm going now," Morgan broke in. "Well, first thing tomorrow anyway."

"By yourself? You don't need to do that, Kid."

Tasmin said, "You're wasting your breath, Phillip. He's as stubborn as a mule. He can barely walk, and he's talking about starting to Texas tomorrow."

Morgan smiled faintly and pointed out, "I'm not going to walk there."

"Yeah, but you don't need to take on those three by yourself," Bearpaw insisted. "I ought to come with you."

"The doctor said you'd be laid up for a month."

"Patrick said the same thing about you. You were up and around in a couple of weeks."

Morgan shook his head. "I can't wait even that long. Lasswell and Harker were going to take Moss home. There's no telling if they stayed there in Diablito. I may have to track them somewhere else."

Bearpaw studied him intently for a moment, then asked, "You think you're ready to go it alone?"

"I went it alone yesterday," Morgan said, "and I'm still alive."

Bearpaw's head went up and down in a slow nod. "I suppose you're right about that. The proof is in the pudding, as they say. But Lasswell's probably the most dangerous of the whole bunch. We don't really know about Harker and Moss."

"Moss is crippled."

"Doesn't mean he's not still dangerous. A broken-backed rattler can still sink its fangs in you, Kid."

Morgan didn't want to continue this argument. He leaned forward in his chair, squeezed Bearpaw's shoulder, and said, "I'll see to it that all your expenses are taken care of while you recuperate, yours and Tasmin's both. And I'll tell you who to wire in San Francisco if you ever need anything after that. When you're ready to travel, the two of you can head back to Sawtooth." He smiled at Tasmin. "It's a good place to live. You'll be able to make a new life for yourself there."

"Where no one will know I used to be a whore?" she asked.

Morgan inclined his head. "Everybody can use a fresh start now and then, I reckon."

"What about you, Kid? When does your fresh start come along?"

"Not yet," he replied, thinking about Clay Lasswell, Ezra Harker, and Vernon Moss. "Not yet."

He stood up. Bearpaw held up a hand and said, "Wait a minute, Kid. I can see that I'd be wasting my time trying to talk you out of this."

Morgan smiled again, signifying agreement.

"I want you to take my Sharps with you," Bearpaw went on. "One of these days, you'll need to make a long shot, and you won't find a sweeter rifle for it than that one."

"The Sharps is yours," Morgan protested.

"That's right. So it's mine to give away if I want to. Take it, Kid. Otherwise, I might just have to follow you to Texas."

"I'll buy a wagon," Tasmin said. "We can load you in it and probably travel now."

"The hell with that," the Kid said sharply. "You try something crazy like that and it's liable to kill you, Phillip."

"Then take the Sharps. Make a loco old redskin feel better."

Morgan sighed. He could see that he wasn't going to win this argument. "All right," he said. "If it'll help, I'll take the Sharps. Between that and the Winchester and my Colt, I reckon I'll be armed for bear."

"My knife, too," the Paiute said. "I want you to have it."

Morgan nodded. "All right." He had already decided

that he would stop at one of Trinidad's general stores and make arrangements to have a new Sharps and the best knife they had in stock delivered to the doctor's house for Bearpaw when he was well away from the settlement.

"You'd better come to see me in the morning before you ride out," Bearpaw warned.

"I can do that . . . as long as you promise not to give me any more trouble."

"Trouble?" Bearpaw repeated with mock indignation. "More often than not, *I'm* the one who's *saved* you from trouble."

"No argument there," Morgan said. "I owe you my life several times over."

He left the room, saying that he needed to take his horse down to the livery stable. Tasmin followed him out onto the porch. It had warmed up quite a bit during the day, and some of the snow had melted. The rest of it would be gone in another day or two, Morgan thought.

"Are you really all right?" Tasmin asked as they paused on the porch.

"I'm fine," Morgan assured her. "My hip is bruised, but that's all."

"And it'll probably be healed up by the time you reach the Rio Grande."

"I'm counting on that," Morgan said.

She folded her arms across her chest. "Did you ever stop to think that all this you're doing won't bring her back, Kid?"

He looked off into the distance and answered honestly.

"Every day of my life."

Chapter 23

Texas was a far cry from Colorado, in more ways than one. Over the course of several weeks, Morgan had traveled more than a thousand miles from those snow-dappled mountains to this hot, dry, dusty plain along the Rio Grande. Though autumn storms continued to bring snow and cold winds to more northern climes, weather like that seldom penetrated to this chaparral-covered border country southeast of Laredo.

If everything he had learned since leaving Colorado was correct, the border village of Diablito was now only a mile or two ahead of him. His journey was almost at an end. That was the good news.

The bad news was that two men were following him.

Morgan had no idea who they were, but they had been back there for a couple of days, never coming too close, always staying far enough back to keep him in sight without crowding him. Bearpaw had taught him to watch his backtrail, and that lesson was paying off now.

Morgan thought about trying to set up an ambush for the men following him, but he had decided that as long as they didn't make a move against him, he would press on toward his destination. They had to have a reason for dogging his trail, and maybe he would find out what it was once he reached Diablito.

In the meantime, and without taking his attention off what was in front of him and behind him, a portion of his thoughts drifted back to Trinidad. He would never forget the look on Bearpaw's face as he gripped the Paiute's hand and bade him farewell. Frank Morgan was his father, and the Kid had come to accept that. But Bearpaw was like the uncle he'd never had.

Nor would he forget the sadness in Tasmin's dark eyes as she stood there on the front porch of the doctor's house, a shawl around her shoulders, her dark hair blowing in the wind. When they were standing there together on the porch, before he mounted up and rode away, she had made a move like she was about to kiss him, then stopped abruptly as if realizing that it wouldn't do any good. It would just deepen the pain for both of them.

"Life has damned bad timing, doesn't it?" she had whispered.

Morgan thought about how things might have been different, first with Eve McNally, then with Tasmin, and knew that was true. Life had damned bad timing, and there wasn't a thing anybody could do about it.

Nothing except ride on and look to the future, not the past.

That is, as soon as the past was laid to rest.

Vernon Moss wheeled himself toward the open door, groaning in pain as he did so. He didn't figure he would ever get used to this damned chair. He was starting to think the agony from his crushed legs would never fade either. But it wasn't quite as bad when he could sit outside in the shade of the vine-covered porch. There might be a little breeze, and maybe the young Mexican girl he paid to take care of the place would rub his useless legs through the blanket that was spread over them. Sometimes that made them feel better.

Moss was still several feet from the door when the tall figure of a man appeared in it, dark and feature-less against the bright sunlight outside. Moss took his hands off the chair's wheels and said, "Who the hell are you?"

"I'm looking for Vernon Moss," the stranger said.

"You found him . . . or what's left of him," Moss said bitterly.

"Where are Clay and Ezra?"

The stranger sounded like he knew them. It was hard for Moss to think because of the pain in his legs, so he said, "They've gone down to the cantina. They'll be back in a little while. You used to ride with them or something?"

The man chuckled, but there wasn't any humor in the sound. Instead, it struck Moss as something that might have come from an open grave. He didn't know why that bizarre thought passed through his mind, but it made him shiver.

"Started in a cantina, and now it's going to end in one," the stranger muttered to himself.

Moss slipped a hand under the blanket. "Damn it, mister, I want to know who you are."

"You don't remember me? From Black Rock Canyon?"

The stranger moved a step into the room, so that

Moss could see him a little better. Moss recognized his face, just like he recognized the reference to Black Rock Canyon. He would never forget that night, or the face of the man who had run him down with that buggy and crippled him for life.

"Damn you!" Moss screamed as he jerked the pistol from under the blanket.

The gun in his hand roared, but not before flame licked from the muzzle of the stranger's Colt, which had appeared with blinding speed. Moss felt a giant fist punch him in the chest. The impact made the chair lurch back. The gun trickled from his fingers and fell onto the blanket. Many's the time he had thought about taking that gun and putting the barrel in his mouth or pressing it to his temple and then pulling the trigger to put himself out of his helpless misery—but in the end, he hadn't been able to do it. He'd been too gutless.

Now, even though blood had begun to fill his mouth, he managed to croak, "Thank you," to the stranger before he died. Those words, and the sudden pound of hoofbeats, were the last things Vernon Moss heard on this earth.

Morgan whirled around as he heard the horses coming up fast behind him. Just as he had expected, the shots had drawn the men who'd been following him into the open. So he wasn't surprised to see the two riders galloping toward him.

He was shocked, though, that he recognized them—and they were two of the last people he would have expected to see here in this sleepy border village.

One was tall and lanky, with a thatch of dark hair under his Stetson. The other was shorter and stockier, with a round face and sandy hair. Despite those obvious differences, they bore a distinct resemblance to each other—and to Morgan's late wife.

They were Rebel's brothers, Tom and Bob Callahan.

As surprised as Morgan was to see them, they appeared to be even more shocked to recognize him as they reined their horses to sliding halts. Bob Callahan, the shorter of the brothers, yelped, "Conrad!" Even in the gunfighter garb, they knew their brother-in-law.

Morgan figured the fight wasn't over. Diablito was small enough so that Lasswell and Harker would have heard those shots and might come to investigate. He replaced the spent cartridge in the Colt and slid a round into the normally empty sixth chamber. Then, as he snapped the cylinder closed, he said, "What are you boys doing here?"

"We've been following you," Tom said as he swung down from the saddle. Beside him, Bob did likewise. Tom went on. "We picked up your trail up in the Four Corners. We were lookin' for the bunch that kidnapped and killed Rebel. Figured if anybody was gonna settle the score for her, it'd have to be us . . . since as far as we knew, you'd killed yourself in Carson City."

Morgan nodded. "That's what everybody was supposed to think."

"Then . . . then, damn it, *you're* the mysterious gunfighter who's been killin' off those bastards one by one?" Bob asked in amazement.

"We knew somebody else was after 'em," Tom added, "but we figured it didn't have anything to do with what happened to Rebel."

"It had everything to do with it," Morgan said. "And it's not over—"

Before he could finish that sentence, a shot blasted from down the street. The bullet whined past his ear and thudded into the adobe wall of Moss's house. Morgan wheeled around and spotted Lasswell and Harker splitting up, taking cover behind buildings on opposite sides of the street as they continued throwing lead at Morgan and the Callahan brothers.

"Hunt some cover!" Morgan snapped as he triggered a shot back at Lasswell and Harker and ducked behind a corner of the adobe shack.

Tom and Bob slapped their horses on the rump and sent the animals running out of the line of fire as they scurried for cover of their own. Slugs kicked up dust around their feet, but they made it to safety, Bob behind the house across the street, Tom behind a shed.

Lasswell and Harker must have moseyed out of the cantina to see what the shooting was about, noticed the three men standing in front of Moss's shack, and figured that trouble had caught up to them at last. Now it was going to be a cat-and-mouse game, the two outlaws against Morgan and his unexpected allies. Morgan had his enemies outnumbered for a change.

He wasn't sure he liked that. He had placed Bearpaw in danger, and the Paiute had paid the price. Tasmin had come close to dying, too. Morgan didn't want anything to happen to Tom and Bob. They had already suffered enough, losing their sister like that.

But he also knew that the Callahan brothers were tough, seasoned hombres who had been in more than one fight. He caught Bob's eye across the street and gestured to him, signaling that he was going to work around behind the buildings and try to get the drop on Lasswell. Bob nodded and motioned that he and Tom would do the same with Harker.

As Morgan moved in a crouching run behind the buildings, he hoped that the people who lived here in Diablito would keep their heads down while this little war was going on. He didn't want any other innocents getting hurt.

The guns had fallen silent for the moment while everyone jockeyed for position. Morgan moved carefully, using every bit of cover he could find and darting across the open areas as fast as he could. Sweat trickled down his back. His heart pounded, either from nerves or from the anticipation that his long quest would soon be over—or both. He jerked a little as shots from across the street suddenly shattered the tense silence.

"Tom!" Bob Callahan yelled in alarm.

Morgan's jaw clenched. Tom must be hit, he thought. He dashed up a narrow alley between two buildings, and reached the street in time to see Ezra Harker drawing a bead on Bob as Bob tried to drag his wounded brother to safety.

"Harker!" Morgan shouted.

The outlaw whirled toward him. Flame stabbed from Harker's gun. At the same time, the Colt in Morgan's fist roared and bucked. Harker staggered, but didn't go down. He fired again, sending shards of adobe flying as the bullet struck the corner of the house next to Morgan.

The next second, Harker was riddled with lead as Morgan fired three more times and both Callahan brothers blazed away at him, too, even the wounded Tom, who lay propped up on one elbow as he fired with his other hand. Harker went backward in a macabre dance with blood exploding from him as the bullets ripped through him.

In the eerie silence that fell as the thunderous echoes rolled away, Morgan heard a gun being cocked behind him.

"That's six," Clay Lasswell said. "You've gotta be empty."

Lasswell didn't realize he had replaced the bullet he had used to kill Moss, Morgan thought as he stiffened. The gunman didn't know that there was still one round in the Colt.

"Turn around," Lasswell went on. "I want to see who I'm about to kill."

Morgan let his arm sag to his side an air of defeat. He turned slowly and faced Lasswell. The ginger-bearded gunman said, "So you're the bastard who's been trackin' down those fellas who rode with me. Yeah, I know about it. I heard through the grapevine about how you killed Baggott and Hooper and Buck and Julio and the rest of 'em. What I want to know is why."

"Take a good look at me," Morgan rasped. "Then you'll know."

Lasswell's eyes narrowed, then widened in shock. "Browning! But you're supposed to be—"

He didn't finish. He pulled the trigger instead.

But even as Lasswell's finger closed on the trigger, Morgan's gun came up again with speed the likes of which he had never achieved before. So fast that it all seemed to happen in the same shaved heartbeat, both Colts roared, Morgan felt the hot breath of a slug as it passed his ear, and Lasswell was rocked back by Morgan's bullet driving into his body.

Now Morgan's gun really was empty, and he couldn't defend himself if Lasswell got off another shot. But Lasswell didn't fire again. He staggered to the side, then dropped his gun and fell to his knees.

Morgan suddenly cried, "Wait! Don't die yet!" and leaped toward him.

Lasswell crumpled onto his left side.

Morgan dropped to his knees as well and grabbed Lasswell's shoulders. "Damn you, don't die!" he said as he shook the outlaw. "Who hired you to kill my wife? Tell me!"

Blood dribbled from the corner of Lasswell's mouth as he looked up at Morgan with an expression that was half smile, half grimace. "You'll . . . never know," he gasped out.

Then his head drooped to the ground and all the life went out of his body.

Morgan looked up at the hot Texas sky and howled, *"Nooooo!"*

It wasn't over.

Maybe it never would be.

Four days later, wearing the fringed buckskin jacket against the dank, chilly wind coming off the Pacific, Kid Morgan walked into the San Francisco building that housed the offices of Turnbuckle and Stafford. A law clerk greeted him, saying, "Mr. Turnbuckle is expecting you, Mister, ah, Kid. He said to show you right into his office when you got here."

"Thanks," Morgan said with a nod. He followed the man to a heavy door of polished, engraved wood. The clerk swung it open, and Morgan stepped inside.

He stopped short at the sight of the two men standing by the window. Claudius Turnbuckle was a stout, balding man with bushy eyebrows and muttonchop whiskers. Morgan expected to see him. It was the other man who came as a surprise.

"Hello, Conrad," Frank Morgan said.

The Drifter was a medium-sized, deceptively powerful man with graying dark hair. He wore range clothes and a holstered six-gun. He stepped forward, put his arms around his son, and gave him a hug that the Kid returned awkwardly.

"Claudius has just been telling me what you've gone through these past few months," Frank went on. "I wish I'd found out sooner. I'd have given you a hand."

"That's . . . all right," the Kid said. "I handled it."

At least, he'd handled it as much as he could, he thought.

"I was up north in timber country. Claudius didn't know where to find me." Frank put a hand on the Kid's shoulder and squeezed. "I'm so sorry about Rebel. She was as fine a gal as anybody will ever see."

The Kid nodded. The pain of his loss was still there inside him, as sharp as ever, but he had learned by now to keep it tamped down, to not acknowledge it unless he had to. That was the only way he could keep going.

After the shoot-out in Diablito, he and the Callahan brothers had ridden to San Antonio, where a real doctor took over caring for the wounded Tom Callahan. Morgan had patched him up as best he could, and the sawbones said that Tom ought to be all right. Then Morgan had sent a wire to Turnbuckle, letting him know what had happened, and gotten a speedy message in return asking him to come to San Francisco as soon as possible. He'd been able to catch a westbound Southern Pacific train in San Antonio, and now here he was in San Francisco, reunited with his father.

"I have a particularly good bottle of brandy I've been

saving," Turnbuckle said. "I'll break it out, and then we can all sit down and you can tell us what you've been doing, Conrad."

"We already know some of what he's been doing," Frank said with a slight smile. "Raising hell from here to Texas. I have to say, Conrad, I knew you'd changed a mite, but . . ." He looked the Kid over. "Maybe not this much."

As glad as he was to see his father, Morgan wasn't in any mood to sit around and reminisce. He still had things to do. But he supposed he owed Frank and Turnbuckle an explanation, so he took off his hat and sat down as the lawyer suggested, accepted a snifter of brandy, and launched into a recitation of everything that had happened in the past few months. It was a dark and bloody tale, and that was reflected in the faces of Frank and Turnbuckle.

"Is Tom going to be all right?" Frank asked when the Kid was finished.

"I think so."

"What about that fella Bearpaw?"

Morgan nodded. "I've already sent a wire to Tasmin and gotten one back from her saying that they're fine. They're still in Trinidad, but they'll be starting back to Nevada soon. She wants me to visit them in Sawtooth . . ." Morgan shrugged. "But I doubt if I ever will. I still have things to do."

"Returning to take over the management of the Browning financial interests, you mean?" Turnbuckle asked.

"No," the Kid replied, not bothering to keep the harshness out of his voice. "Those days are over. Too much has happened for things to ever go back to the way they were before."

The lawyer frowned. "But surely you don't intend to continue with this . . . this . . ." He waved at the Kid's fringed jacket and the buscadero gunbelt and holster. "Masquerade!"

"It's not a masquerade anymore. I'm Kid Morgan now." He paused. "I might have one more use for Conrad Browning, though."

"To help you find out who hired Lasswell to kill Rebel and put you through hell?" Frank guessed.

"That's right." The Kid drained the last of his brandy and reached for his hat. "Whoever sicced Lasswell and his bunch on me has a grudge against Conrad, not Kid Morgan, so if I'm going to draw the bastard out, Conrad has to live again. The Callahan boys told me that Rebel is buried in New Mexico, down close to where she and I first met." He stood up, nodded to Frank and Turnbuckle, and said, "It's time for Conrad Browning to pay a visit to his wife's grave."

Turn the page for an exciting preview of the
USA Today bestselling series SIDEWINDERS!

SIDEWINDERS: CUTTHROAT CANYON
by William W. Johnstone
with J. A. Johnstone

Coming in June 2009
Wherever Pinnacle Books are sold

The wise man avoids trouble,
so as to grow old with grace and dignity.
—Sir Harry Fulton

Nobody ever accused us of bein' smart.
—Scratch Morton

Chapter 1

Scratch Morton dug an elbow into Bo Creel's ribs, nodded toward the building they were passing, and said, "That's new since the last time we were here, ain't it?"

As Bo looked at the building, a nearly naked woman leaned out a second-story window and called to them, "Hey, boys, come on inside and pay me a visit."

Bo ticked a finger against the brim of his black, flat-crowned hat, said politely, "Ma'am," then used his other hand to grasp his trail partner's arm and drag him on past the whorehouse's entrance.

"You'd have to pay, all right, like the lady said," he told Scratch, "and we're a mite low on funds right now."

"Well, then, let's find a saloon and a poker game," Scratch suggested. "There should be plenty of both in El Paso."

Bo didn't doubt that. The border town was famous for its vices. That was the main reason Scratch had insisted on stopping here. They had been on the trail for a long time, and Scratch had a powerful hankering for whiskey and women, not necessarily in that order. They had come home to Texas, and Scratch was of a mind to celebrate.

For most of the past two score years, the two drifters had been somewhere else other than the state where they were born. Of course, Texas hadn't been a state when Bo Creel and Scratch Morton entered the world. It was still part of Mexico then. They had been youngsters when the revolution came along, and after that they'd been citizens of the Republic of Texas for a while.

By the time Texas entered the Union in 1845, Bo and Scratch had pulled up stakes and gone on the drift, due to Scratch's fiddle-footed nature and Bo's desire to put the tragedy of losing his wife and family to sickness behind him. They had been back to the Lone Star State a few times since then, but mostly they'd been elsewhere, seeing what was on the other side of the next hill.

The long years showed in their tanned, weathered faces, as well as in Scratch's shock of silver hair and the strands of gray shot through Bo's dark brown hair, but not in their rangy, muscular bodies that still moved with the easy grace of younger men.

As befitting his deeply held belief that he was God's gift to women, Scratch was something of a dandy, sporting a big, cream-colored Stetson, a fringed buckskin jacket over a white shirt, and tan whipcord pants tucked into high-topped brown boots. The elaborately tooled leather gunbelt strapped around his hips supported a pair of holstered Remington revolvers with long barrels and ivory grips. People had accused him in the past of looking like a Wild West Show cowboy, and he took that as a compliment.

Bo, on the other hand, had been mistaken for a preacher more than once with his sober black suit and vest and hat. His gunbelt and holster were as plain as could be, and so was the lone .45 he carried. Not many preachers, though, had strong, long-fingered hands that could handle a gun and a deck of cards with equal deftness.

Having lived through the chaos of the Runaway Scrape and the Battle of San Jacinto, Bo and Scratch both claimed to want nothing but peace and quiet. Somehow, though, those things had a habit of avoiding them. It seemed that despite their best efforts, wherever they went, trouble soon followed.

Bo was determined that things would be different here in El Paso, since they were back on Texas soil. They would replenish their funds, have a few good meals, sleep under a roof instead of the stars, stock up on supplies, then ride on to wherever the trail took them next.

It was a good plan, but it required money. Bo set his eye on the Birdcage Saloon in the next block as a likely source of those funds.

He recalled the Birdcage from previous visits to the border town. It was run by a big German named August Strittmayer who insisted that all the games of chance there be conducted in an honest fashion. Bo was sure some of the professional gamblers who played at the Birdcage skirted the edge of honesty from time to time, but by and large, Strittmayer's influence kept the games clean.

"You can have a beer at the bar in Strittmayer's place while I see if there's an empty chair at any of the tables," he suggested to Scratch.

"Now you're talkin'," Scratch agreed with a grin. "The scenery's plumb nice in there, too."

Bo knew what Scratch was referring to. On a raised platform on one side of the room sat the big cage that gave the place its name. Instead of a bird perching on the swing that hung inside the cage, one of the saloon girls was always there, in the next thing to her birthday suit. The girls took turns rocking back and forth on that swing. They might not sing like birds, but their plumage was mighty nice.

When Bo and Scratch pushed through the batwings and went inside, they saw that the saloon was doing its usual brisk business. Thirsty cowboys filled most of the places at the bar and occupied all but a few of the tables. A group of men gathered around the bird-cage in the corner, calling out lewd comments to the girl on the swing.

Strittmayer had laid down the law where those girls were concerned. The saloon's bouncers would deal quickly and harshly with any man who so much as set foot inside the cage. He couldn't stop the comments, though, and the girls who worked the cage soon learned to ignore them and continue to wear a placid smile.

The air was full of the usual saloon smells— whiskey, tobacco, sweat, and piss—and the sounds— loud talk, raucous laughter, tinny piano music, the click of a roulette wheel, the whisper of cards being shuffled and dealt. Bo nodded toward the bar and told Scratch, "Go grab a beer."

"I can handle that job," Scratch said.

Bo spotted a dealer he knew at one of the baize-covered tables where poker games were going on. The man wore the elaborate waistcoat and frilly shirt of a professional tinhorn. Close acquaintances knew him as Three-Toed Johnny because of an accident with an ax while splitting some firewood one frosty morning. He was an honest dealer, at least most of the time. Bo hadn't seen him for a couple of years. The last place they had run into each other was Wichita.

The hand was over as Bo came up to the table, and Johnny was raking in the pot. No surprise there. One of the players said in a tone of disgust, "I'm busted. Guess I'm out." He scraped back his chair and stood up.

Johnny stopped him and held out a chip. "No man leaves my table without enough money for a drink, my friend," he said.

The man hesitated, then said, "Thanks," and took the chip. He headed for the bar to cash it in and get that drink.

Bo said, "Some people say that's what got Bill Hickok killed. He busted Jack McCall at cards, then tossed him a mercy chip like that the day before McCall came back into the Number Ten and shot him."

Three-Toed Johnny looked up and grinned. "Bo Creel! I didn't see you come in."

Bo sort of doubted that. Johnny didn't miss much.

"It's good to see you again, amigo," the gambler went on.

Bo gestured toward the empty chair. "You have room for another player?"

"Most assuredly. Sit down."

"Wait just a damned minute," a man on the other side of the table said. He was dressed in an expensive suit, but the big Stetson pushed back on his head, the seamed face of a man who spent most of his life out-doors, and the calluses on his hands all told Bo that he was a cattleman. The suit and the big ring on one

of his fingers said he was probably a pretty successful one. So did the arrogant tone of his voice.

"Is there a problem, Mr. Churchill?" Johnny asked.
Bo could tell that the gambler was keeping his own
voice deceptively mild.

By using the hombre's name, Johnny had also
identified him for Bo. The upset man was Little Ed
Churchill, the owner of one of the largest ranches in
West Texas. Little Ed wasn't little at all, but his pa Big
Ed had been even bigger, Bo recalled, hence the name.

"This fella's a friend of yours," Churchill said as
he jerked a hand toward Bo. "You said as much yourself just now."

"And that's a problem because . . . ?"

"How do the rest of us know that you and him
aren't about to run some sort of tomfoolery on us?"

Johnny's eyes hardened. "You mean you're afraid
we'll cheat you?" he asked, and his soft tone was
really deceptive now. Bo knew how angry Johnny was.

He wasn't too happy about being called a cheater
himself.

"I've seen you play, Fontana," Churchill said. "You
win a lot."

"It's my job to win. But I do it by honest means."

So Johnny was using the last name Fontana now,
Bo thought. Johnny had had half a dozen different
last names at least. Bo wasn't sure Johnny even remembered what name he'd been born with.

"To tell you the truth," Johnny went on, "I don't
need to cheat to beat you, Churchill. All I have to do
is take advantage of your natural recklessness."

One of the other players rested both hands on the
table, in plain sight, and said, "I don't like the way this
conversation is going. I came here for a friendly game,

gentlemen, not a display of bravado. And certainly not for gunplay."

"Shut the hell up, Davidson," Churchill snapped.

The man called Davidson paled and sat up straighter. He was in his thirties, well dressed, with tightly curled brown hair and a mustache that curled up on the tips. As Davidson moved forward a little in his chair, Bo caught a glimpse of a gun holstered in a shoulder rig under the man's left arm. Despite his town suit, Davidson looked tough enough to use the iron if he had to.

"I can go find another game," Bo suggested. He didn't want to sit in on this particular one badly enough to cause a shootout. "I just thought I'd say hello to an old friend."

"There's no need for that, Bo," Johnny said. He gave Churchill a flat, level stare and went on. "Bo Creel is an honest man, and so am I. If you doubt either of those things, Churchill, maybe it's you who had better find another game."

"I won't be stampeded, damn it." Churchill nodded toward the empty chair. "Sit down, Creel. But remember that I'll be watching you." He looked at Johnny. "Both of you."

"It's going to be a distinct pleasure taking your money," Johnny drawled.

"Shut up and deal the cards."

Johnny shut up and dealt.

Chapter 2

Bo wasn't sure what would have happened if he or Johnny had won the first hand after he sat down. Little Ed Churchill might have been more convinced than ever that he was being cheated.

The man called Davidson was the one who raked in that pot, however. In fact, judging by the way what had been a fairly small pile of chips in front of Davidson when Bo sat down began to grow after that, the man's luck appeared to have changed for the better.

Davidson won three out of the next five hands, with Bo taking one and Johnny the other. Bo understood now what Johnny meant about Churchill being reckless. The man was a plunger when he had a decent hand and a poor bluffer when he didn't. Bo wasn't surprised that Churchill lost a considerable amount of money in a short period of time.

The cattleman's face was red to start with, and it flushed even more as he continued to lose. Bo felt trouble building. If not for the fact that he and Scratch needed money, he would have just as soon gotten up from the table and walked away.

Scratch ambled over from the bar and stood there watching the game with a mug of beer in his hand. Churchill glanced at him and glared.

"What two-bit melodrama did you come from?"

Scratch's easy grin didn't hide the flash of anger in his eyes that Bo noted. "I'll let that remark pass, friend," the silver-haired Texan said. "I can see you've got troubles of your own."

"What the hell do you mean by that?"

"Well, from what I've seen so far of your poker playin', my hundred-and-four-year-old grandma could likely whip you at cards."

Churchill slapped his pasteboards facedown on the table and started to stand up. "Why, you grinning son of a—"

"Gentlemen, gentlemen!" The booming, Teutonic tones of August Strittmayer filled the air as the saloon's proprietor loomed over the table. "All the games in the Birdcage are friendly, *nicht wahr?*"

"Don't talk that damned Dutchy talk at me," Churchill snapped. He settled back down in his chair, though. Strittmayer was an imposing figure, two yards tall and a yard wide in brown tweed, with a bald head and big, knobby fists.

"Trouble here, Johnny?" Strittmayer asked.

"Not really," Johnny answered with a casual shrug. "Mr. Churchill is a bit of a poor loser, that's all."

"No one leaves the Birdcage unhappy," Strittmayer declared. "Why don't you come over to the bar and have a drink with me before you go, Herr Churchill? I have some splendid twenty-year-old brandy that I would be pleased to share with you."

"Who said I was going anywhere? I'm staying right here, damn it, until I win back my money!"

"I'm afraid we don't have that much time," Stritt-mayer said.

Johnny added, "Yeah, we'd all grow old and die before then."

For a smart man, Johnny never had learned how to control his mouth, Bo thought. Churchill paled at the insult. He glared at Strittmayer and demanded, "Are you throwing me out, you damned Dutchman?"

Strittmayer looked sorrowful. "Although I regret to say it, yes, I am, Herr Churchill."

"Do you know who I am?"

That was a stupid question, given the fact that Strittmayer had just called the cattleman by name. But Churchill was too angry to be thinking straight, Bo decided.

"Most certainly I do."

"You'll lose a hell of a lot of business if I tell my ranch hands to stay away from this place."

"Then I suppose I shall have to make up that business some other way," Strittmayer said.

Churchill got to his feet. "You'll be sorry about this," he said. "And you can keep your damned twenty-year-old brandy. In fact, you can take the bottle and shove it right up your—"

Strittmayer's hamlike hand closed around Churchill's arm and propelled the rancher toward the door. "I think you have said enough, *nicht wahr?* Good evening, Herr Churchill."

The whole saloon had gone silent now. Everybody in the Birdcage watched as Strittmayer marched Churchill to the door. Even the girl in the cage wasn't swinging back and forth anymore.

Churchill cursed loudly at the humiliation as Stritt-mayer forced him through the batwings. When the rancher had stalked off, Strittmayer stepped back inside, dusted his hands off as if they had gotten dirty, and beamed around at the crowd. "No more trouble, *ja?* The next round of drinks, it is on the house!"

Cheers rang out from the customers as most of them bellied up to the bar for that free drink. Bo had a feeling that the bartenders would be reaching for special bottles full of booze they had watered down especially for such occasional demonstrations of generosity on Strittmayer's part.

"Sorry about that, gents," Three-Toed Johnny Fontana told the other cardplayers at the table. "Poker should be a game of more subtle pleasures."

"I don't know," Davidson said with a smile. "I enjoyed watching that blowhard get thrown out of the place. A man like that gets a little money and power and thinks he owns everything and everybody."

Bo nodded toward the big, affable German who had gone back to the bar and asked Johnny, "Can Churchill really make trouble for Strittmayer?"

Johnny shrugged. "That depends on how badly his pride is wounded. August does enough business so that it won't hurt him much if Churchill orders his men to stay away from the place."

"What if he tries something a little more drastic than that?"

"You mean like coming back here with a bunch of those hardcases who ride for him and trying to wreck the place?" Johnny shook his head. "That seems like a little bit much for a dispute over a few hands of poker."

For once Johnny's ability to judge other men, which was so important in his profession, seemed to be letting him down a mite, Bo thought. He had seen something bordering on madness in Little Ed Churchill's eyes as he was forced out of the saloon. As Davidson had said, some men got that way when most people didn't dare to stand up to them. It enraged them whenever they ran into an hombre who didn't have any back-up in his nature.

But maybe Churchill would show some sense and go back to his ranch to sleep off that rage. Bo hoped that would turn out to be the case. When Johnny said, "Shall we resume the game?" Bo nodded.

Davidson's luck was still the best of anyone's around the table, but Bo won a few hands and was careful to cut his losses in the ones he couldn't win. He had increased their stake enough so that he and Scratch could afford a couple of hotel rooms and some supplies. He was about to call it a night when he heard a lot of hoofbeats in the street outside.

"Strittmayer!" a harsh voice bellowed as the horses came to a stop. "I told you you'd be sorry, you damned Dutchman!"

Bo dropped his cards and started to his feet, but Scratch grabbed his shoulder and forced him back down. "Everybody hit the dirt!" Scratch shouted, his deep voice filling the room.

Even as Scratch called out the warning, the glass in the two big front windows exploded inward as a volley of shots shattered them. The saloon girls screamed and men yelled curses as more shots blasted from the street. Muzzle flashes lit up the night like a lightning storm.

As Bo dived out of his chair he rammed a shoulder into Davidson, knocking the man to the floor out of the line of fire. Bo palmed out his Colt as Scratch overturned the poker table to give them some cover. Scratch crouched behind the table with Bo and drew his long-barreled Remingtons. Everybody in the saloon had either hit the floor or leaped over the bar to hide behind the thick hardwood, so the two of them had a clear field to return the fire of Little Ed Churchill and his men.

Churchill must have gathered up a dozen or more of his ranch hands in some of El Paso's other saloons and gambling dens and brothels and led them back here to Strittmayer's place. Bo didn't know if the cattlemen had spun some wild yarn for his men about how he'd been cheated at cards and then run out of the Birdcage, or if Churchill had simply ordered his men to attack. A lot of cowboys rode for the brand above all, and if the boss man said sic 'em, they skinned their irons and got to work, no questions asked.

Either way, lead now filled the air inside the Birdcage. The mirrors behind the bar shattered, and bottles of liquor arranged along the backbar exploded in sprays of booze and glass as bullets struck them.

Davidson crawled along the floor and got behind the same table where Bo and Scratch had taken cover. He pulled his gun from the shoulder holster Bo had seen earlier and started firing toward the street. He glanced over at Bo and Scratch and said, "I knew Churchill was a little loco, but I didn't think he was crazy enough to come back and lay siege to the place."

From behind the bar, Strittmayer called, "Everyone stay down, *ja?*" The next moment, several shotguns poked over the bar. Each of the weapons let go with a double load of buckshot. That barrage blew out what little glass remained in the windows and ripped into the cowboys in the street. Men and horses went down, screaming in pain.

Anger flooded through Bo. Not only was Churchill trying to kill everybody in the saloon, but now he had led some of his own men to their deaths, all because Churchill was a stubborn, prideful bastard who couldn't admit that he wasn't a very good poker player. What a damned waste, Bo thought.

He could only hope that some of that buckshot had found Churchill as well, so that maybe this fight could come to an end.

That didn't prove to be the case. With an incoherent, furious shout, the rancher leaped his horse onto the boardwalk and then viciously spurred the animal on into the saloon. The horse was terrified, anybody could see that, but Churchill forced the wild-eyed beast on. Men rolled and jumped desperately to avoid the slashing, steel-shod hooves.

Three-Toed Johnny leaped up from somewhere and shouted, "Stop it! For God's sake, stop it!" He had a derringer in his hand that Bo knew had come from a concealed sheath up the gambler's sleeve. Johnny swung it up toward Churchill, but the cattleman was faster. He had a six-gun in his right hand, and as he brought it down with a chopping motion, powder smoke geysered from the muzzle. The slug punched into Johnny's body and threw him backward.

Bo and Scratch fired at the same time, but Churchill was already jerking his horse around. Their bullets whistled harmlessly past his head. Churchill sent his horse crashing into the overturned table. Bo and Scratch threw themselves to the side to get out of the way, but the table rammed into Davidson and knocked him down. His gun flew out of his hand.

"Now I'll get you, you damned four-flusher!" Churchill yelled as he brought his revolver to bear on the helpless Davidson, who lay sprawled on the floor under the rearing horse.

Bo and Scratch fired again, and this time they didn't miss. Their bullets tore through Churchill's body on an upward-angling path, causing him to lean so far back that he toppled out of the saddle. Suddenly riderless, the panic-stricken horse whirled around a couple of times and then leaped out through the one of the already broken front windows.

The shooting from outside had stopped. Churchill's men were all either dead or had lit a shuck out of El Paso. The survivors probably wouldn't stop at Churchill's ranch either. After this brutal attack on the saloon, the men who had lived through it would take off for the tall and uncut and keep going, so that the law would be less likely to catch up to them. With Churchill dead, his wealth and influence couldn't protect them anymore.

A pale and visibly shaken August Strittmayer emerged from behind the bar clutching a reloaded shotgun. "They are all gone, *ja?*" he asked.

"Looks like it," Bo replied. He heard a lot of shouting from outside. The city marshal and some of his deputies were coming toward the Birdcage on the run, he assumed. The sounds of a small-scale war breaking out had been enough to attract the law.

Bo didn't pay any attention to that at the moment, but hurried to the side of Three-Toed Johnny instead. As Bo dropped to a knee, the gambler's eyelids fluttered open. His vest was soaked with blood over the place where Churchill's bullet had ventilated him.

"I think I'm . . . shot, Bo," Johnny gasped out as his eyes tried futilely to focus.

"I'm afraid so, Johnny," Bo agreed.

"Pretty . . . bad . . . huh?"

"Bad enough."

"Well . . . hell . . . we all draw . . . a bad hand . . . sooner or later." Johnny's head rolled from side to side. His eyes still wouldn't lock in on anything. "Ch-Churchill?"

Scratch had knelt on the gambler's other side. "Dead as he can be, pard," Scratch said.

"Good . . . At least I'm . . . not the only one . . . to fold—"

His eyes widened and grew still at last, and the air came out of him in a rattling sigh. Bo waited a moment, then shook his head and reached out to close those staring eyes as they began to grow glassy.

Strittmayer said in a hollow voice, "I never thought . . . I never dreamed that . . . that Churchill would . . . would do such a *verdammt* thing! To come back with his men and open fire on innocent people! The man was insane!"

Bo and Scratch got to their feet and started reloading their guns. "I don't reckon he was loco," Scratch said. "Just poison-mean and too used to gettin' his own way."

That was when several men with shotguns slapped the batwings aside and rushed into the saloon, leveling the Greeners at the two drifters as a gent with a soup-strainer mustache yelled, "Drop them guns, you ring-tailed hellions!"

Chapter 3

The man with the mustache turned out to be Jake Hamlin, the local marshal. The other shotgunners were his deputies, of course. They had seen half a dozen cowboys and a couple of horses shot to pieces in the street, and had no idea what had prompted this bloody massacre, but the busted windows of the Birdcage told them that the fatal shots must have come from inside the saloon. So they had charged in and thrown down on the first two gun-toting gents they had spotted, in this case Bo and Scratch.

It took a good half hour for Strittmayer, Davidson, and the other witnesses in the saloon to convince the lawman that Little Ed Churchill had been responsible for the hell that had broken loose. Churchill had been an important man in West Texas, and now he lay dead on the sawdust-littered floor of the saloon. To Jake Hamlin's mind, that meant somebody was guilty of murder, and who better for that role than a couple of no-account drifters?

"Creel and Morton, eh?" the marshal mused when

he found out their names. "I think I got paper on you two back in my office."

"We're not wanted in Texas," Bo said.

"And any reward dodgers you got on us from other places, well, those charges are bogus," Scratch added. "We're law-abidin' hombres."

"If you put those two fellows in jail, you will be the laughingstock of El Paso, Marshal!" Strittmayer bellowed. "I will see to this myself. Why, for Gott's sake, they saved the life of Herr Davidson here!"

Hamlin frowned. "What the hell'd you say? Here, here?"

"No, Herr here!" Strittmayer said, pointing at Davidson.

Hamlin snarled and sputtered and finally said, "Oh, shut up and lemme think!" After a few moments of visibly painful concentration, he turned to Bo and Scratch and went on. "All right, I reckon you two acted in self-defense. But there'll have to be an inquest to make it official, so don't even think about slopin' outta town until then."

"We were planning to be here for a day or two anyway," Bo said.

"Yeah, well, just remember what I told you!" Hamlin turned back to Strittmayer. "Anybody else killed?"

"Just poor Johnny there," Strittmayer replied as he waved a hand at the fallen gambler. "Several people were wounded, and my beautiful saloon, *ach!* It is shot to pieces!"

"Well, you can talk to Little Ed's lawyer about the estate payin' for the damages, but I wouldn't hold my breath waitin' for it if I was you," Hamlin advised. He looked around the room and raised his voice.

"This saloon's closed for the night! Everybody out! Go home!"

Davidson said to Bo and Scratch, "Do you fellas have a place to stay here in town?"

Bo shook his head, and Scratch said, "Not yet. We'd just rode in and stabled our horses. This was the first place we stopped."

"Come on over to the Camino Real with me, then," Davidson suggested. "That's where I'm staying. We'll see about getting you some rooms and a good hot meal."

"You don't have to do that," Bo said.

"I think I do. Churchill would have killed me, sure as hell, if not for you two."

Bo and Scratch couldn't argue with that, so after saying good night to Strittmayer, who promised to see to it that Johnny Fontana got a proper burial, they headed for the Camino Real Hotel with Davidson.

The Camino Real was El Paso's best hotel, and its rooms didn't come cheap. The fact that Davidson was staying there confirmed that he had plenty of money. As the three men walked along the street, he said, "We were never actually introduced. I'm Porter Davidson."

"Bo Creel," Bo said as he gripped the hand that Davidson put out. "This fancy-dressed drink of water with me is Scratch Morton. But I reckon you already know that since we told our names to the marshal."

"Pleased to meet you, Mr. Davidson," Scratch said as he shook hands with the man. "Too bad there had to be so much gunplay first."

"Yes, it ruined what had been a fairly pleasant evening. But maybe we can make something out of it yet."

Davidson spoke to the clerk at the desk in the hotel

lobby and maybe slipped him a greenback, too. Bo wasn't sure about that. But either way, within minutes the clerk was sliding a pair of keys across the desk to them. Even though the clerk had said originally that the hotel was full up, at Davidson's urging he had somehow found a couple of vacant rooms on the third floor.

"Is the dining room still open?" Davidson asked.

"I believe it's just about to close," the clerk said.

"Would you go out to the kitchen and let the cook know that we'll need two dinners? Whatever's left will be fine, as long as it's hot."

"Yes, sir."

As they went into the empty dining room and sat down at one of the tables, Scratch commented, "You seem to be the big skookum he-wolf around these parts, Mr. Davidson."

"Not really," Davidson said with a laugh. "I guess it doesn't take long for word to get around, though, when you own a gold mine."

Scratch lifted his eyebrows.

Bo wasn't particularly surprised, though. Davidson hadn't struck him as a cattleman, and on the frontier a rich man who didn't run cows was usually mixed up with either the railroad or mining.

"I didn't know there were any gold mines around here," he commented. "There are a few down in the Big Bend, but they're not what I'd call bonanzas."

"The mine's not in Texas," Davidson said.

"New Mexico Territory?"

"No. It's across the border in Mexico, in the mountains. A place called Barranca del Asesino."

Bo and Scratch looked at each other, then back at Davidson. "Cutthroat Canyon," Bo translated.

"That's right."

"Does it live up to its name?" Scratch asked.

Davidson chuckled. "No, most of the time it's a pretty peaceful place." His face grew more serious. "The trouble happens between there and here."

Bo said, "You have trouble, do you?"

"Yes, as a matter of fact. That's one reason I wanted to talk more to you two fellows. That and my gratitude for what you did for me, of course. I'm hoping I can persuade you to do even more. I'd like to hire you both."

Before the discussion could continue, the white-aproned cook came out of the kitchen carrying a couple of plates of food. "The waiters have all gone home already," he explained as he set the plates in front of Bo and Scratch. They contained thick steaks, baked potatoes, and biscuits and gravy. "That's all we got left."

"Looks mighty fine to me," Scratch said with a smile. "We're much obliged, mister."

"Got half a pot of coffee back in the kitchen, too, if you'd like some."

"Bring it on," Bo said.

For the next few minutes they were too busy eating to ask Davidson what he had meant about hiring them. The mine owner sat there with an amused smile on his face as he watched them putting away the food.

"You fellows look like you've been on short rations for a while," he commented.

"We had to stretch our provisions the last few days on the trail," Bo admitted. "I figured we could shoot a jackrabbit or something while we were on our way across the southern part of New Mexico Territory, but game was pretty scarce."

"It's been mighty dry over that way," Scratch put in. "Reckon most of the critters 'cept for the rattlesnakes have gone off lookin' for someplace that's more hospitable. And I've never cared much for eatin' snake, although I've known some hombres who think it's good."

"Well, you won't go hungry if you work for me," Davidson said. "There's a nice little valley right outside the canyon where the Mexicans from a nearby village have their farms. We buy our food from them. And there's a cantina in the village with some pretty girls who work there, too, if you're interested in such things."

"Interested in tequila and señoritas?" Scratch said. "I hope to smile we are!"

Davidson leaned forward and clasped his hands together on the table. "I think we should discuss wages, then."

"Let's talk about the job first," Bo said. "Just what is it that you'd be hiring us to do?"

"That's a fair enough question. Like I said, there's been trouble between El Paso and the mine. I bring the ore here by wagon. There's no way to refine it in the canyon, and this is the closest railroad stop so that I can ship it out. There's been talk of building a spur line down there into the mountains, but the railroad and the Mexican government have to work out all the details first. It's liable to be a long, drawn-out process. In the meantime, I've got ore sitting there that I can't get out because of bandits."

Bo nodded. "I reckoned that was what we were getting to. Your ore shipments have been held up?"

"Several times. I've lost shipments, and men who worked for me have been killed."

Scratch's voice was dry as he drawled, "You ain't makin' the job sound all that appealin', Mr. Davidson."

"We've ridden shotgun on gold wagons before," Bo said. "It's a good way to get killed."

Davidson shook his head. "I'm not asking you to ride shotgun. I thought that if the two of you trailed the wagons at a short distance, when the bandits attack, you'd be able to jump them and take them by surprise."

Bo took a sip of coffee and slowly nodded. "That might work. Once anyway. After that, the hombres who are after your gold would be watching for us."

"Once might be enough to scare them off," Davidson said. "They've had their own way so far, like Churchill, and nobody's been able to stop them. I want to put the fear of God into them. Maybe even wipe them out."

"Bo and me, we're pretty tough," Scratch said, "but even so, I don't reckon the two of us would be any match for a whole gang of *bandidos*."

"I don't expect the two of you to take care of them by yourselves. I have several other men who'll be riding back across the border with me. That's why I came to El Paso, to recruit some good men who can take care of this problem. From what I saw of your abilities in the Birdcage, the two of you will fit right in with the other men I've hired." Davidson looked back and forth between them. "Well, what do you think? Will you take the job? Remember, we haven't even talked about wages yet, but I'm sure we'd be able to reach an agreement on that matter. I believe in paying for the best."

"Give us a minute to ponder on it," Bo said.

"Of course," Davidson replied with a nod. "I need to speak to the hotel clerk anyway. I'll wait for you out in the lobby."

He stood up and walked out of the dining room. Bo and Scratch looked at each other over the remains of their supper, and Scratch said, "What do you think?"

"I don't much cotton to being lumped in with a bunch of hired guns," Bo said. "You know that's what Davidson's talking about."

"Yeah, but he seems like a pretty good fella, and he's got a right to get his gold up here without havin' it stolen. Not to mention the hombres who work for him bein' killed like that. Such things don't sit well with me."

"I know, you never have liked outlaws. Neither do I."

Scratch grinned. "And I'd be lyin' if I said I didn't have a hankerin' to visit Old Mexico again. I ain't as young as I used to be, and the heat down there feels good on these bones o' mine."

"Not to mention the señoritas."

The grin on Scratch's rugged face widened. "They feel pretty good on these bones o' mine, too."

Slowly, Bo nodded. "Well, since we don't have anywhere else we have to be . . ."

"As per usual."

"I don't suppose it would hurt anything if we rode down there with Davidson and had a look around. If we don't like the lay of the land, we can always pull out. Wouldn't be anything stopping us."

"That's right." Scratch drank the last of his coffee. "Be good to spend some time in Mañana-land again."

They found Davidson in the lobby. With an eager expression on his face, the man asked, "Have you made up your minds?"

"We'll ride down there with you," Bo said. "Whether or not we stay depends on what we find there."

"Fair enough," Davidson said with an emphatic nod. He shook hands with them again and added, "I think everything will work out just fine once we get to Cutthroat Canyon."

THE FIRST MOUNTAIN MAN SERIES BY
WILLIAM W. JOHNSTONE